PILGRIM'S PROGRESS

NELSON'S
ROYAL
CLASSICS

PILGRIM'S PROGRESS

JOHN BUNYAN

Publishers since 1798

THOMAS NELSON PUBLISHERS
Nashville

Published in Nashville, Tennessee, by Thomas Nelson, Inc.

Library of Congress Cataloging-in-Publication Data

Bunyan, John, 1628–1688.
    The pilgrim's progress from this world, to that which is to come : delivered under the similitude of a dream / John Bunyan.
        p.   cm.—(Nelson's royal classics series : 1)
    ISBN 0-7852-4222-8
    1. Christian pilgrims and pilgrimages—Fiction.   2. Puritan movements—Fiction.   3. Christian life—Fiction.   I. Title.
II. Series.
[PR3330.A1   1999]
828'.407—dc21   99–19873
                                                                                      CIP

Printed in the United States of America
1 2 3 4 5 6 7 — 04 03 02 01 00 99

PUBLISHER'S PREFACE

S ince the birth of the Christian church, thousands of writers have examined the teachings of the church and chronicled the experience of faith. Yet only a few of these works stand out as true classics—books that had and continue to have a significant impact on the church and the everyday lives of believers. They describe the core of our beliefs and capture the essence of our Christian experience. They remain an essential part of every Christian's library, and they continue to challenge the way we conceive our faith and our world.

Welcome to Nelson's Royal Classics—our commitment to preserving these treasures and presenting them to a new generation of believers. Every book contains an introduction that will detail the life and faith of the author and define why these works have such an important place in the history of our faith. As you read, you'll find that the timeless wisdom of the writers in this series is not only encouraging and enlightening but also very stimulating. These rich resources will strengthen your spiritual growth and show you ways to grow ever closer to God.

Each volume, such as Sheldon's *In His Steps,* Bunyan's *Pilgrim's Progress,* or St. Augustine's *Confessions,* is a treasure to be read and cherished. As a series, they become an heirloom library of invaluable worth. Read them now, and share them with others as a way to pass on the heart of Christianity.

JOHN BUNYAN, 1628–1688

HIS LIFE	1628–1688	WORLD EVENTS
Born in Elstow, Bedfordshire.	1628–1629	Oliver Cromwell becomes a member of the English Parliament (1628); Charles I dissolves Parliament; colony of Massachusetts founded (1629).
Leaves school to follow his father's trade—that of a tinker; travels throughout Bedfordshire selling their goods.	1638–1643	Japan issues edict banning emigration and prohibiting ship building (1638); beginning of the English Civil War (1640).
Bunyan is drafted into the Parliamentary army.	1644–1646	Ming Dynasty in China ends (1644); Oliver Cromwell reorganizes the armies of the English Parliament and captures Charles I. Alexis I becomes the second Russian czar of the house of Romanov (1645).
Discharged from the army, Bunyan meets and marries his first wife, Mary, who influences him to spiritual re-examination.	1647–1648	The Holy Roman Emperor and the King of France sign the Treaty of Westphalia (1648).
Dreams and night visions torment him about his spiritual quest.	1649–1651	Charles I is executed. England is proclaimed a republic. Oliver Cromwell tried to force the Irish off their land.
Buys an orchard in Bedford, converting its barn into a meeting place; joins his wife's church (1653).	1652–1653	Cromwell dissolves Parliament and takes the title of Lord Protector.
Finally accepts his full redemptions; friends encourage him to preach.	1655	Christian Huggens discovered the rings of Saturn.
Publishes first pamphlet defending his faith.	1656	The weird "handles" which Galileo saw on the sides of Saturn are first understood to be rings around the planet.
Publishes second pamphlet defending his faith; takes first assignment as a "field" preacher.	1657	The Accademia del Cimento for scientific research is founded in Florence by Leopoldo de Medici.
Wife Mary dies.	1658	Oliver Cromwell dies.
Bunyan is arrested while preaching.	1660	Charles II is restored to England's throne.
Writes *Grace Abounding to the Chief of Sinners*.	1666	*The Misanthrope* by Molière first performed; the Great Fire destroys London.
Bunyan is released from prison; begins preaching in Bedford.	1672	Peter the Great of Russia is born.
Bunyan is arrested again for his religious views.	1675	Isaac Newton presents "Discourse on Light and Colour" to The Royal Society, containing his suggestion that light is a stream of particles.
Released from prison.	1677	Racine publishes *Phedre*.
Publishes the first part of *Pilgrim's Progress* (1678).	1678–1679	England passes the *habeas corpus* act guaranteeing people protection from arbitrary arrest (1679).

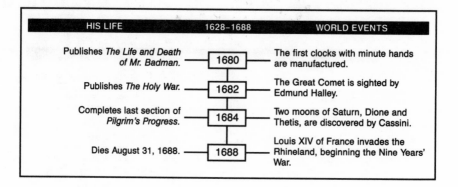

HIS LIFE	1628–1688	WORLD EVENTS
Publishes *The Life and Death of Mr. Badman.*	1680	The first clocks with minute hands are manufactured.
Publishes *The Holy War.*	1682	The Great Comet is sighted by Edmund Halley.
Completes last section of *Pilgrim's Progress.*	1684	Two moons of Saturn, Dione and Thetis, are discovered by Cassini.
Dies August 31, 1688.	1688	Louis XIV of France invades the Rhineland, beginning the Nine Years' War.

INTRODUCTION

The preacher had been riding all night, his clothes and hair soaked by the cold, relentless rain. It was not the worst hardship he had ever known, having spent much of his life in poverty and having been in prison for more than twelve years. Also, he felt compelled to make this ride, a mission to visit one of the judges who had, in fact, been responsible for those long years of imprisonment. The judge had been long estranged from his son, who now sought the preacher's help in reconciling with his father. The preacher, however, was already ill, and the strain of the ride weakened him beyond recovery. His mission was a success, but, a few days later, on August 31, 1688, John Bunyan died, leaving behind an unparalleled legacy of service to God.

No one who knew him was surprised that John Bunyan had made that last, determined ride to help a friend. For most of his life, Bunyan had pushed himself to the limits, driven from within by a passion for life, and, following his conversion, for God. Although he had received an elementary education, Bunyan left school at the age of 10 in order to learn his father's trade and help support the family. As tinkers, father and son traveled throughout the Bedfordshire countryside, making pots and other metal utensils. This early familiarity with the people and the geography around Bedfordshire would later help Bunyan the preacher as he sought to help the people who lived around him.

As a young man, however, Bunyan was more passionate about fun than ministry. Wild and coarse as a teenager, he was known for the boisterous antics he and his friends frequently pulled. This reputation followed him as he joined the Parliamentary Army in 1644.

John Bunyan lived at a time of great political and social unrest. The English civil war began in 1640, undermining the monarchy and bringing Oliver Cromwell to power. The seeds of change were also being planted in Bunyan's life, starting with the traumatic deaths of his mother and sister when he was sixteen. His father had remarried quickly, providing Bunyan with an even stronger impetus than patriotism for joining the army. However, strictly enforced devotional times were a part of the Cromwellian army, which put Bunyan upon a spiritual path that would continue after his discharge in 1647. At that time, Bunyan also married his first wife, Mary, whose reliance upon God and the teachings of Scripture had a strong influence on her new husband.

Bunyan read the Bible eagerly, searching for the deepest meaning. He started to have a series of increasingly disturbing dreams and night visions, which left him miserable and unsure of his own redemption, even though he accepted Christ and joined the Baptist church in 1653. Expanding his study of Scripture with the writings of Martin Luther, he was feeling more content by 1655, and, encouraged by friends who had benefited from his plain way of explaining scriptural messages, he began preaching throughout Bedfordshire.

His deep devotion to God and simple way of speaking soon made him one of the most popular preachers around. However, in 1660, the monarchy was restored, Charles II returned to Britain's throne, and the time was a dangerous one for dissenting preachers. Bunyan was arrested on November 12, 1660, and would remain in prison for the next twelve years.

Although he used much of his time in prison to further his study of the Bible, he also had to work making shoelaces in order to eat and to provide some support for his family. He had had four children with Mary, who had died in 1658. Bunyan had remarried, and his new wife Elizabeth worked for his release, even as she remained devoted to her husband's children. His eldest child, a daughter who was born blind, spent time in prison with her father, helping him as he studied and wrote the first of his literary masterpieces, *Grace Abounding to the Chief of Sinners.* This spiritual autobiography, which detailed his early struggles with poverty, doubt, and redemption, was published in 1666.

Despite the deprivation of his imprisonment, Bunyan remained incredibly resourceful and creative. He ministered to his jailers and fellow prisoners, bringing many of them to Christ. He continued to write and study, producing nine books before his release in 1672, including the first part of his best-known work, *Pilgrim's Progress,* which would be published in 1678.

Bunyan published more than 30 books after *Pilgrim's Progress,* but the popularity of *Pilgrim's Progress* spread rapidly, with more than eleven editions being published during his lifetime. Only the Bible would outsell the simply written allegory about the pilgrim Christian and his search for the Celestial City. The hero, who was remarkably similar to Bunyan, captured the hearts of readers worldwide, and gave us the lasting images of the City of Destruction, the Valley of Humiliation, and the immortal Vanity Fair. The book was immediately successful, and its dominance in western culture continues even today, having influenced the work of such writers as Nathaniel Hawthorne, George Bernard Shaw, and William Makepeace Thackeray.

It also, in its own odd way, led to Bunyan's death. The book made him one of the most sought-after preachers in the country. He responded gladly to such demands, pushing himself hard to meet the needs of God's children. One of these needs was the old judge who had imprisoned Bunyan. Having read *Pilgrim's Progress,* his heart had been changed toward his son, a fervent support of John Bunyan. It was this mission that took Bunyan forty miles through the cold rain, ending the life of the most influential writer in the English language.

Rudyard Kipling once referred to Bunyan as the father of the English novel. Although Bunyan never intended for *Pilgrim's Progress* to be a novel, his work completely changed the way we view fictional characters and the impact they have on the reader. He took a lofty goal and made it completely accessible to the average person. More importantly, John Bunyan made it clear that our spiritual journey—and our personal relationship with God—is the most vital part of our human existence.

Contents

Part I

Part II

THE
PILGRIM'S
PROGRESS

PART I

THE AUTHOR'S APOLOGY
FOR HIS BOOK
Part I

WHEN at the first I took my pen in hand
Thus for to write, I did not understand
That I at all should make a little book
In such a style: no, I had undertook
To make another; which, when almost done,
Before I was aware I this begun.
And thus it was: I, writing of the way
And race of saints in this our gospel-day,
Fell suddenly into an allegory
About their journey, and the way to glory,
In more than twenty things which I set down
This done, I twenty more had in my crown,
And they again began to multiply,
Like sparks that from the coals of fire do fly.
No, then, thought I, if that you breed so fast,
I'll put you by yourselves, lest you at last
Should prove ad infinitum, and eat out
The book that I already am about.
Well, so I did; but yet I did not think
To show to all the world my pen and ink
In such a style; I only thought to make
I knew not what: nor did I undertake
Thereby to please my neighbor; no, not I;
I did it my own self to gratify.
Neither did I but vacant seasons spend
In this my scribble; nor did I intend
But to divert myself, in doing this,
From worse thoughts, which make me do amiss.
Thus I set pen to paper with delight,

And quickly had my thoughts in black and white;
For having now my method by the end,
Still as I pull'd, it came; and so I penned
It down; until it came at last to be,
For length and breadth, the bigness which you see.
Well, when I had thus put mine ends together
I show'd them others, that I might see whether
They would condemn them, or them justify:
And some said, let them live; some, let them die:
Some said, John, print it; others said, Not so:
Some said, It might do good; others said, No.
Now was I in a strait, and did not see
Which was the best thing to be done by me:
At last I thought, Since you are thus divided,
I print it will; and so the case decided.
For, thought I, some I see would have it done,
Though others in that channel do not run:
To prove, then, who advised for the best,
Thus I thought fit to put it to the test.
I further thought, if now I did deny
Those that would have it, thus to gratify;
I did not know, but hinder them I might
Of that which would to them be great delight.
For those which were not for its coming forth,
I said to them, Offend you, I am loath;
Yet since your brethren pleased with it be,
Refrain judging, till you do further see.
If you will not read, let it alone;
Some love the meat, some love to pick the bone.
Yes, that I might them better palliate,
I did too with them thus expostulate:
May I not write in such a style as this?
In such a method too, and yet not miss
My end—your good? Why may it not be done?

Dark clouds bring waters, when the bright bring
   none.
Yes, dark or bright, if they their silver drops
Cause to descend, the earth, by yielding crops,
Gives praise to both, and not object to either,
But treasures up the fruit they yield together;
Yes, so commix both, that in their fruit
None can distinguish this from that; they suit
Her well when hungry; but if she is full,
She spews out both, and makes their blessing null.
You see the ways the fishermen take
To catch the fish; what engines does he make!
Watch how he engages all his wits;
Also his snares, lines, angles, hooks, and nets:
Yet fish there be, that neither hook nor line,
Nor snare, nor net, nor engine can make thine:
They must be groped for, and be tickled too,
Or they will not be caught, whatever you do.
How does the fowler seek to catch his game
By various means! all which one cannot name.
His guns, his nets, his lime-twigs, light and bell:
He creeps, he goes, he stands; yea, who can tell
Of all his postures? yet there's none of these
Will make him master of what fowls he please.
Yea, he must pipe and whistle, to catch this;
Yet if he does so, that bird he will miss.
If that a pearl may in toad's head dwell,
And may be found too in an oyster-shell;
If things that promise nothing, do contain
What better is than gold; who will disdain,
That have an inkling of it, there to look,
That they may find it. Now my little book,
(Though void of all these paintings that may make
It with this or the other man to take),

Is not without those things that do excel
What do in brave but empty notions dwell.
"Well, yet I am not fully satisfied
That this your book will stand, when soundly tried."
Why, what's the matter? "It is dark." What though?
"But it is feigned." What of that? I trust
Some men by feigned words, as dark as mine,
Make truth to spangle, and its rays to shine.
"But they want solidness." Speak, man, your mind.
"They drown the weak; metaphors make us blind."
Consistency, indeed, becomes the pen
Of him that writes things divine to men:
But do I need solidness, because
By metaphors I speak? Were not God's laws,
His gospel laws, in olden time held forth
By types, shadows, and metaphors? Yet loath
Will any sober man be to find fault
With them, lest he be found for to assault
The highest wisdom! No, he rather stoops,
And seeks to find out what, by pins and loops,
By calves and sheep, by heifers, and by rams,
By birds and herbs, and by the blood of lambs,
God speaks to him; and happy is he
That finds the light and grace that in them be.
But not too forward, therefore, to conclude
That I want solidness—that I am rude;
All things solid in show, not solid be;
All things in parable despise not we,
Lest things most harmful lightly we receive,
And things that good are, of our souls bereave.
My dark and cloudy words they do but hold
The truth, as cabinets incase the gold.
The prophets used much by metaphors
To set forth truth: yes, who so considers

Christ, his apostles too, shall plainly see,
That truths to this day in such disguises be.
Am I afraid to say, that holy writ,
Which for its style and phrase puts down all wit,
Is everywhere so full of all these things,
Dark figures, allegories? Yet there springs
From that same book, that luster, and those rays
Of light, that turn our darkest nights to days.
Come, let my frivolous objections to his life now look,
And find there darker lines than in my book
He finds any; yes, and let him know,
That in his best things there are worse lines too.
May we but stand before impartial men,
To his poor one I would adventure ten,
That they will take my meaning in these lines
Far better than his lies in silver shrines.
Come, truth, although in swaddling-clothes, I find
Informs the judgment, rectifies the mind;
Pleases the understanding, makes the will
Submit, the memory too it does fill
With what does our imagination please;
Likewise it tends our troubles to appease.
Sound words, I know, Timothy is to use,
And old wives' fables he is to refuse;
But yet grave Paul him nowhere does forbid
The use of parables, in which lay hid
That gold, those pearls, and precious stones that were
Worth digging for, and that with greatest care.
Let me add one word more. O man of God,
Art you offended? Do you wish I had
Put forth my subject in another dress?
Or that I had in things been more express?
Three things let me propound; then I submit
To those that are my betters, as is fit.

1. I find not that I am denied the use
Of this my method, so I no abuse.
Put on the words, things, readers, or be rude
In handling figure or similitude,
In application; but all that I may
Seek the advance of truth this or that way.
Denied, did I say? No, I have leave,
(Example too, and that from them that have
God better pleased, by their words or ways,
Than any man that breathes now-a-days),
Thus to express my mind, thus to declare
Things unto you that excellent are.
2. I find that men as high as trees will write
Dialogue-wise; yet no man does them slight
For writing so. Indeed, if they abuse
Truth, cursed be they, and the craft they use
To that intent; but yet let truth be free
To make her sallies upon you and me,
Which way it pleases God: for who knows how,
Better than he that taught us first to plow,
To guide our minds and pens for his designs?
And he makes base things usher in divine.
3. I find that holy law, in many places,
Appears with this method, where the cases
Do call for one thing to set out another:
Use it I may then, and yet nothing smother
Truth's golden beams: no, by this method may
Make it shine forth its rays as light as day.
And now, before I do put up my pen,
I'll show the profit of my book; and then
Commit both you and it unto that hand
That pulls the strong down, and makes weak ones
    stand.
This book is drawn out before your eyes

The man that seeks the everlasting prize:
It shows you from where he comes, where he goes,
What he leaves undone; also what he does:
It also shows you how he runs, and runs,
Till he unto the gate of glory comes.
It shows, too, who set out for life amain,
As if the lasting crown they would obtain;
Here also you may see the reason why
They lose their labor, and like fools do die.
This book will make a traveler of thee,
If by its counsel you will ruled be;
It will direct you to the Holy Land,
If you will its directions understand.
Yes, it will make the slothful active be;
The blind also delightful things to see.
Are you for something rare and profitable?
Or would you see a truth within a fable?
Are you forgetful? Would you remember
From New-Year's day to the last of December?
Then read my fancies; they will stick like burs,
And may be, to the helpless, comforters.
This book is writ in such a dialect
As may the minds of listless men affect:
It seems a novelty, and yet contains
Nothing but sound and honest gospel strains.
Would you divert yourself from melancholy?
Would you be pleasant, yet be far from folly?
Would you read riddles, and their explanation?
Or else be drowned in your contemplation?
Do you love picking meat? Or would you see
A man in the clouds, and hear him speak to thee?
Would you be in a dream, and yet not sleep?
Or would you in a moment laugh and weep?
Would you lose yourself and catch no harm,

And find yourself again without a charm?
Would you read yourself, and read you know not
    what,
And yet know whether you art blest or not,
By reading the same lines? O then come hither,
And lay my book, your head, and heart together.

JOHN BUNYAN

THE FIRST STAGE

As I walked through the wilderness of this world, I lighted on a certain place where was a den, and laid me down in that place to sleep; and as I slept, I dreamed a dream. A man, dressed in rags, was standing with his back toward his house. A book was in his hand; a great burden was on his back (Is. 64:6; Luke 14:33; Ps. 38:4). I saw him open the book and read. He wept and trembled. Unable to control himself he gave a pathetic cry, "What shall I do?" (Acts 2:37; 16:30; Hab. 1:2–3).

He went home and attempted to hide his feelings from his wife and children. But the troubles increased and he could not keep silent. "My dear wife and children of my flesh, I, your dear friend, am doomed by a burden that lies heavy on me. I know that our city will be burned with fire from heaven. I fear that you, my wife, and you, my sweet children, will miserably come to ruin unless a way of escape that I can not see, is found."

They did not believe him. They thought he was unbalanced. Since it was late, they forced him to bed hoping a night's sleep would calm him. But he was as troubled at night as he had been during the day. Instead of sleeping, he moaned and wept. In the morning the family asked how he was, "Worse and worse." He tried to talk. They attempted to drive his insanity away with harshness, ridicule, admonishment, and neglect. He went to his bedroom to pray for them and to find comfort from his misery. He spent time walking alone in the fields, sometimes reading and sometimes praying.

I saw him walking in the fields reading his book. He was deeply distressed, he shouted, "What must I do to be saved?" (Acts 16:30–31).

I also saw that he looked this way and that way, as if he would run. Yet he stood still because (as I perceived) he could not tell which way to go. I looked again and saw a man named Evangelist approach him. He asked, "Why are you crying?"

"Sir, I perceive from the book in my hand that I am condemned to die, but after this the judgment (Heb. 9:27). I find I am not willing to do the first (Job 10:21–22), nor able to do the second" (Ezek. 22:14).

Evangelist asked, "Why are you not willing to die, since this life is full of many evils?"

The man answered, "Because I fear the burden on my back will sink me lower than the grave and I will fall into Tophet (Is. 30:33). If I am not ready to go to prison, I am not ready for judgment and execution. This makes me weep."

Evangelist responded, "If this is your condition, why are you standing still?"

"Because I do not know where to go."

Then Evangelist gave him a scripture verse, "Flee from the wrath to come" (Matt. 3:7).

The man read it, looked carefully at Evangelist, and asked, "Where can I flee?"

Evangelist pointed to a wide field, "Do you see the narrow gate?" (Matt. 7:13–14).

The man answered, "No."

"Do you see the shining lamp?" (Ps. 119:105; 2 Pet. 1:19).

"I think so."

Evangelist said, "Keep that light in your eye, go directly toward it and you will see the narrow gate. When you knock, you will be told what to do."

I saw in my dream that the man began to run. He had not run far from his door when his wife and children realized it. They began to cry for him to return. The man put his fingers in his ears and ran crying, "Life! Life! Eternal life!" (Luke 14:26). He did not look back (Gen. 19:17), but fled toward the middle of the plain.

The neighbors watched (Jer. 20:10), some mocked, others threatened, and some yelled for him to return. Obstinate and Pliable resolved to bring him back by force. The man had gone a good distance but they were determined to catch him, and they did. The man asked, "Neighbors, why did you chase me?"

"To persuade you to come back with us."

"No," said he, "you live in the city of Destruction, the place where I was born. This is how I see it, sooner or later, you will sink lower than the grave into a place that burns with fire and brimstone. Good neighbors, come with me."

OBST. What, said Obstinate, and leave friends and comfort behind!

CHR. Yes, said Christian (for that was his name), everything you forsake is not worthy of being compared with what I am seeking to enjoy (2 Cor. 4:18). If you will come with me, and hold steady, we will prosper. For where I go, there is enough and to spare (Luke 15:17). Come with me, and prove my words.

OBST. What are the things you seek, since you leave all the world to find them?

CHR. I seek an inheritance incorruptible, undefiled, that does not fade away (1 Peter 1:4). It is reserved and safe in heaven (Heb. 11:16), to be given at the time appointed to them that diligently seek it. Read it, if you want, it is in my book.

OBST. Never, away with your book. Will you or won't you go back?

CHR. No, because I have put my hand to the plow (Luke 9:62).

OBST. Come then, neighbor Pliable, let us go home without him. There is a group of these superficial pretenders that, when they have an idea, are wiser in their own eyes than any seven reasonable men.

PLI. Don't castigate him. If what the good Christian says is true, the things he looks for are better than ours. My heart favors going with my neighbor.

OBST. What, more fools! Listen, come back. Who knows where such an unbalanced fellow will lead you? Go back, go back, and be wise.

CHR. Come with your neighbor, Pliable! The things I spoke about are available, plus many more glories. If you do not believe me, read it in this book where the truth is stated and confirmed by the blood of Him that made it (Heb. 9:17–21).

PLI. Well, neighbor Obstinate, said Pliable, I am beginning to understand. I intend to go with this good man and cast my lot with him. But, my good companion, do you know to get to this desired place?

CHR. A man named Evangelist directed me. He said to hurry to the narrow gate where we will receive instructions about the way.

PLI. Come, good neighbor, let us go. They went together.

OBST. I will go back to my place. I will not be a companion of such misled, fanatical people.

I saw in my dream that after Obstinate left, Christian and Pliable began to talk.

CHR. Neighbor Pliable, I am glad you agreed to come. If Obstinate felt what I felt, the powers and terrors of what is unseen, he would not have so readily turned his back on us.

PLI. Neighbor Christian, since there are only two of us, tell me the things we will enjoy where we are going.

CHR. I conceive them in my mind better than I speak them with my tongue. Since you want to know, however, I will read them in my book.

PLI. Do you think the words in your book are true?

CHR. Yes, indeed, they were made by Him who cannot lie (Titus 1:2).

PLI. Well said! What things are they?

CHR. There is an endless kingdom to be inhabited, and everlasting life to be given that we may live there forever (Isa. 65:17; John 10:27–29).

PLI. Well said! What else?

CHR. There are crowns of glory and garments that will make us shine like the sun in the firmament of heaven (2 Tim. 4:8; Rev. 22:5; Matt. 13:43).

PLI. This is very pleasant. What else?

CHR. There will be no crying and no sorrow; for He, the owner of the place, will wipe all tears from our eyes (Is. 25:8; Rev. 7:16, 17; 21:4).

PLI. What fellowship will we have there?

CHR. We will be with seraphim and cherubim (Is. 6:2; 1 Thess. 4:16,17; Rev. 5:11), creatures that will dazzle your eyes. You will meet ten thousand times ten thousand, and thousands of thousands that have gone before us. None are harmful; all are loving and holy. Every one walking in the sight of God, forever accepted in His presence. We will see the elders with crowns of gold on their heads (Rev. 4:4). We will see the holy virgins playing their golden harps (Rev. 14:1–5). We will see men that the world cut in pieces, burned in flames, gave to wild beasts, and drowned in the seas because of their love for the Lord of the place (John 12:25). All will be dressed in the radiance of immortality (2 Cor. 5:2).

PLI. This is enough to delight one's heart. Can we enjoy these things? Can we share in it?

CHR. The Lord, the governor of the country, has recorded this in His book (Is. 55:1,2; John 6:37; 7:37; Rev. 21:6; 22:17). If we are willing to have it, he will freely give it to us.

PLI. Well, my good companion, I am glad to hear these things. Come, hurry, let us increase our pace.

CHR. I cannot go any faster because of the burden on my back.

Now I saw in my dream, that just as they ended the conversation, they came close to a miry swamp in the middle of the plain. Not paying attention, they unexpectedly fell into the swamp named Despond. They wallowed, totally covered with muck. Christian, because of the burden on his back, began to sink in the mire.

PLI. Neighbor Christian, where are you?

CHR. Really, I do not know.

PLI. Pliable was offended and angrily said, Is this the happiness you have been telling me about? If we are having this much trouble early in our pilgrimage, what can we expect between here and our journey's end? If I escape from here with my life, you can keep the brave country. He gave two desperate pushes and got out of the mire on the side of the swamp closest to his house. He left, and Christian never saw him again.

Christian was now alone in the Swamp of Despond. He struggled to the side of the swamp that was farthest from his house, and closest to the narrow gate. He could not get out because of the burden on his back. Then I saw in my dream a man, whose name was Help. He came to Christian and asked what he was doing there.

CHR. Sir, I was told to go this way by a man named Evangelist. He directed me to that distant gate to escape the coming wrath. I was going there when I fell in.

HELP. Why did you not look for the steps?

CHR. Fear followed me so hard that I fled and fell in.

HELP. Give me your hand. So he gave him his hand and was pulled out (Ps. 40:2), set on solid ground, and sent on his way.

Then I approached Help and said, "Sir, since this is the way from the city of Destruction to the narrow gate, why is this swamp not filled in? Poor travelers need more security to pass." He answered, "This miry swap cannot be filled in. It contains scum and filth that continually run with the frequent conviction of sin. This is why it is called the Swamp of Despond. As the sinner wakes to his lost condition, fears, doubts, and discouraging apprehensions arise in his soul. All of these settle in this place. This is why the ground is so dangerous.

"It is not the King's pleasure for this place to remain dangerous (Is. 35:3,4). Under the direction of his Majesty's surveyors, his laborers have been working on this patch of ground for sixteen hundred years. To my knowledge," said he, "there has been at least twenty thousand cartloads and millions of wholesome instructions brought here from all the places in the King's dominions. (Knowledgeable people say this is the best material for making good ground). It should have been filled, but this is the Swamp of Despond. It will be filled when they have done what they can.

"Under the direction of the Lawgiver, good, substantial steps have been placed through the middle of this swamp. But when this place spews filth, the steps are difficult to see, men miss the steps, and are dragged in. The ground, however, is good when they enter through the gate" (1 Sam. 12:23).

Now I saw in my dream that when Pliable returned home, his neighbors came to visit. Some called him wise for returning. Some called him a fool for putting himself in jeopardy with Christian. Others mocked him as a coward, "I would not have been so worthless as to quit after a few difficulties." Pliable sat silently, gaining more confidence. Then they changed their stories and ridiculed poor Christian behind his back.

Christian was walking alone when he saw someone cross the field to meet him. It was Mr. Worldly Wiseman, who lived in the great town of Carnal Policy, close to Christian's home. He had heard about Christian, (for Christian's leaving the city of Destruction was common talk in many communities). Mr. Worldly Wiseman thought it was Christian as he watched his laborious walk, sigh, and groan. He began to talk with him.

WORLD. Excuse me, good fellow, where are you going with this burden?

CHR. A burden indeed, it is as heavy as ever a poor creature carried! Since you asked me where I am going, I will tell you. I am going to that distant narrow gate. There, I have been informed that I will be relieved of my heavy burden.

WORLD. Do you have a wife and children?

CHR. Yes, but my burden is so heavy that I take no pleasure in them, as I once did. It is as if I have no family (1 Cor. 7:29).

WORLD. Will you listen to me if I give you counsel?

CHR. If it is good. I need some good counsel.

WORLD. I would advise you to hurry and get rid of your burden. Your mind will never be settled, nor will you enjoy the benefits of the blessings God has given until you do.

CHR. I want to get rid of this heavy burden, but I can not get it off by myself. There is no man in our country that can take it off my shoulders. I told you, I am going this way to get rid of my burden.

WORLD. Who told you to go this way to get rid of your burden?

CHR. A man, a great and honorable person, as I remember, his name is Evangelist.

WORLD. A curse on his counsel! This is the most dangerous way. You will find that out if you follow his advice. You have already met with something, I can tell from the muck of the Swamp of Despond that is on you. This is just the beginning of the sorrows of those who go that way. Listen to me. I am older than you. If you go this way, you will likely meet weariness, pain, hunger, peril, nakedness, sword, lions, dragons, darkness, and, in a word, death. These things are certainly true, confirmed by many testimonies. Why should a man carelessly throw himself away listening to a stranger?

CHR. Sir, this burden on my back is more terrible than anything you mentioned. I do not care what I meet on the way if I can find deliverance from my burden.

WORLD. How did you get the burden?

CHR. Reading this book.

WORLD. I thought so. It has happened to you and other weak men. You meddle with things too high and suddenly you fall into distractions that emasculate you. They force you into desperate ventures to obtain who knows what.

CHR. All I want is my heavy burden lifted.

WORLD. Why do you seek relief this way since there are so many dangers? Especially since (had you the patience to hear me) I could direct you to obtain what you want without the dangers. Yes, the remedy is at hand. Instead of those dangers, you will meet with safety, friendship, and contentment.

CHR. Sir, please tell me this secret.

WORLD. In the village of Morality, lives a gentleman named Legality. He is judicious, has a good name, and the skill to help men lift burdens off their shoulders. To my knowledge, he has done a great deal of good. He has the expertise to cure those that are somewhat deranged from their burdens. As I said, you may go to him and be quickly helped. His house is not quite a mile from here. If he is not home, he has a son, Civility, who can lift your burden as well as the old gentleman. If you do not want to go back home (as indeed I would not), send for your wife and children. In this village there are empty houses, one of which you may have for a reasonable rate. Provisions are cheap and good. Things that will make your life happy are there. The neighbors are reputable and well-behaved.

Now Christian was undecided, but he eventually concluded that if what this gentleman said was true, his wisest action would be to take his advice.

CHR. Sir, how do I reach this honest man's house?

WORLD. Do you see that high hill in the distance?

CHR. Yes, clearly.

WORLD. Go to that hill, the first house will be his.

So Christian turned from his way and started toward Mr. Legality's house. When he got close, the hill seemed so high that the side next to the road hung over it. Christian would not go any closer for fear that the hill would fall on him. He stood still. He did not know what to do. His burden seemed heavier than when he was in the way. Flashes of fire (Ex. 19:16, 18) came out of the hill. Christian feared that he might be burned. He was exceedingly afraid, he trembled (Heb. 12:21). He began to be sorry that he had taken Mr. Worldly Wiseman's counsel. Then he saw Evangelist coming to meet him. He began to blush with shame. Evangelist came closer and closer, looking at him with a severe and dreadful expression. He began to reason with Christian.

EVAN. What are you doing here? Christian did not know how to answer; he stood speechless. Are you the man I found crying outside the walls of the city of Destruction?

CHR. Yes, dear sir, I am the man.

EVAN. Did I direct you to the narrow gate?

CHR. Yes, dear sir.

EVAN. Why did you so quickly turn aside? You are now out of the way.

CHR. I met a gentleman, when I got past the Swamp of Despond, who persuaded me to find a man in this village who could take my burden off.

EVAN. What was he?

CHR. He looked like a gentleman, talked much, and got me to come here. When I saw this hill, and how it hangs over the road, I suddenly stopped for fear it would fall on me.

EVAN. What did that gentleman say?

CHR. He asked me where I was going. I told him.

EVAN. What did he say?

CHR. He asked if I had a family; I told him. I also said that I am so loaded with the burden on my back that I could no longer take pleasure in my family.

EVAN. What did he say?

CHR. He wished me speed to get rid of my burden. I told him ease was what I sought. I was going to the distant gate to receive further directions on how to reach the place of deliverance. He said that he would show me a better way. One that did not have so many difficulties as the way, sir, you sent me. He directed me to a house where a gentleman lives who has the skill to take this burden off. I believed him and turned from the way to be relieved. But when I came to this place, and saw things as they are, I stopped from fear (as I said) of danger. Now I do not know what to do.

EVAN. Stand a moment so I may show you the words of God. Christian stood trembling as Evangelist said, "See that you do not refuse Him who speaks. For if they did not escape who refused Him who spoke on earth, much more shall we not escape if we turn away from Him who speaks from heaven" (Heb. 12:25). He also said, "Now the just shall live by faith; but if anyone draws back, My soul shall have no pleasure in him" (Heb. 10:38). He then applied these words: You are the man running into this misery. You have begun to reject the counsel of the Most High, to draw your foot back from the way of peace, and risk damnation.

Christian fell at his feet as dead, crying, Woe is me, I am undone!

Evangelist caught him by the right hand and said, "Every sin and blasphemy will be forgiven men" (Matt. 12:31). "Do not be unbelieving, but believe" (John 20:27). Then Christian revived and stood trembling before Evangelist.

Evangelist continued, Pay serious attention to the things I tell you. I will show who deluded you and whom it was he sent you to. The man that met you is Worldly Wiseman. His name is partly accurate because he speaks as the world (1 John 4:5) (therefore he always goes to church in the town of Morality), and partly because he loves that doctrine best. It saves him from persecution for the cross of Christ (Gal. 6:12). Because he is carnal, he seeks to pervert my ways. Now there are three things in this man's counsel that you must completely abhor.

1. His turning you from the way.
2. His working to make the cross odious to you.
3. His setting your feet in the way that leads to death.

First, you must abhor his turning you from the way, and your consenting to it. This rejects the counsel of God for the counsel of a Worldly Wiseman. The Lord says, "Strive to enter through the narrow gate" (Luke 13:24), the gate I send you to. "Because narrow is the gate and difficult is the way which leads to life, and there are few that find it" (Matt. 7:13,14). This wicked man has turned you from the narrow gate and from the way. He almost brought you to destruction. Hate his turning you from the way; abhor yourself for listening to him.

Second, you must detest his attempts to make the cross despicable. Prefer the cross above the treasures of Egypt (Heb. 11:25, 26). Besides, the King of glory has told you, He who loves his life will lose it, and he who hates his life in this world will keep it for eternal life. And if anyone comes to Him and does not hate his father and mother, wife and children, brothers and sisters, yes, and his own life also, he cannot be His disciple (Mark 8:38; John 12:25; Matt. 10:39; Luke 14:26). Therefore, for a man to work at persuading you that this will be your death, that you can not have eternal life, you must abhor this doctrine.

Third, you must hate his sending you in the way that leads to death.

Consider whom he sent you to; how that person was unable to deliver you from your burden.

Legality, to whom you were sent for ease, is the son of the bond-woman and is in bondage with her children (Gal. 4:21–27). Legality is, in a mystery, Mount Sinai, which you fear will fall on you. Now if she and her children are in bondage, how can you expect them to make you free? Thus, Legality is unable to free you from your burden. Legality has never lifted a burden from anyone, nor will he ever. The works of the law cannot justify you; by the deeds of the law no man living can be rid of his burden: Therefore Mr. Worldly Wiseman is an alien and Mr. Legality is a cheat. His son Civility, despite his good looks, is only a hypocrite. He cannot help you. Believe me, there is nothing in all that you have heard about these foolish men, except a strategy to cheat you of your salvation by turning you from the way I sent you. Evangelist called to the heavens for confirmation of what he had said. Then there came words and fire out of the mountain where poor Christian was. The hair on his flesh stood up. The words were pronounced: "As many as are of the works of the law are under the curse; for it is written, Cursed is everyone who does not continue in all things which are written in the book of the law to do them" (Gal. 3:10).

Now Christian looked for nothing but death. He began to mournfully cry, cursing the time he met Mr. Worldly Wiseman, calling himself a thousand fools for listening to his counsel. He was greatly ashamed to think that this gentleman's arguments, flowing only from the flesh, prevailed and caused him to leave the right way. This done, he applied Evangelist's words and wisdom.

CHR. Sir, what do you think? Is there any hope? May I now go to the narrow gate? Will I be abandoned and sent back ashamed? I am sorry that I listened to this man's counsel. Will my sin be forgiven?

EVAN. Your sin is great. You have committed two evils. You have forsaken the way that is good, to walk in forbidden paths. Yet the man at the gate will receive you. He has goodwill toward men. But be careful that you do not turn aside again, lest "you perish in the way, when His wrath is kindled but a little" (Ps. 2:12).

THE SECOND STAGE

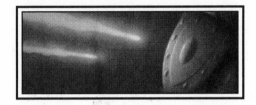

T hen Christian decided to return. Evangelist kissed him, smiled, and wished him Godspeed. He left in a hurry, speaking to no one, even if they asked for an answer. He moved like one walking on forbidden ground. He knew that he was not safe until he returned to the way that he had left. In the process of time, Christian reached the gate. Over the gate was written, "Knock, and it will be opened to you" (Matt. 7:7).

He knocked, more than once or twice, saying,

> May I now enter here? Will he within
> Open to sorry me, though I have been
> An undeserving rebel? Then shall I
> Not fail to sing his lasting praise on high.

Finally, Goodwill, a solemn person, came to the gate. He asked who was there, where he came from, and what he wanted?

CHR. Here is a poor burdened sinner from the city of Destruction. I am going to Mount Zion to be delivered from the wrath to come. I would, sir, since I am informed that this gate is the way to that place, know if you are willing to let me in.

GOOD. I am willing with all my heart, he said, and with that he opened the gate.

As Christian stepped forward, Goodwill pulled him in. Christian asked, Why did you do that? Goodwill answered, A little distance from this gate is a strong castle where Beelzebub is the captain. From there, Beelzebub, and those that are with him, shoot arrows at those that come to this gate in an attempt to kill them before they can enter. Christian said, I rejoice and tremble. When he was inside the Gate, Goodwill asked who sent him.

CHR. Evangelist told me to come here and knock. He said that you, sir, would tell me what I must do.

GOOD. An open door is set before you, and no man can shut it.

CHR. Now I begin to reap the benefits of my dangers.

GOOD. Why did you come alone?

CHR. None of my neighbors saw the danger as I did.

GOOD. Did any of them know your plans?

CHR. Yes, my wife and children, they called me to return. Some of my neighbors stood crying and called for me to come back. But I put my fingers in my ears and continued on my way.

GOOD. Did anyone follow you to persuade you to go back?

CHR. Yes, Obstinate and Pliable. When they saw that they could not prevail, Obstinate went back complaining. Pliable came a short distance with me.

GOOD. Why did he not come through?

CHR. We were together until we came to the Swamp of Despond, where we suddenly fell in. My neighbor Pliable became discouraged and would not go any farther. He got out of the swamp on the side closest to his house. He told me to possess the brave country alone. He went his way after Obstinate and I came to this gate.

GOOD. Alas, the poor man, is the celestial glory of so little esteem that he did not consider it worth running the hazard of a few difficulties to obtain?

CHR. I have told the truth about Pliable. I will also tell you all the truth about me. I am no better than he. It is true that he went back to his house, but I turned aside to go in the way of death. Mr. Worldly Wiseman persuaded me with his carnal arguments.

GOOD. Oh, did he light on you? He would have you seek comfort at the hands of Mr. Legality! Both of them are cheats. Did you take his counsel?

CHR. Yes, as far as I dared, I went to find Mr. Legality. I thought the mountain that stands by his house would fall on me. I was forced to stop.

GOOD. That mountain has been the death of many, and will be the death of many more. It is well you escaped being dashed to pieces.

CHR. Honestly, I do not know what would have happened if Evangelist had not met me again while I was deliberating in the midst of my despair. It was God's mercy, or else I would never have come here. I deserved death by that mountain, more than talking with my Lord. Oh, what a favor that I am granted entrance!

GOOD. We make no objections against anyone, despite anything they may have done before they arrived here. They will by no means be cast out (John 6:37). Good Christian, come a little way with me, I will teach you about the way you must go. Look, do you see this narrow way? That is the way. The patriarchs, prophets, Christ, and His apostles built it. It is as straight as a ruler can make it. This is the way you must go.

CHR. Are there any turns or curves where a stranger can lose his way?

GOOD. Yes, there are many ways to lose the mark and they are all crooked and wide. You may distinguish right from wrong, the right is always straight and narrow (Matt. 7:14).

Then I saw in my dream that Christian asked Goodwill if he would help him take off the burden that was on his back.

He answered, "As for your burden, be content to carry it until you come to the place of deliverance. There it will fall from your back by itself."

Christian tightened his belt and thought about the journey. Goodwill said that after some distance from the gate, he would come to the house of the Interpreter. There he should knock on the door and be shown excellent things. Christian left his friend, wishing him Godspeed.

He went until he came to the house of the Interpreter. There he knocked again and again. At last someone came to the door, and asked who was there.

CHR. Sir, I am a traveler, who was told by an acquaintance of the good man of this house to call here for my improvement. I would speak with the master of the house.

He called the master of the house. After a little time he came to Christian and asked what he wanted.

CHR. Sir, I am a man that has come from the city of Destruction on my way to Mount Zion. The man that stands at the entrance gate told me that if I stopped here you would show me excellent things to help me on my journey.

INTER. Come in. I will show you what will be useful. He commanded his servant to light a candle and asked Christian to follow. They went into a private room, a door was opened, and Christian saw the picture of a serious person hanging on the wall. The eyes were lifted up to heaven, the best of books was in his hand, the law of truth was written on his lips, the world was behind his back. He stood as if pleading with men. A crown of gold hung over his head.

CHR. What does this mean?

INTER. The man whose picture this is, is one of a thousand. He can father children (1 Cor. 4:15), labor in birth with children (Gal. 4:19), and nurse them when they are born. You see him with his eyes lifted up to heaven, the best of books in his hand, and the law of truth written on his lips. This shows that his work is to know and unfold dark things to sinners. You see him standing as if he was pleading with men. The world behind him, a crown hanging over his head. This shows that by neglecting and despising present things for the love that he has for his Master's service, he is sure to have glory for his reward in the next world. Now, said the Interpreter, I have shown you this first because the man whose picture this is, is the only one whom the Lord of the place where you are going has authorized to be your guide. He will be with you in all the difficult places along the way. Pay close attention to what I have shown you. Keep in mind all you have seen, lest in your journey you meet with some that pretend to lead you right, but their way goes down to death.

Then he took him by the hand and led him into a very large parlor that was never swept. It was full of dust. After he looked at it for a little while, the Interpreter called a man to sweep. When he began to sweep, the abundant dust started to fly. Christian almost choked. The Interpreter said to a girl that stood by, "Bring water and sprinkle the room". She did and the room was swept and cleaned with pleasure.

CHR. What does this mean?

INTER. This parlor is the heart of a man that was never sanctified by the sweet grace of the Gospel. The dust is his original sin and inner corruption. It has defiled the entire man. He that first started to sweep, is the law. She that brought water, and sprinkled it, is the Gospel. Now you saw that when the first began to sweep, the dust flew so that the room could not be cleaned. You almost choked. This is to show that the law, instead of cleaning the heart (by its working), revives sin (Rom. 7:9), puts strength in it (1 Cor. 15:56), and increases it in the soul (Rom. 5:20), even as it discovers and forbids it. The law does not give power to subdue sin. You saw the girl sprinkle the room with water and it was cleaned with pleasure. This is to show that when the Gospel comes in sweet and precious influences to the heart, just as you saw the girl keep the dust down by sprinkling the floor with water, so sin is vanquished and subdued. The soul is made clean through faith and consequently is prepared for the King of glory to inhabit (John 15:3; Eph. 5:26; Acts 15:9; Rom. 16:25, 26).

I saw in my dream that the Interpreter took him by the hand and put him in a small room where two little children sat, each in his chair.

The name of the oldest was Passion and the other was Patience. Passion seemed dissatisfied; Patience was quiet. Christian asked, "Why is Passion dissatisfied?" The Interpreter answered, "His administrator wants him to stay for his own good until the beginning of next year. But he wants it all now. Patience is willing to wait."

Then one came to Passion, brought him a bag of treasure, and poured it at his feet. He picked it up, rejoiced, and they all laughed at Patience. I watched as he wasted it all. He had nothing left but rags.

CHR. Explain this more fully.

INTER. These two lads are figures. Passion represents the men of this world. Patience represent the men of what is to come. As you see, Passion will have everything now, this year, in this world. Like the men of this world, they must have all their good things now. They cannot wait until next year, until the next world, for their portion of good. The proverb, "A bird in the hand is worth two in the bush," carries more weight with them than all the divine testimonies of the good of the world to come. But as you saw, he quickly wasted everything. All he has left is rags. So it will be with all such men at the end of this world.

CHR. Now I see that Patience has the best wisdom for several reasons. 1. He waits for the best things. 2. He will have glory, when the other has nothing but rags.

INTER. You may add another, the glory of the next world will never wear out, but these are suddenly gone. Passion had no reason to laugh at Patience because he had his good things first. Patience will yet laugh at Passion because he had his best things last. The first must give way to the last, because the last must have their time. The last gives place to nothing, for there is not another to succeed. He who has his portion first, needs time to spend it. But he that has his portion at the end, will have it forever. It was said of a certain rich man, "Remember that in your lifetime you received your good things, and likewise Lazarus evil things; but now he is comforted and you are tormented" (Luke 16:25).

CHR. Then I perceive that it is not best to want things now, but to wait for things to come.

INTER. You speak the truth. Things which are seen are temporary, but things which are not seen are eternal (2 Cor. 4:18). Though this is so, things present and our fleshly appetite are close neighbors. Things to come and temporary senses are strangers to each other. Things which are seen suddenly become friends with fleshly appetites, and that distance is continued with things eternal.

Then I saw in my dream that the Interpreter took Christian by the hand and led him to where there was a fire burning against a wall. Someone was standing by it, throwing water on it to extinguish it. But the fire burn higher and hotter.

Christian said, What does this mean?

The Interpreter answered, This fire is the work of grace in the heart. He that pours water on it to extinguish it, is the devil. Because you see the fire burning higher and hotter, you also see the reason. He turned Christian to the back side of the wall. There he saw a man, with a container of oil in his hand, continually (but secretly) throwing it on the fire.

Christian asked, What does this mean?

The Interpreter answered, This is Christ, who continually with the oil of His grace maintains the work already begun in the heart. Despite what the devil can do, the souls of His people are still gracious (2 Cor. 12:9). You saw the man standing behind the wall to maintain the fire. This is to teach that it is hard for the tempted to see how this work of grace is maintained in the soul.

I also saw that the Interpreter took him by the hand and led him into a pleasant place, a stately palace, beautiful to look at. The scene greatly delighted Christian. He saw on the top of the palace, people walking. They were clothed in gold.

Christian asked, May we go in?

The Interpreter led him to the palace door. A great company of men stood there wanting to enter, but not daring to. A man, a little distance from the door, sat at a table with a book and pen, to take the names of those that would enter. He also saw that many men in armor stood guarding the doorway. They were resolved to do harm and damage to any that would enter. Christian was amazed. Finally, after every man fell back in fear, Christian saw a courageous man approach the table. He said, "Write my name down, sir." When he finished writing, the man drew his sword, put a helmet on his head, and rushed toward the door. The armed men attacked him with deadly force. The man, not at all discouraged, fiercely cut and hacked. After he had received and given many wounds to those who attempted to keep him out (Matt. 11:12; Acts 14:22), he cut his way through and pushed into the palace. Immediately a pleasant voice from inside the palace was heard,

> Come in, come in,
> Eternal glory you will win.

He went in and was clothed with garments like theirs. Then Christian smiled, and said, I think I know the meaning of this.

Now, said Christian, let me go there. No, said the Interpreter, stay until I have shown you a little more. Then you may go. He took him by the hand and led him into a dark room where a man sat in an iron cage.

The man seemed sad. He sat with his eyes looking down to the ground, hands folded, and sighed as if his heart would break. Christian asked, What does this mean? The Interpreter invited him to talk with the man.

Christian said, What are you? He answered, I am what I was not once.

CHR. What were you once?

MAN. I once was a promising and prospering believer (Luke 8:13), both in my eyes and in the eyes of others. I once was, as I thought, ready for the Celestial City. I rejoiced at the thoughts that I would get there.

CHR. Well, what are you now?

MAN. I am a man of despair. Shut up in this iron cage. I cannot get out. I cannot!

CHR. What put you in this condition?

MAN. I stopped watching and being sober. I laid the reins on the neck of my lusts. I sinned against the light of the word, and the goodness of God. I grieved the Spirit, and he is gone. I tempted the devil, and he came to me. I provoked God to anger, and he left me. I hardened my heart so that I cannot repent.

Christian asked the Interpreter, Is there any hope for a man like this? Ask him, said the Interpreter.

CHR. Is there no hope? Must you be kept in the iron cage of despair?

MAN. No hope, none at all.

CHR. Why? The Son of the Blessed is very merciful.

MAN. I have crucified him to myself again (Heb. 6:6). I have despised his person (Luke 19:14). I have despised his righteousness. I have counted his blood as an unholy thing. I have disdained the spirit of grace (Heb. 10:29). I have shut myself out of all the promises. There now remains for me nothing but threats, dreadful threats, faithful threats of certain judgment and fiery indignation that will devour me as an adversary.

CHR. How did you get in this condition?

MAN. I promised myself great delight in the lusts, pleasures, and profits of this world. Now every one of those things bite and gnaw like a burning worm.

CHR. Can you repent and turn?

MAN. God has denied me repentance. His word gives me no encouragement to believe. He, Himself, has locked me in this iron cage and all the men in the world cannot get me out. Oh eternity! eternity! How will I grapple with the misery that I must meet in eternity?

INTER. Remember this man's misery and let it be an everlasting caution to you.

CHR. This is fearful! God help me to watch, be sober, and pray that I may avoid the cause of this man's misery. Sir, is it time for me to leave?

INTER. Stay until I show you one thing more. Then you will be on your way.

He took Christian by the hand again and led him into a bedroom where one was getting out of bed. As he put on his clothes, he shook and trembled. Christian asked, Why does this man tremble? The Interpreter told him to answer Christian's question.

He began, "One night, in my sleep, I dreamed that the heavens grew exceeding black. Frightful thunder and lightening put me in agony. I looked up in my dream and saw the clouds twisting. I heard the great sound of a trumpet and saw a man sitting on a cloud. He was escorted by the thousands of heaven. They were all in flaming fire. The heavens were a burning flame. I heard a voice, 'Arise, you dead, and come to judgment.' With that the rocks split, the graves opened, and the dead came out. Some were exceeding glad and looked up. Some sought to hide under the mountains.

Then I saw the man that sat on the cloud open the book. He ordered the world to come near. An unquenchable flame was in front of him. It kept a distance between him and them, as between the judge and the prisoners at the bar (1 Cor. 15; 1 Thess. 4:16; Jude 15; John 5:28, 29; 2 Thess. 1:8–10; Rev. 20:11–14; Isa. 26:21; Micah 7:16, 17; Ps. 5:4; 50:1–3; Mal. 3:2, 3; Dan. 7:9,10). I heard this proclaimed to those that escorted the man that sat on the cloud, 'Gather the tares, the chaff, and stubble, and throw them into the burning lake' (Matt. 3:12; 18:30; 24:30; Mal. 4:1). With that the bottomless pit opened, just about where I stood. Out of the pit's mouth came heavy smoke, coals of fire, and hideous noises. It was also said to the same people, 'Gather my wheat into the barn' (Luke 3:17). With that I saw many caught up and carried into the clouds, but I was left behind (1 Thess. 4:16, 17). I tried to hide. I could not. The man who sat on the cloud kept his eye on me. My sins came to mind; my conscience accused me on every side (Rom. 2:14, 15). With this I woke."

CHR. What made you so afraid?

MAN. Why, I thought the judgment day had come, and I was not ready. But this frightened me the most; the angels gathered several people, and left me behind. Then the pit of hell opened her mouth where I stood. My conscience afflicted me. The Judge always had his eye on me; there was indignation in his expression.

Then the Interpreter said to Christian, "Have you considered all these things?"

CHR. Yes, and they put me in hope and fear.

INTER. Keep these things in mind. Let them be a goad in your side, forcing you forward in the way you must go. Then Christian tightened his belt and prepared for the journey. The Interpreter said, "The Comforter will always be with you, good Christian, to guide you in the way that leads to the city." So Christian went on his way, saying,

> Here I have seen things rare and profitable,
> Things pleasant, dreadful, things to make me stable
> In what I have begun to take in hand:
> Then let me think on them, and understand
> Wherefore they showed me were, and let me be
> Thankful, O good Interpreter, to thee.

THE THIRD STAGE

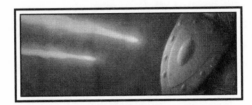

I saw in my dream that the highway Christian traveled was enclosed by a wall on both sides. The wall was called Salvation (Isaiah 26:1). Christian ran with great difficulty because of his burden.

He ran until he came to a peak where a cross stood; a little below, in the bottom, was a tomb. When Christian reached the cross, his burden became loose, fell from his back, and tumbled into the tomb. I never saw the burden again.

Christian was delighted. He spoke with a happy heart, "He has given me rest through his sorrow, and life by his death." He stood in wonder. It was surprising that the sight of the cross could lift his burden. He looked, and looked again, until the springs that were in his head sent water down his cheeks (Zech. 12:10). As he stood looking and weeping, three Shining Ones approached and greeted him. "Peace," the first said, "Your sins are forgiven" (Mark 2:5). The second removed his filthy rags and dressed him in rich clothing (Zech. 3:4). The third put a mark on his forehead (Eph. 1:13) and gave him a sealed roll. He told Christian to look at the roll as he ran and to leave it at the celestial gate. Then the Shining Ones went their way. Christian gave three leaps for joy and left singing,

> Thus far did I come loaded with my sin,
> Nor could anything ease the grief that I was in,
> Till I came here. What a place is this!
> Must here be the beginning of my bliss?
> Must here the burden fall from off my back?
> Must here the strings that bound it to me crack?
> Blest cross! blest sepulchre! blest rather be
> The Man that there was put to shame for me!

I saw in my dream that he went on until he came to the bottom. There, a little out of the way, he saw three men sound asleep. They had chains on their feet. The names were Simple, Sloth, and Presumption.

Christian went over to wake them. He cried, You are like one who lies at the top of the mast (Prov. 23:34). The Dead Sea is under you, a gulf without a bottom. Wake up! Come with me. If you are willing, I will help you take your irons off. If he that walks about like a roaring lion (1 Pet. 5:8) comes by, you will certainly be victim to his teeth. They just looked at him. Simple said, I see no danger. Sloth said, Just a little more sleep. Presumption said, Every tub must stand on its own bottom. And so they laid down again to sleep, and Christian went his way.

Yet he was troubled to imagine that men in danger would think so little of his kindness to help them take off their chains. As he thought about this, he saw two men tumble over the wall on the left side of the narrow way. They ran up to him. The name of one was Formalist, and the other Hypocrisy. So, as I said, they chased him to have a conversation.

CHR. Gentlemen, where did you come from? Where are you going?

FORM. AND HYP. We were born in the land of Vain-glory. We are going to Mount Zion for praise.

CHR. Why didn't you come in at the gate? Do you not know it is written, "He who does not enter the sheepfold by the door, but climbs up some other way, the same is a thief and a robber" (John 10:1)?

FORM. AND HYP. Going to the gate for admission is too far. Our usual way is to take a short cut and climb over the wall.

CHR. Are you not trespassing against the Lord of the city where we are going? Are you not violating his revealed will?

FORM. AND HYP. Do not trouble your head about it. What we did is our practice. We can produce, if necessary, testimony that it has been done for more than a thousand years.

CHR. Can you prove it in court?

FORM. AND HYP. This custom is more than a thousand years old. It would doubtless be admitted as legal by an impartial judge. Besides, as long as we get in, what difference does it make how we get in? If we are in, we are in. You are in the way. You, as we perceive, came in at the gate. We also are in the way even though we came tumbling over the wall. Now is your condition any better than ours?

CHR. I walk by the rule of my Master. You walk by the imprudent working of your imagination. The Lord of the way already considers you thieves. Therefore, I doubt that you will be found true men at the end. You came in by yourselves, without his direction. You will go out by yourselves, without his mercy.

They had little answer. They told him to look to himself and went on their way without much conferring. The two men told Christian that as to laws and ordinances, they were as conscious as he. They said, You are not different from us, except for the coat that you are wearing. We believe that it was given you by your neighbors, to hide the shame of your nakedness.

CHR. You will not be saved by laws and ordinances because you did not come in by the door (Gal. 2:16). As for this coat, the Lord of the place where I am going gave it to me. You say it is to cover my nakedness. I consider it an act of kindness, for I had nothing but rags, and it gives me comfort. Surely, when I come to the gate of the city, the

Lord will know me because I have his coat on. A coat he freely gave me the day he took my rags. I also have a mark on my forehead, perhaps you did not notice it. One of my Lord's most intimate associates put it there the day the burden fell off my shoulders. Let me tell you something else, I was given a sealed roll to read and comfort me as I travel along the way. I was also told to leave it at the celestial gate as a sign of assurance that I would be admitted. These things you do not have, because you did not come in at the gate.

They gave no answer. All they did was look at each other and laugh. They all went on, but Christian talked only to himself, sometimes with sighs, and sometimes in comfort. He often read from the roll that one of the Shining Ones gave him; this refreshed him.

They continued until they came to the bottom of the hill Difficulty. There was a spring there and two other ways beside the straight road from the gate. One turned left and the other right. The narrow way ran directly up the hill called Difficulty. Christian first went to the spring (Isa. 49:10), drank, refreshed himself, and then started up the hill, saying,

> The hill, though high, I covet to ascend;
> The difficulty will not me offend;
> For I perceive the way to life lies here:
> Come, pluck up heart, let's neither faint nor fear.
> Better, though difficult, the right way to go,
> Than wrong, though easy, where the end is woe.

The other two came to the foot of the hill and saw that it was steep and high. There were two other ways to go; they assumed these roads would meet the narrow way on the other side of the hill. Thus, they decided to take those ways. The name of one way was Danger. The name of the other was Destruction. One took the way called Danger; it led to a great forest. The other took the way to Destruction; it led to a wide field, full of dark mountains. There he stumbled, fell, and never rose again.

I watched Christian go up the hill. The steep slope slowed him from running to walking, to crawling on his hands and his knees. About half way to the top was a pleasant arbor, made by the Lord of the hill for the refreshment of weary travelers. When Christian arrived at the arbor, he sat down to rest. He pulled out his roll and read it for comfort. He thought about the coat that was given him when he stood near the cross. Greatly pleased, he fell into a slumber, and then into a fast sleep that almost lasted until night. The roll fell from his hand. While he was sleeping one came and woke him, "Go to the ant, you sluggard! Consider her ways, and be wise" (Prov. 6:6). Christian suddenly jumped up and sped on his way until he reached the top of the hill.

Now when he reached the top, two men arrived running hard. The name of one was Timorous and the other was Mistrust. Christian asked them, Sirs, what's the matter? You run the wrong way. Timorous answered that they were going to the city of Zion and got up that difficult place. But, said he, the farther we went, the more danger we met. So we turned around and are going back.

Yes, said Mistrust, just ahead are a couple of lions. We did not know if they were asleep or awake. We thought if we came within their reach, they would tear us to pieces.

CHR. You make me afraid. Where can I go to be safe? If I go back to my country, fire and brimstone await, and I will certainly perish. If I reach the celestial city, I am safe. I must keep going. To return is death. To go forward is fear of death with everlasting life beyond. I will go forward. Mistrust and Timorous ran down the hill, and Christian went on his way.

Thinking about what he heard, he looked for his roll to read it for comfort. He could not find it. Christian was in great distress. He did not know what to do. He needed the roll for comfort, and it was his pass to the celestial city. He was greatly perplexed. Then he thought, I slept in the arbor on the side of the hill. Falling to his knees, he asked God forgiveness for that foolish act. Then he went back to look. Who can sufficiently tell the sorrow of Christian's heart? Sometimes he sighed, sometimes he wept, and often he chided himself for being so foolish as to fall asleep in the arbor that was built to offer a little refreshment from weariness. Thus, he went back, carefully looking on this side and that, to find the roll that had been his comfort so many times in the journey. He went on until he came to the arbor. This increased his sorrow by reminding him of the evil of sleeping unto his mind (Rev. 2:4; 1 Thess. 5:6–8). He continued to regret his sinful sleep, saying, O wretched man to sleep in the daytime, to sleep in the middle of difficulty, to indulge the flesh by using that rest for my contentment. The Lord of the hill erected that arbor only for the relief of the spirits of pilgrims! How many steps have I taken in vain! It happened to Israel, because of their sin they were sent back again by the way of the Red Sea. I am made to tread those steps with sorrow. I might have walked them with delight had it not been for this sinful sleep. How far might I have been by now! I am forced to walk these steps three times; I needed only to walk them once. Now I am likely to be overtaken by night, for the day is almost over. O that I had not slept!

When he reached the arbor, he sat down and wept. But (as Providence would have it), he looked under the seat and saw the roll. He picked it up with trembling and haste and put it inside his robe. Who can tell how joyful this man was? His roll was the assurance of life and acceptance at the desired haven. He held it next to his heart and gave thanks to God for directing his eye to the place where it lay. With joy and tears he again started his journey. O how nimbly he went up the rest of the hill! Yet before he reached the top, the sun had set. This made him again recall the folly of sleeping. He began to sympathize with himself. Oh sinful sleep, for your sake night has overtaken me! I must walk without the sun, darkness covers the path, and I hear the noise of the wretched creatures.

He remembered the story that Mistrust and Timorous told about two lions that frightened them. Christian said to himself, These beasts roam at night for prey. If they should meet me in the dark, how can I defeat them? How can I escape being torn to pieces? He went his way fretting about his unhappy failure. He looked up and there, in front of him, was a stately palace named Beautiful. It stood by the side of the road.

I saw in my dream that he hurried forward to obtain lodging. Before he had gone far, he entered a narrow passage about a furlong off the Porter's lodge. He saw two lions. Now, thought he, I see the danger that drove Mistrust and Timorous back. (The lions were chained, but he could not see the chains.) He was afraid and thought about going back, judging that nothing but death was ahead. The Porter at the lodge, whose name is Watchful, perceived that Christian had stopped, as if to go back. He cried out, Is your strength so small? (Mark 4:40). Do not fear the lions. They are chained and put there for a trial of faith. Keep in the middle of the path; no harm will come to you.

He went on, trembling with fear of the lions, but paying attention to the Porter's directions. He heard the lions roar, but they did not harm him. He clapped his hands and went on until he stood before the gate where the Porter was. Christian said to the Porter, Sir, what house is this? May I lodge here tonight? The Porter replied, This house was built by the Lord of the hill for the pilgrims' relief and security. The Porter asked where he had been and where he was going.

CHR. I have come from the city of Destruction, and am going to Mount Zion. Because the sun has set, I desire lodging here tonight.

PORT. What is your name?

CHR. My name is Christian, but it use to be Graceless. I am from the race of Japheth, whom God will persuade to dwell in the tents of Shem (Gen. 9:27).

PORT. Why do you come so late? The sun has set.

CHR. I would have been here sooner but, wretched man that I am, I slept in the arbor on the hillside! No, I would have been here much sooner, but while asleep I lost my evidence. When I came to the top of the hill, I looked for it. Not finding it, I was forced with sorrow of heart to go back to where I slept. There I found it. Now I am here.

PORT. I will call one of the virgins of this place. According to the rules of the house, if she likes your talk, she will bring you in to meet the rest of the family. Watchful, the Porter, rang a bell. At the sound, a solemn, beautiful lady, named Discretion, came out and asked why she was called.

The Porter answered, This man is on a journey from the city of Destruction to Mount Zion. He is weary and night has overtaken him. He asked if he might lodge here. I told him that I would call you and that after you talked with him, you would do whatever is good, according to the law of the house.

She asked where he was from and where he was going. He answered her. She asked how he got into the way. He told her. Then she asked what he had seen and met in the way. He told her. Finally, she asked his name. He answered, It is Christian. I have a great desire to stay here tonight because the Lord of the hill built this place for the relief and security of pilgrims. She smiled, but water stood in her eyes. After a little pause she said, I will call two or three more family members. She ran to the door and called Prudence, Piety, and Charity. After a short conversation they invited him in. Many of the family met him at the door. They said, Come in, you blessed of the Lord. The Lord of the hill built this house to entertain pilgrims like you. He bowed his head and followed them. He sat down and they gave him something to drink. They agreed that until supper was ready, some of them would have a discussion with Christian. They appointed Piety, Prudence, and Charity to talk with him.

PIETY. Come, good Christian, since we have been loving enough to receive you into our house tonight, let us, in order to better ourselves, talk with you about all the things that have happened in your pilgrimage.

CHR. Indeed, with good will, I am glad that you are so inclined.

PIETY. What made you a pilgrim?

CHR. I was driven out of my native country by a dreadful sound in my ears. Unavoidable destruction was mine if I stayed.

PIETY. What made you leave your country this way?

CHR. When I was trembling and weeping under the fear of destruction, I did not know where to go. As God would have it, a man named Evangelist directed me to the narrow gate. I could never have found it. He set me in the way that led directly to this house.

PIETY. Did you pass the house of the Interpreter?

CHR. Yes, and there I saw things that I will remember as long as I live. Three things especially. How Christ, despite Satan, maintains his work of grace in the heart. How a man had sinned himself out of the hope of God's mercy. How a man in his dream thought the day of judgment had come.

PIETY. Did he tell you his dream?

CHR. Yes. It was dreadful. It made my heart ache, but I am glad I heard it.

PIETY. Was that all you saw at the house of the Interpreter?

CHR. No, he showed me a stately palace and the people dressed in gold. An adventurous man cut his way through armed men that stood in the door to keep him out. He was asked to come in, and win eternal glory. Those things ravished my heart. I would have stayed at that good man's house a year, but I had farther to go.

PIETY. What else did you see in the way?

CHR. See? I went just a little farther and I saw One, as I thought in my mind, hang bleeding on a tree. I groaned under a heavy burden. The very sight of him made my burden fall off my back. It was strange; I never saw such a thing before. While I stood looking up (for I could not help looking), three Shining Ones came to me. One of them testified that my sins were forgiven, another took my rags and gave me this embroidered coat, and the third put this mark in my forehead and gave me this sealed roll (and with that he pulled it out of his robe).

PIETY. You saw more than this, did you not?

CHR. The things that I have told you about were the best. Yet I saw other things: three men, Simple, Sloth, and Presumption, lying asleep, a little out of the way, with chains on their feet. Do you think I could awake them? I saw Formality and Hypocrisy tumble over the wall, pretending to go to Zion. They were quickly lost; I told them but they would not believe. Above all, I found it hard work to get up this hill and equally difficult to pass the lions' mouths. If it had not been for the good man, the porter that stands at the gate, I might have turned back. But I thank God that I am here and thank you for receiving me.

Then Prudence wanted to ask some questions.

PRU. Do you ever think about the country you came from?

CHR. Yes, with shame and revulsion. If I had been truly mindful of that country, I might have had the opportunity to return. But now I desire a better country, a heavenly one (Heb. 11:15, 16).

PRU. Do you still carry some of the familiar things?

CHR. Yes, but greatly against my will, especially my inner and fleshly thoughts that delighted all my countrymen and me. Now all those things are my grief. I would choose never to think of those things again. But when I would do what is best, that which is worst is with me (Rom. 7:15, 21).

PRU. Do you sometimes feel as if those things were vanquished, while at other times they are your bewilderment?

CHR. Yes, but only seldom. They are golden hours when these things happen.

PRU. Can you remember what makes your annoyances disappear?

CHR. Yes! When I think about what I saw at the cross, that will do it. When I look at my embroidered coat, that will do it. When I read the roll that I carry in my robe, that will do it. When my thoughts grow warm about where I am going, that will do it.

PRU. What makes you want to go to Mount Zion?

CHR. I hope to see Him alive that hung dead on the cross. I hope to get rid of all those things in me that to this day are an annoyance. There, they say, is no death (Isa. 25:8; Rev. 21:4). There I will dwell with the company that I like best. To tell you the truth, I love Him because he lifted my burden. I am weary of my inner sickness. I want to be where I will die no more, and with the company that continually cries, Holy, holy, holy.

Then Charity asked Christian, Do you have a family? Are you a married man?

CHR. I have a wife and four small children.

CHAR. Why did you not bring them?

CHR. Christian wept and said, Oh, how willingly I would have done it! But they were utterly averse to my going on this pilgrimage.

CHAR. You should have talked to them and tried to show them the danger of staying behind.

CHR. I did. I told them that God had shown me the destruction of our city. I seemed to them as one that mocked; they did not believe me (Gen. 19:14).

CHAR. Did you pray that God would bless your counsel to them?

CHR. Yes, with much affection, my wife and poor children are precious to me.

CHAR. Did you tell them about your sorrow and fear of destruction? I suppose that destruction was visible enough to you.

CHR. Yes, over, and over, and over. They could see my fears in my appearance, in my tears, and in my trembling under the apprehension of the judgment that hung over our heads. Yet it was not sufficient to prevail on them to come.

CHAR. What did they say? Why didn't they come?

CHR. Why? My wife was afraid of losing this world. My children were given to the foolish delights of youth. So by one thing and another, they left me to wander alone.

CHAR. Did you, with your empty life, use all methods of persuasion to bring them?

CHR. I cannot commend my life. I am conscious of many failings. I know that a man, by his conversation, argument, or persuasion may soon overthrow what he works to give others for their good. Yet this I can say, I was wary of giving them a reason by any improper action to make them averse to going on a pilgrimage. Yes, for this very thing, they would say I was too precise. I denied myself things (for their sakes) in which they saw no evil. No, I think I may say that if what they saw in me hindered them, it was my great tenderness in sinning against God, or doing any wrong to my neighbor.

CHAR. Indeed, Cain hated his brother because his works were evil, and his brother's works were righteous (1 John 3:12). If your wife and children have been offended by this, they are implacable to good, but you have delivered your soul (Ezek. 3:19).

Now I saw in my dream that they talked until supper was ready. Then they sat down to eat. The table was loaded with good things and wine that was well refined. Their table talk was about the Lord of the hill, what he had done, why he had done it, and why he had built that house. From what they said, I perceived that he had been a great warrior and had fought and destroyed him who had the power of death (Heb. 2:14, 15). But not without great danger to himself; this made me love him all the more.

They said, and Christian agreed, that he did it with a great loss of blood. Yet what put the glory of grace into this was that he did it out of pure love for his country. There were some in the household that had been with him and had spoken to him since he died on the cross. They attested that they heard it from his lips. He is such a lover of poor pilgrims that his equal is not found from east to west. They gave an example of what they affirmed: he stripped himself of his glory that he might do this for the poor. They heard him say that he would not dwell in the mountain of Zion alone. They also said that he had made many pilgrims princes, though by nature they were beggars born on a garbage heap (1 Sam. 2:8; Ps. 113:7).

They talked until late at night. Then, after committing themselves to their Lord for protection, they went to bed. They put Christian in a large upper bedroom with windows that opened toward the sunrise. The name of this room was Peace. Here he slept until daybreak, when he woke and sang,

> Where am I now? Is this the love and care
> Of Jesus, for the men that pilgrims are,
> Thus to provide that I should be forgiven,
> And dwell already the next door to heaven!

They all arose in the morning and after more conversation told Christian that he should not leave until they had shown him the treasures of the place. First they took him into the study where they showed him ancient records. As I remember my dream, they showed him the lineage of the Lord of the hill. He was the Son of the Ancient of days and came by eternal generation. Here also was fully recorded all the acts that he had done and the names of many hundreds that he had taken into his service. And how he had placed them in a habitations that could neither by length of days, nor decay of nature, be dissolved.

They read him worthy acts that some of his servants had done. How they subdued kingdoms, worked righteousness, obtained promises, stopped the mouths of lions, quenched the violence of fire, escaped the edge of the sword, out of weakness were made strong, became valiant in battle, and turned to flight the armies of the aliens (Heb. 11:33,34).

They read another part of the record. It showed how willing their Lord was to receive into his favor anyone, even though in time past they offended him. Here also were several histories of famous things, all of which Christian looked at. Things both ancient and modern, prophecies and predictions that have been accomplished, both to the horror and amazement of enemies and to the comfort and consolation of pilgrims.

The next day they took him into the armory. They showed him all kinds of equipment that their Lord had provided for pilgrims: sword, shield, helmet, breastplate, all-prayer, and shoes that would not wear out. There was enough of this to equip as many men for the service of their Lord as there are stars in the heavens.

They showed him some of the instruments that his servants had done wonderful things with. They showed him Moses' rod, the hammer and nail that Jael slew Sisera with, the pitchers, trumpets, and lamps that Gideon used to put the armies of Midian to route. They showed him the ox-goad that Shamgar used to kill six hundred men. They showed him the jawbone that Samson used to do such mighty feats. They showed him the sling and stone with which David slew Goliath of Gath, and the sword with which their Lord will kill the man of sin in the day that he rises up. They showed him many excellent things, and Christian was delighted. This done, they again went to their rest.

Then I saw in my dream that he got up to leave, but they wanted him to stay another day. They said, If the day is clear, we will show you the Delectable Mountains. These will add to your comfort because they are closer to the desired haven. He agreed to stay. When morning arrived, they had him on the top of the house and told him to look south. There, at a great distance, he saw a pleasant, beautiful, mountainous country with woods, vineyards, fruit, flowers, springs, and fountains. All most pleasant to see (Is. 33:16,17). He asked the name of the country. They said it was Immanuel's land. It is as common, said they, as this hill to all the pilgrims. When you arrive there, you will see the gate of the celestial city and the shepherds that live there will appear.

Now he planned to leave, and they agreed that he should. But first, they said, let us go back to the armory. There they equipped him from head to foot with what was necessary should he be assaulted in the way. Fully equipped, he walked with his friends to the gate. He asked the Porter if he saw any pilgrim pass. The Porter answered, Yes.

CHR. Did you know him?

PORT. I asked his name; he told me it was Faithful.

CHR. I know him. He is my townsman, my close neighbor. He comes from the place where I was born. How far ahead do you think he is?

PORT. By now he is below the hill.

CHR. Good Porter, the Lord be with you. May he add to all your blessings an increase for the kindness you have shown me.

THE FOURTH STAGE

He started to leave. Discretion, Piety, Charity, and Prudence accompanied him down the hill. They reiterated previous conversations. Christian said, It was difficult coming up, but so far as I can see, it is dangerous going down. Yes, said Prudence, it is. It is hard for a man to go down in the valley of Humiliation and not slip. That is why we are accompanying you. He began to cautiously descend, still he slipped once or twice.

Then I saw in my dream that Christian reached the bottom of the hill. His good companions gave him a loaf of bread, a bottle of wine, a cluster of raisins, and he went his way,

> While Christian is among his godly friends,
> Their golden mouths make him sufficient mends
> For all his grief; and when they let him go,
> He's clad with northern steel from top to toe.

Christian was hard pressed in this valley of Humiliation. He had gone only a short distance before he saw an abominable fiend, named Apollyon, crossing the field to meet him. Christian began to be afraid and wondered if he should go back, or stand his ground. He had no armor for his back, so if he turned it would give Apollyon an advantage to pierce him with darts. He resolved to stand his ground. He thought, if I had no more in my eye than to save my life, this is the best way to stand.

He continued on and Apollyon met him. The monster was hideous, covered with scales like a fish, wings like a dragon, feet like a bear, and from his belly came fire and smoke. His mouth was like the mouth of a lion. He looked at Christian with disdain and began to question him.

APOL. Where are you coming from? Where are you going?

CHR. I came from the city of Destruction, the place of all evil. I am going to the city of Zion.

APOL. I think you are one of my subjects because that country is mine. I am the prince and god of it. Why have you run from your king? Were it not that you could give me more service, I would hit you with a blow that would knock you to the ground.

CHR. I was born in your dominion, your service was hard, and your wages not enough to live on. The wages of sin is death (Rom. 6:23). Therefore, when I became of age, just as other considerate people have done, I tried to improve myself.

APOL. No prince will lightly lose his subjects. Nor will I lose you. You complain of your service and wages, be content to go back. Whatever our country can afford, I promise to give you.

CHR. I have given myself to another, to the King of princes. How can I, in all fairness, go back with you?

APOL. You are like the proverb, "changed bad for worse." It is common for those that profess to be his servants to give him the slip and return to me. If you do the same, all will be well.

CHR. I have given him my faith and sworn my allegiance to him. How can I go back and not be hanged as a traitor?

APOL. You did the same to me. Yet I am willing to forget if you go back.

CHR. I promised you before I became of age. Besides, the Prince, under whose banner I now stand, is able to forgive me. Yes, and pardon what I did as I complied with you. O destroying Apollyon, to tell you the truth, I like his service, his wages, his servants, his government, his company, and his country. It is better than yours; stop trying to persuade me. I am his servant. I will follow him.

APOL. Think again, before your blood gets hot. What are you likely to meet in the way that you are going? You know that for the most part his servants come to an unhealthy end because they are transgressors against me and my ways. Many of them have been put to shameful deaths! You count his service better than mine. He never came from where he is to save any of his servants from their enemies. As for me, how many times, as the world well knows, have I delivered by power or fraud those that faithfully serve me. And so I will deliver you.

CHR. His not immediately delivering them is to test their love, to see if they will cling to him to the end. As for the unhealthy end you say they come to, that is most glorious by their account. They do not expect present deliverance. They stay for their glory, and they will have it when their Prince comes in his glory and in the glory of the angels.

APOL. You have already been unfaithful in his service. How do you expect to be paid by him?

CHR. Where, O Apollyon, have I been unfaithful to him?

APOL. You fainted when you started. You almost choked in the swamp of Despond. You did the wrong things to get rid of your burden; you should have stayed until your Prince had taken it off. You sinfully slept and lost your most precious things. You were almost persuaded to go back at the sight of the lions. When you talk about your journey, what you have seen and heard, you want glory in everything that you say or do.

CHR. All this, and much more, is true. But the Prince I serve and honor is merciful and ready to forgive. Infirmities controlled me in your country. I groaned under them. I am sorry for them, and I have obtained a pardon from my Prince.

APOL. Apollyon broke into a disturbing rage. I am an enemy of this Prince. I hate his person, his laws, and his people. I am here on purpose to oppose you.

CHR. Apollyon, beware, I am in the King's highway, the way of holiness. Consider what you are saying.

APOL. Apollyon straddled the entire width of the way. He said, I have no fear in this matter. Prepare to die. I swear by my infernal den, you will go no further. Here I will spill your soul. He threw a flaming dart at his breast, but Christian had a shield in his hand that caught the flaming dart.

Christian knew it was time to move. Apollyon came at him fast, throwing darts as thick as hail. It was all that Christian could do to avoid them. Apollyon wounded him in the head, hand, and foot. This forced Christian back. Apollyon quickly followed. Christian took courage and resisted as manfully as he could. This terrible combat lasted more than half a day. Christian was almost exhausted. He was growing weaker and weaker from his wounds.

Apollyon, seeing his opportunity, closed in. He wrestled Christian to the ground with a dreadful fall. Christian's sword flew out of his hand. Apollyon said, I have you now, and almost pressed him to death. Christian began to despair of life. But, as God would have it, while Apollyon was readying his last blow to kill this good man, Christian nimbly reached out and grabbed his sword. He said, Do not rejoice over me, my enemy, when I fall I will rise (Mic. 7:8). He gave Apollyon a deadly thrust and went at him again, saying, Yet in all these things we are more than conquerors through Him who loved us (Rom. 8:37). Apollyon spread his dragon wings and flew away. Christian never saw him again (James 4:7).

No one could imagine this combat, unless they had seen and heard it, as I did. What yelling and hideous roaring Apollyon made during the fight. He spoke like a dragon. On the other side, what sighs and groans burst from Christian's heart. He never gave so much as one pleasant look, until he had wounded Apollyon with his two-edged sword. Then he smiled and looked up! Still it was a dreadful sight.

When the battle was over, Christian said, I will give thanks here to him who has delivered me from the lion's mouth, to him who has helped me against Apollyon. And so he did, saying,

> Great Beelzebub, the captain of this fiend,
> Designed my ruin; therefore to this end
> He sent him harnessed out; and he, with rage
> That hellish was, did fiercely me engage:
> But blessed Michael helped me, and I,
> By dint of sword, did quickly make him fly:
> Therefore to Him let me give lasting praise,
> And thank and bless his holy name always.

A hand came to him and gave him some leaves from the tree of life. Christian took the leaves and applied them to his wounds. He was immediately healed. He then sat down to eat bread and drink from the bottle that had been given to him. Refreshed, he continued the journey with his sword drawn. He said, I do not know but some other enemy may be at hand. He had no further encounter with Apollyon.

The end of this valley turned into the Valley of the Shadow of Death. Christian had to go through it, for the way to the Celestial City lay via its center. This valley was isolated. The prophet Jeremiah described it. "A wilderness, a land of deserts and pits, a land of drought and the shadow of death, a land that no one [but a Christian] crossed, and where no one dwelt" (Jer. 2:6).

Here, as you will see, Christian was worse off than in his fight with Apollyon.

I saw in my dream that when Christian reached the borders of the Shadow of Death, two men met him. They were the children of them that gave a bad report of the good land (Num. 13:32). They told him to hurry back. Christian spoke,

CHR. Where are you going?

MEN. Back, back. We would have you do the same if life or peace is valued by you.

CHR. Why, what's the matter?

MEN. Matter! We were going the same way as you. We went as far as we dared. We were almost past the point of no return. Had we gone a little farther, we would not be able to bring back the news to you.

CHR. What did you see?

MEN. We were almost in the Valley of the Shadow of Death. We looked, by chance, and saw the danger before we reached it (Ps. 44:19; 107:19).

CHR. What did you see?

MEN. The valley is as dark as pitch. We saw monsters, half men and half goats, and dragons from the pit. We heard continuous howling and yelling, like people in unutterable misery bound in affliction and chains. Over that valley hangs the discouraging clouds of confusion. Death spread his wings over it. In a word, it is totally dreadful and completely without order (Job 3:5; 10:22).

CHR. From what you have said, this is my way to the desired haven (Ps. 44:18, 19; Jer. 2:6).

MEN. It can be your way, but we will not choose it for ours.

They separated. Christian went on with a drawn sword, concerned that he might be assaulted.

I saw in my dream that as far as this valley reached there was a deep ditch on the right where the blind has led the blind in all ages, and both miserably perished. On the left was a dangerous quagmire where even if a good man falls, he finds no bottom for his feet to stand on. King David fell in that mire and would have suffocated, had not He that is able lifted him out (Ps. 69:14).

The pathway was exceeding narrow. Good Christian had to be most cautious for it was dark. He had to avoid the ditch on his right and the mire on his left. When he tried to avoid the mire he had to be most careful for he could readily fall into the ditch. I heard him sigh bitterly. Beside the dangers mentioned above, the pathway was so dark that when he lifted his foot to go forward, he did not know where, or on what, he would next set it.

About in the middle of this valley was the mouth of hell. It stood close to the wayside. Now, thought Christian, what will I do? The flame, smoke, sparks, and hideous noises (things that Christian's sword could not attack), came out in such abundance that he was forced to put his sword away and take another weapon, All-prayer (Eph. 6:18). He cried, O Lord, I implore You, deliver my soul (Ps. 116:4). He continued on with the flames reaching toward him. He heard mournful voices and rushing to and fro. He sometimes thought he would be torn to pieces, or pounded down like mire in the streets. For several miles he saw this frightful sight and heard these dreadful noises. He thought he heard a company of fiends coming to meet him. He began to deliberate. Sometimes he had half a thought to go back. Then he thought he might be halfway through the valley. He also remembered how he had already conquered many dangers. The hazard of going back might be much greater than going forward; he resolved to go on. Yet the fiends seemed to be coming closer and closer. When they were almost on him, he cried with a fervent voice, I will walk in the strength of the Lord God. The fiends retreated and came no farther.

One thing I must say, poor Christian was so confused that he did not know his voice. As he reached the mouth of the burning pit, one of the wicked ones got behind him and softly whispered disturbing blasphemies. Christian thought they were from his own mind. Just to think that he would blaspheme Him that he loved disturbed Christian more than anything he had met. Yet if he could help it, he would not have done it. He lacked the discretion to stop his ears, or to know where these blasphemies came from.

Christian traveled in this distressed condition for a considerable time. He thought he heard the voice of a man ahead of him, Though I walk through the Valley of the Shadow of Death, I will fear no evil, for You are with me (Ps. 23:4).

Then he was glad for these reasons:

First, some who feared God were in this valley with him.

Second, God was with them even though it was dark and dismal. And why not, if He goes by me, I do not see Him; if He moves past, I do not perceive Him (Job 9:11).

Third, he hoped (if he could overtake them) to have company.

He moved on calling to him that was ahead, but there was no answer. He thought he was alone. Then the day broke and Christian said, "He turns the shadow of death into the morning" (Amos 5:8).

Now that morning had arrived he looked back, not to return but to see by the light of day the dangers he had passed through in the dark. He clearly saw the ditch on one side, the quagmire on the other side, and the narrow way between them. He also saw frightful apparitions, monsters, and dragons of the pit from a distance. After daybreak they would not come close. Yet they were uncovered as it is written, "He uncovers deep things out of darkness, and brings the shadow of death to light" (Job 12:22).

Now Christian was greatly affected by his deliverance from the dangers of his solitary way. Though he feared the danger, he saw it more clearly because the light made it conspicuous. About this time the sun was rising. This was another mercy; though the first part of the Valley of the Shadow of Death was dangerous, this second part was, if possible, far more so. The place where he now stood, clear to the end of the valley, was full of snares, traps, engines of torture, nets, pits, pitfalls, deep holes, and inclines. If it was still dark, as when he came the first part of the way, and if he had a thousand souls they would have been lost. But, as I said, the sun was rising. Christian uttered, "His lamp shone upon my head, and by His light I walked through darkness" (Job 29:3).

In this light he reached the end of the valley. I saw in my dream that at the end of the valley lay blood, bones, ashes, and mangled bodies of men, even pilgrims that had passed this way. While I was thinking about this, I saw a cave where two giants, Pope and Pagan, lived in times passed. It was through their power and tyranny that the men, whose bones, blood, and ashes lay there, were cruelly put to death. Christian passed without much danger. I have since learned that Pagan had been dead a long time. As for the other, though he is alive, he is old. He has grown so crazy and stiff in his joints that he can do little more than sit at the cave's mouth, grinning at pilgrims as they pass, and biting his nails because he cannot attack them.

When Christian saw the old man sitting at the mouth of the cave, he did not know what to think. Especially when the old man said, You will never mend, until you are burned. He held his peace, set a good face, and passed unharmed. Then Christian sang,

> O world of wonders (I can say no less),
> That I should be preserved in that distress
> That I have met with here! O blessed be
> That hand that from it has delivered me!
> Dangers in darkness, devils, hell, and sin,
> Did surround me, while I this vale was in;
> Yes, snares, and pits, and traps, and nets did lie
> My path about, that worthless, silly I
> Might have been caught, entangled, and cast down;
> But since I live, let Jesus wear the crown.

THE FIFTH STAGE

Now, as Christian went on his way, he came to a little ascent that had been placed there so the pilgrims could see what was ahead. Looking forward Christian saw Faithful. He hollered, Ho, ho, so-ho, wait, I will be your companion. Faithful looked back. Christian yelled again, Wait, wait, until I catch you. Faithful answered, No, I run for my life. The avenger of blood is behind me.

Christian was somewhat moved by this comment. Using all his strength, he quickly caught Faithful and then passed him. Now, the last was first. Christian's pride smiled because he was ahead of his brother. Not paying attention, he unexpectedly stumbled, fell, and could not get up until Faithful came to help.

Then I saw in my dream that they went lovingly on together. They had sweet conversations about all the things that happened to them in their pilgrimage. Christian began,

CHR. Faithful, my honored and well-beloved brother, I am glad that I have overtaken you and that God has made our spirits so that we can walk as companions in this pleasant path.

FAITH. I had hoped, my dear friend, to have your company from our town, but you got ahead of me. Thus, I was forced to come much of the way alone.

CHR. How long did you stay in the city of Destruction before you followed me?

FAITH. Until I could stay no longer. There was great talk after you left that our city would shortly be burned to the ground with fire from heaven.

CHR. Did your neighbors talk that way?

FAITH. Yes, for a while it was in everyone's mouth.

CHR. Are you the only one who left to escape the danger?

FAITH. Though there was much talk, I do not think they firmly believed it. In the heat of the discussion, I heard some laughingly speak of you and your desperate journey; they called it your pilgrimage. I believe, and still do, that our city will end with fire and brimstone from above. So I escaped.

CHR. Did you hear anything about neighbor Pliable?

FAITH. Yes, Christian, I heard that he followed you until he came to the swamp of Despond, where, as some say, he fell in. The only reason we know is that he was completely covered with dirt from the swamp.

CHR. What did the neighbors say to him?

FAITH. Since going back, he has been greatly ridiculed by all sorts of people. Some mock and despise him, and no one will give him any work. He is seven times worse than if he had never left the city.

CHR. Why should they be against him since they despise the way?

FAITH. Oh, they say, hang him. He is a turncoat. He was not true to his profession! God has stirred up His enemies to hiss at him, and make him a proverb, because he left the way (Jer. 29:18, 19).

CHR. Did you talk with him before you left?

FAITH. I met him once in the street. He crossed to the other side, ashamed of what he had done, I did not speak to him.

CHR. Well, when I first started, I had hopes for that man. Now I fear he will perish in the overthrow of the city. What has happened to him is according to the true proverb, A dog returns to his own vomit, and a sow having washed to her wallowing in the mire (2 Pet. 2:22).

FAITH. These are my fears too, but who can hinder what is to be?

CHR. Well, neighbor Faithful, let us forget him and talk about things that more immediately concern us. What have you met with? I know you have met with some things, or else it will make me wonder.

FAITH. I escaped the swamp that you fell in and reached the gate without danger. Only I met Wanton, she would like to have done me mischief.

CHR. It was well you escaped her net. She hard pressed Joseph, but he escaped as you did. Still it almost cost him his life (Gen. 39:11–13). What did she do to you?

FAITH. You know that she sometimes has a flattering tongue. She came hard to turn me aside, promised all kinds of contentment.

CHR. She did not promise the contentment of a good conscience.

FAITH. You know what I mean, flesh and carnal contentment.

CHR. Thank God you escaped. The mouth of an immoral woman is a deep pit; he who is abhorred by the Lord will fall there (Prov. 22:14).

FAITH. I do not know if I totally escaped her.

CHR. Why, I trust you did not give in to her desires?

FAITH. No, not to defile myself, I remembered an old writing that said, "Her steps lay hold on Hell" (Prov. 5:5). So I shut my eyes, not to be charmed with her looks (Job 31:1). Then she turned her back, and I went on my way.

CHR. Did you meet any other assailants?

FAITH. When I came to the foot of the hill called Difficulty, I met an old man. He asked me who I was and where I was going. I told him I was a pilgrim, going to the Celestial City. Then he said, You look like an honest fellow. Would you be content to live with me if I paid you? I asked his name and where he lived. He said his name was Adam the First and that he lived in the town of Deceit (Eph. 4:22). I asked him what his work was and what he would pay. He said that his work was many delights, and for wages, I would be his heir. I further asked what was in his house and what other servants he had. He told me that his house was maintained with all the luxuries of the world and that his servants were his children. I asked how many children he had. He said three daughters, the Lust of the Flesh, the Lust of the Eyes, and the Pride of Life (1 John 2:16), and that I could marry them if I wanted to. Then I asked how long he wanted me to live with him. He answered, as long as he lived.

CHR. What conclusion did you and the old man reach?

FAITH. I found myself inclined to go with him. I thought he was honest. But when I looked at his forehead, I saw written, "Put off the old man with his deeds."

CHR. Then what happened?

FAITH. This thought came burning into my mind. Regardless of what he said, or how flattering he was, when he got me to his house I would be sold as a slave. So I ordered him to stop talking. I would not go close to the door of his house. Then he berated me; said that he would send someone after me to make the way bitter to my soul. I turned to leave, he grabbed me and gave me a deadly pinch. I thought he had taken a piece out of me. I cried, "O wretched man" (Rom. 7:24) and went on my way up the hill.

When I was about halfway up, I looked behind and someone was chasing me, swift as the wind. He overtook me about the place where the arbor is.

CHR. It was there that I sat down to rest, fell asleep, and lost this roll.

FAITH. Good brother, listen to me, as soon as he overtook me, it was a word and a blow. He knocked me down in an attempt to kill me. When I came to, I asked him why he treated me like this. He said it was because I was inclined to go with Adam the First. Then he struck another deadly blow to my chest knocking me backwards. I lay at his feet as dead. When I regained consciousness, I cried to him for mercy. He said, I do not know how to show mercy and he knocked me down again. He would have killed me, but one came by and ordered him to stop.

CHR. Who ordered him to stop?

FAITH. I did not know at first. But as he passed by, I noticed the holes in his hands and in his side. I concluded that he was our Lord. So I went up the hill.

CHR. The man that attacked you was Moses. He spares none. He does not know how to show mercy to transgressors of the law.

FAITH. I know that well. It was not the first time we met. He came to me when I lived securely at home and said that he would burn my house over my head if I stayed.

CHR. Did you see the house on the top of the hill?

FAITH. Yes, and the lions before I reached it. I think the lions were asleep. It was about noon and because so much of the day was left, I passed the Porter and came down the hill.

CHR. He said that he saw you go by. I wish you had stopped at the house. They would have showed you so many wonders that you would not have forgotten them to the day you died. Tell me, did you meet anyone in the Valley of Humility?

FAITH. Yes, I met Discontent. He would willingly have persuaded me to go back with him. His reason was that the valley was without honor. He told me that to go there would offend my friends, Pride, Arrogance, Self-Conceit, Worldly Glory, and others. They would be greatly insulted if I made a fool of myself by wading through this valley.

CHR. How did you answer him?

FAITH. I told him that although they might claim a relationship to me (for indeed they were my relations according to the flesh), since I had become a pilgrim they had disowned me and I had rejected them. Thus, they were no more to me than if they had never been relatives. I also told him that he had misrepresented this valley, for humility is before honor, and a haughty spirit before a fall. I would rather go through this valley for the honor that was accounted by the wisest, than choose what he thought was most worthy of our affections.

CHR. Did you meet anything else in that valley?

FAITH. Yes, I met Shame. Of all the men I met on my pilgrimage, he has the wrong name. The others say no after a little argument, but bold-faced Shame would never do that.

CHR. Why, what did he say to you?

FAITH. Why? What? He objected to religion; said it was a pitiful, low, sneaking business for a man to mind religion. He said that a tender conscience was an unmanly thing. If a man watched over his words and ways, so as to be tied from the liberty that the brave spirits of the times are accustomed to, this would make him the ridicule of the times. He said that only a few of the mighty, rich, or wise, agreed with my position. That none of them, before they were persuaded to be fools, would voluntary risk the loss of all, for who knows what (1 Cor. 1:26; 3:18; Phil. 3:7–9; John 7:48).

He further claimed that the majority of the pilgrims were crude, ignorant, and lacked understanding in all natural science. Yes, he said a great deal more. It was a shame to sit complaining and grieving under a sermon and come home sighing and groaning. It was a shame to ask my neighbor forgiveness for small things, or to make restitution when I have wrongfully taken from any. He claimed that religion made a man grow strange to the great, because of a few vices that he called by their finer names. This made a pilgrim acknowledge and respect the ignorant because of the same religious fraternity: And is not this, said he, a shame?

CHR. What did you say to him?

FAITH. At first, I did not know what to say. The way he put it, the blood flushed in my face. Finally, I realized that what is highly valued among men is an abomination in the sight of God (Luke 16:15). Shame tells me what men are; it tells me nothing about God or the word of God. At the day of doom we will not be doomed to death or life according to the spirits of this world, but according to the wisdom and law of the Highest. Therefore, what God says is best. It is indeed best, even if all the men in the world are against it. Seeing that God prefers his religion; seeing God prefers a tender conscience; seeing the wise make themselves fools for the kingdom of heaven; seeing the poor man who loves Christ is richer than the greatest man in the world that hates him, Shame departed.

Shame, you are an enemy to my salvation. Will I entertain you instead of my sovereign Lord? How will I look him in the face at his coming? (Mark 8:38). If I am ashamed of his ways and servants now, how can I expect the blessing? Shame was a bold villain. I could scarcely get rid of him. He continued to haunt me and whisper in my ear some of the infirmities that accompany religion. I told him that it was useless to press this business any farther. The things he disdained, I saw the most glory in. Finally, I shook off and got past this unrelenting one. Then I began to sing,

> The trials that those men do meet withal,
> That are obedient to the heavenly call,
> Are manifold, and suited to the flesh,
> And come, and come, and come again afresh;
> That now, or some time else, we by them may
> Be taken, overcome, and cast away.
> O let the pilgrims, let the pilgrims then,
> Be vigilant, and quit themselves like men.

CHR. I am glad, my brother, that you bravely withstood this villain. As you say, he has the wrong name. He is so bold that he follows us in the streets and tries to put us to shame in front of everyone. He tries to make us ashamed of what is good. If he was not so audacious, he would never attempt it. Resist him, despite all his bravadoes he promotes the fool and nothing else. "The wise shall inherit glory," said Solomon, "but shame shall be the legacy of fools" (Prov. 3:35).

FAITH. I think we must pray for help against Shame, that would make us valiant for truth on the earth.

CHR. What you say is true. Did you meet anyone else in that valley?

FAITH. No, no. I had sunshine the rest of the way, even through the Valley of the Shadow of Death.

CHR. It was different with me. I had a hard time almost as soon as

I entered that valley, a dreadful combat with that foul fiend Apollyon. I thought he was going to kill me, especially when he pinned me under him. He almost crushed me to pieces. When he threw me down the sword flew out of my hand. He said he had me. I cried to God and he heard and delivered me from all my troubles. When I entered the Valley of the Shadow of Death, there was no light almost half way through it. I thought I would be killed. Finally the day broke, the sun rose, and I came the rest of the way with ease and quiet.

I saw in my dream that Faithful looked to one side and saw a man named Talkative, walking beside them. There was room enough here for all of them to walk. Talkative was a tall man, better looking at a distance than up close. Faithful spoke to him.

FAITH. Friend, are you going to the heavenly country?

TALK. I am going to the same place.

FAITH. Great. I hope we will have your good company?

TALK. With goodwill I will be your companion.

FAITH. Come on, let us go together and spend our time discussing things that are profitable.

TALK. To talk of things that are good, with you or with anyone else, is most acceptable. I am glad that I have met those who are inclined to good. To tell you the truth, most travelers spend their time talking of things that have no profit. This troubles me.

FAITH. Indeed, that is a thing to regret. For what is as worthy of the tongue and mouth as the things of the God of heaven?

TALK. I like you wonderful well. Your saying is full of conviction. Let me add, What thing is so pleasant, and what is so profitable, as to talk about the things of God? If a man has any delight in things that are wonderful, it is pleasant. For example, if a man delights to talk of the history, or the mystery of things; or if a man loves to talk of miracles, wonders, or signs, where can he find things recorded so delightful, and penned so sweetly, as in the holy Scripture?

FAITH. That is true. Our chief objective should be to profit from these things in our conversation.

TALK. That's what I said, to talk about these things is profitable.

We gain knowledge of many things, such as the vanity of earthly things and the benefit of things above. We learn the necessity of the new birth, the insufficiency of our works, the need of Christ's righteousness, etc. Besides, a man may learn what it is to repent, to believe, to pray, and to suffer. Also, a man may learn, for his own comfort, the great promises and consolations of the Gospel. Further, a man may learn to refute false doctrines, vindicate the truth, and instruct the uninformed.

FAITH. All this is true and I am glad to hear it.

TALK. This is the reason so few understand the need of faith and the need of a work of grace in their soul to inherit eternal life. They live ignorantly in the works of the law, and no one can obtain the kingdom of heaven through the law.

FAITH. Excuse me, heavenly knowledge of these is the gift of God. No one attains them by human effort or by talking about them.

TALK. I know this, a man can receive nothing unless it is given from heaven. It is grace, not works. I could give you a hundred scriptures to confirm this.

FAITH. Well, what is the one thing that we will talk about?

TALK. Whatever you want. I will talk of things heavenly, earthly, moral, evangelical, sacred, profane, past, future, foreign, domestic, essential, or circumstantial. Provided it is done for our profit.

FAITH. Now Faithful began to wonder, going to Christian (for he was walking by himself), he said softly, What a brave companion we have! This man will make an excellent pilgrim.

CHR. Christian modestly smiled, This man, with whom you are so taken, will deceive with his tongue.

FAITH. Do you know him?

CHR. Know him? Yes, better than he knows himself.

FAITH. What is he?

CHR. His name is Talkative. He lives in our town. The only reason you do not know him is that our town is so big.

FAITH. Whose son is he? What is his address?

CHR. He is the son of Say-well. He lives in Prating-Row. He is known to all that are acquainted with him by the name of Talkative of Prating-Row. Despite his fine tongue, he is a sorry fellow.

FAITH. He seems to be a handsome man.

CHR. Only to those who do not know him well. He is at his best away from home. Close to home he is ugly. Your calling him handsome, reminds me of a painter whose pictures show best at a distance. Close up they are not pleasing.

FAITH. I think you jest because you smiled.

CHR. God forbid that I should jest (though I smiled), or that I should falsely accuse anyone. I will give you further information. This man fits in any company and any conversation. As he talks with you, so will he talk when he is at the ale-bench. The more drinks he has, the more things he has in his mouth. Religion has no place in his heart, or house, or conversation. Everything is in his tongue. His religion is to make a noise.

FAITH. Really? Then I am greatly deceived by this man.

CHR. Deceived! You can be sure of it. Remember the proverb, "They say, and do not do"; for the kingdom of God is not in word but in power (Matt. 23:3; 1 Cor. 4:20). He talks of prayer, repentance, faith, and the new birth. But he only knows how to talk about them. I have been with his family and have observed him at home and away. I know what I say about him is true. His house is as empty of religion as the white of an egg is of flavor. There is no prayer or sign of repentance from sin. An animal, in his own way, serves God far better.

He is the stain, reproach, and shame of religion to all that know him (Rom. 2:24, 25). There is hardly a good word for him in the end of the town where he lives. The common people that know him say, "A saint abroad, and a devil at home." His poor family finds it this way. He is such a wretch! So unreasonable with his servants that they do not know how to speak to him. Men that have dealings with him say, It is better to deal with a Turk! Talkative (if it is possible) will defraud, deceive, and cheat. He raises his sons to follow in his steps. If he finds in any of them foolish cowards (for this is what he calls the first appearance of a tender conscience), he calls them fools and blockheads. He will not employ them in much, or speak well of them before others. I am of the opinion that he has, by his wicked life, caused many to stumble and fall. If God does not prevent it, he will be the ruin of many more.

FAITH. Well, my brother, I believe you. Not just because you say you know him, but because, like a Christian, you give an honest report. I do not think you speak these things from ill-will, but because it is so.

CHR. If I did not know him so well, I might have thought as you did. If I had received this report from the enemies of religion, I would have thought it slander that often falls from bad men's mouths on good men's names and professions. I have my own knowledge of all these things, yes, and a great many more equally as bad. I can prove him guilty. Good men are ashamed of him. They can neither call him brother or friend. If they know him, his very name makes them blush.

FAITH. I see that saying and doing are two different things. Hereafter, I will better observe this distinction.

CHR. They are two things as diverse as the soul and the body. The body without the soul is a dead carcass. The soul of religion is the practical part. "Pure and undefiled religion before God and the Father is this: to visit orphans and widows in their trouble, and to keep oneself unspotted from the world" (James 1:27; see also verses 22–26). Talkative is not aware of this. He thinks that hearing and saying will make a good Christian. He deceives his soul. Hearing is just sowing the seed; talking is not sufficient proof that fruit is in the heart and life.

Remember, at the day of doom, men will be judged according to their fruits (Matt. 13:23). It will not be said, Did you believe? But were you doers, or only talkers? They will be judged accordingly. The end of the world is compared to our harvest (Matt. 13:30), and men at harvest think only of the fruit. Not that anything can be accepted that is not of faith. I say this to show you how insignificant his profession will be on that day.

FAITH. This reminds me of Moses when he described the animals that may be eaten (Lev. 11; Deut. 14): Whatever divides the hoof, having cloven hooves and chewing the cud, you may eat. These you shall not eat among those that chew the cud or those that have cloven hooves.

The hare because it chews the cud but does not have cloven hooves is unclean. This truly resembles Talkative. He chews the cud, he seeks knowledge, he chews on the word, but he does not divide the hoof. He does not leave the way of sinners. Like the hare, he retains the foot of the dog or bear. Therefore he is unclean.

CHR. You have spoken the true sense of these gospel texts. Let me add one more. Paul calls some men, including those who are great talkers, sounding brass and clanging cymbals (1 Cor. 13:1, 3). He expounds them in another place as things without life (1 Cor. 14:7). Things without life are without the true faith and the grace of the gospel. Consequently, these things will never be placed in the kingdom of heaven among the children of life, even if they sound like they were spoken by an angel.

FAITH. I was not so fond of his company at first, but now I am sick of it. What can we do to get rid of him?

CHR. Take my advice and do as I tell you. He will soon be sick of your company, unless God touches him and turns his heart.

FAITH. What do you want me to do?

CHR. Get into a serious discussion about the power of religion. Ask him plainly (when he has agreed with you, for he will), if this thing is set up in his heart, house, or conversation.

Faithful stepped forward and said to Talkative, How is it now?

TALK. Thank you, well. I thought we would have had talked a great deal by this time.

FAITH. If you wish, we will now. Since you left it to me to state the question, here it is. How is the saving grace of God discovered when it is in the heart of man?

TALK. I gather that our talk will be about the power of things. It is a good question and I am willing to give you a brief answer. First, when the grace of God is in the heart, it causes a great outcry against sin. Second—

FAITH. No, hold it. Let's consider only one at a time. I think you should rather say, God's grace shows itself by making the soul abhor its sin.

TALK. Why? What difference is there between an outcry against sin, and abhorring sin?

FAITH. A great deal! A man may cry against sin, but can only abhor it by the virtue of a godly antipathy against it. I have heard many cry against sin from the pulpit but keep it in their heart, house, and conversation (Gen. 39:15). Joseph's mistress cried out with a loud voice as if she had been holy, but she would willingly have committed uncleanness with him. Some cry against sin, just as a mother cries against her child when she calls it naughty, and then hugs and kisses it.

TALK. I perceive that you are trying to catch me in a lie.

FAITH. No, not I, I only want to set things right. What is the second thing that you would prove discovers a work of grace in the heart?

TALK. Great knowledge of gospel mysteries.

FAITH. This sign should have been first. But first or last it is false. Knowledge, great knowledge, may be obtained in the mysteries of the Gospel, but still not work grace in the soul. Yes, though I understand all knowledge, but have not love, I am nothing, and, consequently, not a child of God (1 Cor. 13:2). When Christ said, "Do you know all these things?" and the disciples answered, Yes, he added, "Blessed are you if you do them." He does not give a blessing in knowing them, but in doing them. "He that knows his Master's will, and does not do it." A man may have the knowledge of an angel, and not be a Christian. Thus, your sign is not true.

Knowledge is a thing that pleases talkers and boasters. Doing it pleases God. Not that the heart can be good without knowledge, for without knowledge the heart is nothing. There are two kinds of knowledge: knowledge that resists the speculation of things, and knowledge that is accompanied with the grace of faith and love. The second makes us do God's will from the heart. The first serves the talker, but without the second the true Christian is not content. "Give me understanding, and I shall keep Your law; indeed, I shall observe it with my whole heart" (Ps. 119:34).

TALK. You are trying to catch me in a lie! This is not for edification.

FAITH. Well, if you please, give me another sign of how this work of grace is discovered.

TALK. Not I. We will not agree.

FAITH. Well, if you will not, will you allow me?

TALK. Use your liberty.

FAITH. A work of grace in the soul discovers itself, either to him that has it, or to those who watch.

To him who has it, there is a conviction of sin, especially the defilement of his nature. To him who has the sin of unbelief, he will be damned unless he finds mercy at God's hand through faith in Jesus Christ. This sight and sense of things work in him sorrow and shame for sin (Ps. 38:18; Jer. 31:19; John 16:8; Rom. 7:24; Mark 16:16; Gal. 2:16; Rev. 1:6). He finds, revealed in him the Savior of the world and the absolute necessity of being with him for life. Then he hungers and thirsts after him; to this hungering and thirsting the promise is made.

Now, according to the strength or weakness of his faith in his Savior, is his joy and peace, is his love of holiness, is his desire to know him more, and to serve him in this world. Though it reveals itself to him, he is seldom able to conclude that this is a work of grace because corruption and abused reasoning makes his mind misjudge the matter. Thus, in him that hates this work there is required sound judgment before he can conclude that this is a work of grace (John 16:9; Gal. 2:15, 16; Acts 4:12; Matt. 5:6; Rev. 21:6).

To others it is discovered:

1. By an experimental confession of his faith in Christ. 2. By a life answerable to that confession. A life of holiness, heart-holiness, family-holiness (if he has a family), and conversation-holiness in the world teaches him to abhor both his sin and himself for that sin. It teaches him to suppress sin in his family and to promote holiness in the world. Not just by talking, like a hypocrite or a talkative person, but by a practical subjection in faith and love to the power of the word (Job 42:5, 6; Ps. 50:23; Ezek. 20:43; Matt. 5:8; John 14:15; Rom. 10:10; Ezek. 36:25; Phil. 1:27; 3:17–20). Now, sir, as to this brief description of the work

of grace and its discovery, if you have reason to object, object. If not, then allow me to propound a second question to you.

TALK. No, my part is not to object now, but to listen. Let me have your second question.

FAITH. Do you experience the first part of this description? Does your life and conversation testify to it? Or is your religion in word or tongue rather than deed and truth? Please, if you are inclined to answer, say no more than God above will say Amen to, and only what your conscience can justify. He that commends himself is not approved, but only he whom the Lord commends. Besides, to say I am thus and thus, when my conversation and all my neighbors tell me I lie, is great wickedness.

TALK. Talkative began to blush, but recovering his composure he replied, You come now to experience, to conscience, and to God. You appeal to him for justification of what is spoken. This kind of conversation I did not expect, nor am I willing to answer these questions. I do not count myself bound to answer them, unless you consider yourself one who instructs by asking questions. Even if you do, I refuse to make you my judge. Tell me, why do you ask such questions?

FAITH. I saw that you wanted to talk, and I did not know that you had anything else but an opinion. Besides, to tell you all the truth, I have heard that you are a man whose religion lies in talk and that your conversation gives your mouth-profession the lie. They say you are a spot among Christians and your religion fares worse. Because of your ungodly conversation, some have already stumbled in your wicked ways and more are in danger of being destroyed. Your religion is an ale house: covetousness, uncleanness, swearing, lying, and vain company-keeping, etc. The proverb about a harlot is true of you, "She is a shame to all women", and you are a shame to all believers.

TALK. Since you are so ready to take up reports and judge me so rashly, I must conclude you are a complaining or a depressed man, not fit to talk with. Adieu.

Christian came up to his brother and said, I told you what would happen. Your words and his lusts could not agree. He would rather leave your company than reform his life. He is gone, and as I said, let him go. The loss is his. He has saved us the trouble of leaving him. He would have been a blot on our company. Besides, the apostle says, "From such withdraw."

FAITH. I am glad we had this talk with him. He may think of it again. I have dealt honestly with him and am clear of his blood if he perishes.

CHR. You did well to talk honestly. There is little faithful dealing with men today. This makes religion smell in the nostrils of many. These talking fools, whose religion is only in word, are perverted and useless in their conversation. When they are admitted into Christian fellowship, they puzzle the world, blemish Christianity, and grieve the sincere. I wish all men would deal with them as you have. Then they would either conform, or the company of saints would be too hot for them. Faithful said,

> How Talkative at first lifts up his plumes!
> How bravely did he speak! How he presumes
> To drive down all before him! But so soon
> As Faithful talks of heart-work, like the moon
> That's past the full, into the wane he goes;
> And so will all but he that heart-work know.

Thus they went on, talking of what they had seen. This made the way easy, otherwise it would have been tedious. Now they went through a wilderness.

THE SIXTH STAGE

Now when they were almost out of this wilderness, Faithful looked back and saw someone coming. He knew him. Oh, said Faithful to his brother, look who is coming. Christian turned and said, It is my good friend Evangelist. My good friend too, said Faithful, he set me on the way to the gate. Evangelist greeted them.

EVAN. Peace be with you, dearly beloved, and peace to your helpers.

CHR. Welcome, welcome, my good Evangelist, the sight of your face brings memories of your ancient kindness and unwearied labors for my eternal good.

FAITH. A thousand times welcome. Your company, sweet Evangelist, is desirable to poor pilgrims!

EVAN. How has it gone, my friends, since we were last together? What have you met? How have you behaved?

Christian and Faithful told him of all the things that had happened to them. How, and with what difficulty, they had arrived in this place.

I am happy, said Evangelist, not that you met with trials but that you have been victors. You have, despite many weaknesses, continued in the way to this day.

Happy, for my sake and yours, I have sown and you have reaped. The day is coming, when "he who sows and he who reaps may rejoice together" (John 4:36). If you hold out "in due season we shall reap if we do not lose heart" (Gal. 6:9). The incorruptible crown is before you, "run in such a way that you may obtain it" (1 Cor. 9:24–27). There are some that start for this crown, but after they have gone a distance another takes it from them: "hold fast what you have, that no one may take your crown" (Rev. 3:11).

You are still in the devil's gunshot range. "You have not yet resisted to bloodshed, striving against sin." Let the kingdom always be before you. Steadfastly believe the things that are invisible. Let nothing from this side of the world get in you. Above all, look to your hearts and its lusts for they are "deceitful above all things, and desperately wicked." Set your faces like a flint. All power in heaven and earth is on your side.

Christian thanked Evangelist for the exhortation. They needed his words to help them the rest of the way. They knew he was a prophet and could tell them what would happen and how they might resist and overcome. Faithful also agreed and so Evangelist began.

EVAN. My sons, you have heard in the truth of the Gospel that you must "through many tribulations enter the kingdom of God". And again that, "the Holy Spirit testifies in every city, saying that chains and tribulations await you." Therefore you cannot expect a pilgrimage without them. You have found some of the truth of these testimonies already, and more will immediately follow. As you can see, you are almost out of this wilderness. You will soon come to a town. In that town, enemies will trouble you. Make sure that you seal your testimony with blood. "Be faithful until death and the King will give you the crown of life." He that will die there, although his death will be unnatural and perhaps his pain great, will have the best of his fellow. Not only because he will arrive at the Celestial City first, but he will escape many of the miseries that the other will meet on the rest of the journey. When you have come to the town, and find what I have related is true, then remember your friend. Act like men, and "commit your souls to Him in doing good, as to a faithful Creator."

I saw in my dream they left the wilderness and came to the town called Vanity. The town has a fair, named Vanity Fair. It runs all year long. It is called Vanity Fair because the town is lighter than vapor (Ps. 62:9), and because all that is sold there, or comes there, is vanity. It is the saying of the wise, "All that is coming is vanity" (Eccl. 11:8; see also 1:2–14; 2:11–17; Is. 40:17).

This fair is not new; it is ancient. I will show you its origin.

Almost five thousand years ago, two honest pilgrims were walking to the Celestial City. Beelzebub, Apollyon, and Legion, with their companions, perceived the pilgrims' path as they went through Vanity. They constructed a fair to last all year and sell all sorts of vanity. Merchandise like houses, land, trades, places, honors, privileges, titles, countries, kingdoms, lusts, and pleasures are sold there. Pleasures of all types, such as harlots, wives, husbands, children, masters, servants, lives, blood, bodies, souls, silver, gold, pearls, precious stones, and what-not are also sold there.

At this fair there is always frauds, games, plays, fools, apes, villains, and rascals of every kind.

Here can be seen in blood red color, thefts, murders, adulteries, and perjury.

Like many smaller fairs there are several rows and streets with proper names where certain wares are sold. Here, you have the proper places, rows, streets (namely, countries and kingdoms), where the wares of this fair are found. Here is the Britain Row, the French Row, the Italian Row, the Spanish Row, and the German Row, where different types of vanities are sold. Like other fairs, there is one main commodity. Rome's wares and merchandise are highly promoted. Only our English nation, with some others, have taken a dislike to it.

Now, as I said, the way to the Celestial City lies through the town where this lusty fair is held. If you want to go to the Celestial City, and not go through this town, "you must leave this world" (1 Cor. 4:10).

The Prince of princes himself, when here, went through this town. Yes, as I think, it was Beelzebub, the chief lord of the fair, that invited him to buy vanities. He would have made him lord of the fair if he would pay him reverence as he went through town. Yes, he was such a person of honor that Beelzebub took him from street to street. He offered him all the kingdoms of the world to allure the blessed One to buy some vanities. He paid no attention to the merchandise and left the town without laying so much as one penny on these vanities (Matt. 4:8, 9; Luke 4:5–7). This fair is ancient, long standing, and great.

Now, the pilgrims had to go through this fair. As they entered the fair the people became inquisitive about them for several reasons.

First, the Pilgrims were dressed in clothing that was different from any garments sold at the fair. The people studied them. Some said they were fools (1 Cor. 4:9, 10); some said they were insane; some said they were eccentric.

Second, while people wondered about their clothing they also wondered about their speech. Few could understand what they said. The Pilgrims naturally spoke the language of Canaan, but the people who worked at the fair were men of this world. From one end of the fair to the other, they thought the pilgrims were barbarians (1 Cor. 2:7,8).

Third, the sales people were not amused when the pilgrims had no interest in their goods. They didn't even look at them. If they were asked to buy, they put their fingers in their ears and cried, "Turn away my eyes from looking at worthless things" (Ps. 119:37). Then, they looked up, to signify their trade and traffic was in heaven (Phil. 3:20, 21).

One mocked the pilgrims, "What will you buy?"

They looked at him seriously and said, "We buy the truth" (Prov. 23:23). This was reason to despise them all the more. Some mocked, some taunted, some spoke reproachfully, and some called for their death. Finally, a riot started that had consequential confusion. The great one of the fair was informed and quickly came. He deputized some of his most trusty friends to arrest the men that threw the fair into confusion. They were interrogated. They were asked where they came from, where they were going, and why they were dressed in such unusual garb. The men replied that they were pilgrims and strangers in the world. They were going to their own country, the heavenly Jerusalem (Heb. 11:13–16). They had done nothing to the men of the town, or to the merchants to be abused. All they wanted was to continue their journey.

The difficulty began when a seller asked what they wanted to buy. The truth, they replied. The interrogator did not believe them. He thought they were either troublemakers or insane. They took them, beat them, covered them with dirt, and put them in a cage as a spectacle for all at the fair to see. They stayed in the cage for some time and were made the objects of sport, malice, and revenge. The great one of the fair continued to laugh at what happened. But the pilgrims were patient, "not returning reviling for reviling, but on the contrary blessing," giving good words for bad, and kindness for injuries.

Some at the fair, who were more observing and less prejudiced, began to blame the baser sort for the continued abuse of the men. This enraged the tormenters, who counted them as bad as the men in the cage. They said they seemed to be confederates and should suffer the same misfortunes.

The others replied that the men were quiet, sober, and intended no harm. Many, who traded at the fair, were more worthy to be put into the cage and even into the pillory. Thus, after many words had passed on both sides (the pilgrims behaved very wisely and soberly), the men fought among themselves and did harm to each other.

These two poor men were again brought before the examiners. They were found guilty of starting a riot. They were pitifully beaten, placed in irons, and led in chains around the fair, as an example to others not to speak on their behalf or join them.

Christian and Faithful behaved even more wisely. They received the disgrace and shame that was put on them with meekness and patience. This won some to their side (though only a few by comparison). It put the examiners in a rage. They concluded the two men should die for the abuse they had done and for deceiving the men of the fair.

Then were again placed in the cage with their feet secured in the stocks.

They then recalled what they had heard from their faithful friend, Evangelist. They were made more secure in their way and suffering by what he had told them and comforted each other with the thought that whoever died would have the best of it. Each man secretly wished to be the one to die. They committed themselves to the all-wise disposal of Him that rules everything and were fully content in this condition.

They were taken before their enemies and arraigned. The judge's name was Lord Hate-good. The indictment: "They were enemies and disturbers of the trade who caused a commotion and division in the town, swayed several to their dangerous opinions, and were in contempt of the law of their prince."

Faithful began to answer. He had only set himself against what was against Him who is higher than the highest. And, said he, as for disturbance, I made none. I am a man of peace. The parties that were won to us, were won by seeing our truth and innocence. They are only turned from the worse to the better. As for the king you talk about, he is Beelzebub, the enemy of our Lord. I defy him and all his angels.

Then a proclamation was made. Any who had something to say for their lord the king against the prisoner at the bar, should appear and give their evidence. Three witnesses came, Envy, Superstition, and Pickthank. They were asked if they knew the prisoner at the bar, and what they had to say for their lord the king against him.

Envy stood and said, My lord, I have known this man a long time. I will attest on my oath before this honorable bench that he is . . .

JUDGE. Hold it. Give him his oath.

So they swore him in. Then he said, My lord, this man, despite his hypocritical name, is one of the vilest men in our country. He does not regard prince or people, law or custom. He does all he can to give all men his disloyal notions, which he calls principles of faith and holiness. In particular, I heard him once affirm that Christianity and the customs of our town of Vanity were diametrically opposite and could not be reconciled. By this, my lord, he immediately condemned not only all our laudable doings, but us as well.

The judge asked, Do you have any more to say?

ENVY. My lord, I could say much more, but I would not be tiresome to the court. Yet, if need be, when the other gentlemen have given their evidence, if anything is missing to dispatch him, I will expand my testimony. So he was asked to stand by.

Then they called Superstition and asked him to look at the prisoner. They also asked what he could say for their lord the king against him. They swore him in and he began.

SUPER. My lord, I have no great acquaintance with this man, nor do I want to have any further knowledge of him. However, this I know from a discussion I had with him the other day, he is a pestilent fellow. I heard him say that our religion was nothing! It was such that a man could not please God. Your lordship well knows what must necessarily follow. We worship in vain; we are still in our sins; we finally will be damned. This is all that I have to say.

Then Pickthank was sworn in and asked what he knew on behalf of their lord the king against the prisoner at the bar.

PICK. My lord and gentlemen, this fellow I have known for a long time. I have heard him say things that should not be spoken. He has scoffed our noble prince Beelzebub and has spoken contemptibly of his honorable friends, the Lord Old Man, the Lord Carnal Delight, the Lord Luxurious, the Lord Desire of Vain Glory, my old Lord Lechery, Sir Having Greedy, and the rest of our nobility. He has said, moreover, that if all men were like him, not one of these noblemen would remain in this town. Besides, my lord, he has not been afraid to speak against you, his judge. He called you an ungodly villain, and many other vilifying terms. He has stained most of the gentry of our town.

When Pickthank finished his tale, the judge spoke to the prisoner at the bar. You rebel, fugitive, heretic, and traitor, have you heard what these honest gentlemen have witnessed against you?

FAITH. May I speak a few words in my defense?

JUDGE. You vile character, you vile character, you deserve to live no longer. You will be slain immediately. But so that all men may see our gentleness, let us hear what you, a vile fugitive, has to say.

FAITH. 1. In answer to what Mr. Envy has spoken, I said only this. The rules, laws, customs, or people that are flat against the word of God, are diametrically opposite to Christianity. If I am wrong in this, convince me of my error, and I am ready to recant.

2. As to Mr. Superstition and his charge against me, I said only this. The worship of God requires a divine faith, but there can be no divine faith without a divine revelation of God's will. Therefore, whatever is placed into the worship of God that does not agree with divine revelation, is done by a human faith that does not bring eternal life.

3. As to what Mr. Pickthank said, (avoiding terms that I am a rebel and the like), I say that the prince of this town, with all the rabble and his attendants that this gentleman named, are more fit for being in hell than being in this town and country. The Lord have mercy on me.

The judge spoke to the jury (who stood nearby to hear and observe). Gentlemen of the jury, you see this man about whom so great an uproar has been made in this town. You have also heard what these worthy gentlemen have testified against him. You have also heard his reply and confession. It lies now in your hearts to hang him, or save his life. But I think you need instruction in our law.

There was an act made in the days of Pharaoh the Great, servant to our prince, to prevent those of a contrary religion from multiplying and growing too strong: Their males should be thrown into the river (Exod. 1:22). There was also an act made in the days of Nebuchadnezzar, the Great, another of his servants: Whoever would not fall down and worship his golden image, should be thrown into a fiery furnace (Dan. 3:6). There was also an act made in the days of Darius: Whoever called on any god but him, should be thrown into the lion's den (Dan. 6:7). The substance of these laws this rebel has broken, not only in thought (which is not to be considered), but also in word and deed. This must be considered, it needs to be intolerable.

Pharaoh's law was made on a supposition to prevent mischief with no apparent crime. Here the crime is apparent. Concerning the second and third charges, you see he disputed our religion, to that treason he has already confessed. He deserves to die the death.

Then the jury went out. Their names were Mr. Blindman, Mr. No-good, Mr. Malice, Mr. Love-lust, Mr. Live-loose, Mr. Heady, Mr. High-mind, Mr. Enmity, Mr. Liar, Mr. Cruelty, Mr. Hate-light, and Mr. Implacable. Everyone gave their private verdict and unanimously concluded to bring a guilty finding before the judge. Mr. Blindman, the foreman, said, I clearly see that this man is a heretic. Then said Mr. No-good, Away with such a fellow from the earth. Yes, said Mr. Malice, I hate his looks. Then Mr. Love-lust said, I could never stand him. Nor I, said Mr. Live-loose, he would always be condemning my way. Hang him, hang him, said Mr. Heady. A sorry scrub, said Mr. High-mind. My heart rises against him, said Mr. Enmity. He is a rogue, said Mr. Liar. Hanging is too good for him, said Mr. Cruelty. Let us dispatch him out of the way, said Mr. Hate-light. Then Mr. Implacable said, If I have the world given me, I could not be reconciled to him. Let us immediately find him guilty of death.

And they did. He was presently condemned to be taken from the place where he was, to the place from where he came, and there to be put to the most cruel death that could be invented.

They brought him out, to do with him according to their law. First they scourged him, then they beat him, and lanced his flesh with knives. After that they stoned him, pierced him with their swords, and burned him to ashes at the stake. Thus Faithful came to his end.

Now I saw, behind the multitude, a chariot with a couple of horses waiting for Faithful. As soon as his adversaries dispatched him, he was put into the chariot and swiftly carried up through the clouds, with the sound of a trumpet, to the celestial gate. As for Christian, he had some relief. He was remanded back to prison and remained there for a while. But he who overrules all things, having the power of their rage in his own hand, worked it so that Christian escaped and went on his way.

As he went, he sang,

Well, Faithful, thou has faithfully professed
Unto thy Lord, with whom thou shalt be blest,
When faithless ones, with all their vain delights,
Are crying out under their hellish plights:
Sing, Faithful, sing, and let thy name survive;
For though they killed thee, thou art yet alive.

THE SEVENTH STAGE

Now I saw in my dream that Christian did not go alone. Hopeful (from watching Christian and Faithful in their words, actions, and sufferings) went with Christian. They entered a brotherly covenant and agreed to be companions. One died testifying to the truth but another rose from his ashes to be Christian's pilgrimage companion. Hopeful told Christian that many more at the fair would, in time, follow them.

Shortly after they left the fair, they overtook a man, By-ends. They asked, What country are you from, sir? How far are you going? He was from the town of Fair-speech, going to the Celestial City. He did not give them his name.

From Fair-speech, said Christian, does any good live there? (Prov. 26:25).

BY. Yes, said By-ends, I hope so.

CHR. Tell me, sir, what may I call you?

BY. I am a stranger to you, and you to me. If you are going this way, I will be glad to have your company. If not, then I will be content.

CHR. This town of Fair-speech, I have heard about it. As I remember, it's a wealthy place.

BY. Yes, it is. I have many rich relatives there.

CHR. Who are your relatives, if I may be so bold?

BY. Most of the town, my closest relatives are Lord Turn-about, Lord Time-server, and Lord Fair-speech, from whose ancestors the town took its name. I am also related to Mr. Smooth-man, Mr. Facing-both-ways, and Mr. Any-thing. The parson of our parish, Mr. Two-tongues, was my mother's brother. To tell you the truth, I am a gentleman of good quality. Yet my great-grandfather owned a ferry, looking one way and rowing another. I got most of my estate from the same occupation.

CHR. Are you married?

BY. Yes, my wife is a virtuous woman, the daughter of a virtuous woman. She was Lady Feigning's daughter, so she is from an honorable family. She has reached such a pinnacle of breeding that she knows how to mix with everyone, from prince to peasant. It's true, we differ somewhat in religion from the stricter sort, but only in two small points. First, we never strive against wind and tide. Second, we are always most zealous when Religion walks about in his silver slippers. We love to walk with him in the streets when the sun shines and the people applaud him.

Christian stepped aside and said to Hopeful, It runs in my mind that this man is By-ends, from Fair-speech. If it is, we have as big a scoundrel in our company as lives in all these parts. Hopeful said, Ask him! He should not be ashamed of his name. Christian went up to him and said, Sir, you talk as if you know more than all the world does, if I do not miss my mark, I can guess your name. Is it Mr. By-ends of Fair-speech?

BY. That is not my name. That is a nickname given by some that cannot stand me. I must be content to bear it as a reproach, just as others have lived with theirs.

CHR. Did you ever give people a reason to call you this?

BY. Never, never! The worst I ever did to give them a reason to call me this was I always had the luck to jump with the present ways and get there. If things are thrown at me, let me count them a blessing. I will not let the malicious load me with reproach.

CHR. I thought you were the man. Let me tell you what I think. This name more properly belongs to you than you are willing to admit.

BY. If you want to imagine it, I cannot help it. You will find me fair company if you allow me to associate with you.

CHR. If you go with us, you must go against wind and tide. This, I perceive, is against your opinion. You must also accept Religion in rags as well as silver slippers. You must stand by him, when bound in irons, as well as when he walks the streets with applause.

BY. You must not impose, nor lord it over my faith, leave me to my liberty. Let me go with you.

CHR. Not a step farther, unless you do what I propose.

BY. I will never desert my old principles. They are harmless and profitable. If I may not go with you, I will do as I did before you met me: go by myself until someone overtakes me who will be pleased to have my company.

Now I saw in my dream that Christian and Hopeful left him and kept their distance. Looking back, they saw three men following Mr. By-ends. As they caught up with him, he warmly greeted them for he knew them well. They were Mr. Hold-the-world, Mr. Money-love, and Mr. Save-all. In their youth they were students of Mr. Gripeman, a schoolmaster in Lovegain, a market town in the county of Coveting, in the North. Their Schoolmaster taught them the art of getting by violence, chicanery, flattering, lying, or putting a guise on religion. These four gentlemen learned so well from their master that anyone of them could have taught the class.

After they greeted each other, Mr. Money-love said to Mr. By-ends, Who is ahead of us on the road? For Christian and Hopeful were still in view.

BY. A couple of far country-men going on a pilgrimage.

MONEY. Why didn't they wait? We could have enjoyed their good company? For they, we, and you, sir, I hope, are all going on a pilgrimage.

BY. We are indeed. But the men ahead of us are so rigid, so love their own ideas, and so lightly esteem the opinions of others, that if a godly man does not agree with them in all things, they push him out of their company.

SAVE. That is bad. We read of some that are overly righteous, unyielding, and judge and condemn all but themselves. What did you disagree about?

BY. Why, their headstrong manner, they concluded that it is their duty to rush the journey in all weather. I wait for wind and tide. They are willing to risk all for God on a whim. I am for taking every advantage to secure my life and estate. They are for holding their ideas, even when all others are against them. I am for religion when time and safety will bear it. They are for religion even when in rags and contempt. I am for religion when he walks in his silver slippers, in the sunshine, and with applause.

HOLD-THE-WORLD. Yes, provided he keeps you there in the sunshine and the applause. I count him a fool that has the liberty to keep what he has, but is so unwise as to lose it. Let us be wise as serpents. It is best to make hay in the sunshine. You see how the bee lies still in winter and stirs only when she can have profit with pleasure. God sometimes sends rain and sometimes sunshine. If they are fools enough to go through the first, let us be content to take the fair weather. I like religion that will stand with the security of God's good blessing. Who, ruled by his reason, can not imagine that since God has given us the good things of this life, God would also have us keep them for his sake? Abraham and Solomon grew rich in religion. Job says that you will lay your gold in the dust. He is not like the men ahead of us, if they are as you have described.

SAVE. I think we are agreed. There is no need for any more words about it.

MONEY. No more words about it indeed. He that does not believe Scripture or reason (and we have both on our side), neither knows his liberty nor seeks his safety.

BY. My brethren, we are on a pilgrimage. As a diversion from bad things, let me propose a question.

Suppose a man, a minister, or a tradesman, has an opportunity to get the good blessings of this life. But he can not secure this opportunity unless he becomes extraordinarily zealous in some points of religion that he never meddled with before. Can he use this to obtain his goal and still be honest?

MONEY. I see the bottom of your question. With your permission I will endeavor to develop an answer. First, to speak to your question as it concerns the minister. Suppose he is a worthy man with only a small parish and his eye on a much larger one. He now has an opportunity to get it if he becomes more studious and preaches more frequently and zealously. Because the mood of the people requires it, he alters some of his principles. I see no reason why a minister may not do this, provided he has a call and a great deal more. Why?

1. His aspiration for a larger parish is lawful (this cannot be contradicted) because it is put in front of him by Providence without a question of conscience.

2. His desire for that parish makes him more studious and a more zealous preacher. This makes him a better man. Yes, it makes him improve, and this is in accord with the mind of God.

3. Now, as for complying with the mood of his people by abandoning some of his principles, this is his argument, 1. His disposition is self-denying. 2. His deportment is sweet and winning. Thus, 3. he is more suitable for the ministerial function.

4. I conclude that a minister who exchanges a small for a great should not be considered covetous. Rather, he has improved. He is counted as one that pursues his call with an opportunity put his hand to do good.

The second part of the question, about the tradesman, supposes he is poorly employed. If by becoming religious he improves his market, perhaps get a rich wife, or more and better customers for his shop, I see no reason why this is not lawful. Why?

1. To become religious is a virtue by any means.

2. It is lawful to get a rich wife, or more customers for my shop.

3. The man that gets these by becoming religious, gets what is good from them that are good, by becoming good himself. Here then is a good wife, good customers, and good gain, all from becoming religious, which is good. Thus, to become religious to get these is a good and profitable plan.

Mr. Money-love's answer to Mr. By-ends' question was highly applauded. They concluded that it was wholesome and advantageous because they thought no man could contradict it. Since Christian and Hopeful had opposed Mr. By-ends, they agreed to test them with this question as soon as they overtook them. They decided that old Mr. Hold-the-world, not Mr. By-ends, should propound the question because there would be less heat kindled than between Mr. By-ends and them. They called Christian and Hopeful and they stopped.

They came up to each other. After a short greeting, Mr. Hold-the-world propounded the question to Christian and Hopeful. He asked them to answer it, if they could.

CHR. A baby in religion may answer ten thousand such questions. It is unlawful to follow Christ for loaves (John 6:26), so how much more abominable is it to make him and religion a stalking-horse to get and enjoy the world! We find only heathens, hypocrites, devils, and wizards are of this opinion.

1. Heathens: When Hamor and Shechem wanted Jacob's daughter and cattle, they realized there was no way to get them unless they were circumcised. They said to their companions, If every male among us is circumcised as they are circumcised, will not their livestock, their property, and every animal of theirs be ours? They used their religion as the stalking-horse to obtain what they wanted. Read the whole story (Gen. 34:20–24).

2. This is the religion of hypocritical Pharisees. Long prayers were their pretence, but getting the widows' houses was their intent. Greater damnation from God was their judgment (Luke 20:46, 47).

3. Judas, the devil, belonged to this religion. He was religious for the moneybag, to possess what was in it. But he was lost, was thrown away, and was the very son of perdition.

4. Simon, the magician, was a member of this religion. He wanted the Holy Spirit to get money. His words are recorded in Scripture (Acts 8:19–22).

5. This will not leave my mind, the man who takes up religion for the world, will throw away religion for the world. As surely as Judas appropriated the world in becoming religious, he surely sold religion and his Master for the world. To answer the question affirmatively, as I perceive you have done, and to accept such answers as authentic, is heathenish, hypocritical, and devilish. Your reward will be according to your works.

They stood staring at one another, but had no answer. There was a great silence among them. Mr. By-ends and his company staggered and stayed behind Christian and Hopeful. Hopeful agreed with the soundness of Christian's answer. Christian said to his friend, If these men cannot stand before the sentence of men, what will they do with the sentence of God? If they are silent when they argue with vessels of clay, what will they do when they are rebuked by the flames of a devouring fire?

Christian and Hopeful went on with great contentment until they came to a smooth plain, called Ease. The plain was narrow, so they quickly crossed it. On the far side was a little hill, called Lucre. In that hill was a silver mine that some had gone to see. Going too close to the rim of the pit, the ground broke under them, some were killed and others injured. The injured never fully recovered.

Then I saw in my dream that a little off the road, close to the silver mine, stood Demas (gentleman-like). He called to the pilgrims to come and see. Ho! Turn aside and I will show you a thing.

CHR. What thing deserves our turning from the way?

DEMAS. A silver mine, come dig for treasure. You may richly provide for yourselves with little effort.

HOPE. Let us go and look.

CHR. Not I! I have heard of this place. There are many that have been killed here. The treasure is a snare to those that seek it. It hinders their pilgrimage.

Christian called to Demas, Is the place dangerous? Has it hindered others in their pilgrimage? (Hosea 9:6).

DEMAS. Not very dangerous, unless you are careless. He blushed as he spoke.

CHR. Let us not go a step closer. Let us keep on our way.

HOPE. I will guarantee you that when By-ends arrives, if he has the same invitation, he will turn in there.

CHR. No doubt about it, his principles will lead him that way. A hundred to one he dies there.

DEMAS. Come and see?

CHR. Demas, you are an enemy to the Lord of this way. You are already condemned by one of his Majesty's judges for turning aside (2 Tim. 4:10). Why do you want to bring us into condemnation? If we turn aside, our Lord the King will certainly hear about it and put us to shame. Then we could not boldly stand before him.

Demas cried again that he was one of their fraternity. If only they would wait, he would walk with them.

CHR. What is your name? Is it not what I called you?

DEMAS. Yes, my name is Demas, I am the son of Abraham.

CHR. I know you. Gehazi was your great-grandfather, Judas your father, and you walk in their steps. It is a devilish prank that you use. Your father was hung as a traitor. You deserve no better reward (2 Kings 5:20–27; Matt. 26:14, 15; 27:3–5). Be assured, when we come to the King we will tell him about your behavior. Then they went their way.

His companions were now within sight. At the first call they approached Demas. Whether they fell into the pit by looking over the brink, or whether they went down to dig, or whether they were suffocated in the bottom by the fumes, I am not certain. But this I observed, they were never seen in the way again. Then Christian sang,

> By-ends and silver Demas both agree;
> One calls, the other runs, that he may be
> A sharer in his lucre: so these two
> Take up in this world, and no farther go.

On the other side of this plain the pilgrims came to a place, close to the highway, where an old monument stood. They were both concerned for it seemed as if it had been a woman changed into the shape of a pillar. They looked, but did not know what to make of it. At last Hopeful saw strange writing above the head. Not being a scholar, he called Christian (for he was learned) to see if he could pick out the meaning. After careful study he determined that it said, "Remember Lot's wife." They both agreed that this was Lot's wife who looked back and became a pillar of salt as she left Sodom for safety (Gen. 19:26). This sudden and amazing sight gave them reason to have the following conversation.

CHR. My brother, this is an appropriate sight after Demas' invitation to view the hill Lucre. Had we done as he wished, and as you were inclined, we would be like this woman, a spectacle for all who follow to look at.

HOPE. I am sorry that I was so foolish. It is a wonder that I am not like Lot's wife. What was the difference between her sin and mine? She only looked back. I had a desire to go and see. Let grace be adored. Let me be ashamed that ever such a thing was in my heart.

CHR. Let us remember what we see here. This woman escaped one judgment, she did not fall by the destruction of Sodom, but another destroyed her. As we see, she was turned into a pillar of salt.

HOPE. True! She should be both caution and example. Caution that we shun her sin, or a sign of judgment will overtake us. Just as Korah, Dathan, Abiram, and the two hundred and fifty men that perished in their sin became an example to others (Numb. 16:31, 32; 26:9, 10).

But above all, I ponder one thing, how can Demas and his fellows confidently stand and look for that treasure? While this woman, for just looking behind (we do not read that she stepped one foot out of the way) was turned into a pillar of salt. Especially since her judgment is an example within their sight. They cannot help but see her if they look up.

CHR. It is a thing to wonder at. It argues that their hearts have grown desperate. I do not know who to compare them with. They are like thieves that pick pockets in the presence of the judge, or cut purses under the gallows. The men of Sodom were "exceedingly wicked and sinful against the Lord." That is, in his eyesight, despite the kindness he had shown them, for the land of Sodom was now like the garden of the Lord (Gen. 13:10–13). This provoked him all the more to jealousy. It made their plague as hot as the fire of the Lord out of heaven could be. It is rational to conclude that those who sin, despite examples that are continually placed before them for caution, must be partakers of the severest judgments.

HOPE. Doubtless you say the truth. What a mercy that neither you, but especially I, am not made this example! This ministering occasion causes us to thank God, to fear him, and to always remember Lot's wife.

I saw then that they went on their way to a pleasant river. A river that David the king called "the river of God", but John called it, "the river of water of life" (Ps. 65:9; Rev. 22:1; Ezek. 47:1–9). Now their way ran along the bank of this river. Here, Christian and his companion walked with great delight. They drank the water of the river; it was pleasant and encouraging to their weary spirits. On both banks were green trees with all kinds of fruit. They ate the leaves to help digestion and to prevent other diseases common to those that heat their blood by travel. On both sides of the river were meadows, curiously beautiful with lilies. It was green all year long. Here, they lay down and slept, for the needy will lie down in safety (Ps. 23:2; Is. 14:30). When they woke they picked fruit from the trees, drank the water of the river, and slept. They did this for several days and nights. Then they sang;

> Behold, how these Crystal Streams do glide,
> To comfort pilgrims by the highway side.
> The meadows green, besides their fragrant smell,
> Yield dainties for them; And he that can tell

What pleasant fruit, yes, leaves these trees do yield,
Will soon sell all, that he may buy this field.

When they were ready to go (for they were not at their journey's end), they ate, drank, and departed.

I saw in my dream that they had not journeyed far when the river and the way parted. They were more than a little sorry to see this. Yet they would not leave the way. Now the way from the river was rough and their feet tender from their travels. The souls of the pilgrims were discouraged because of the way (Num. 21:4). As they went on, they wished for a better way. Ahead of them, on the left side of the road, was a meadow and a stile to enter it. That meadow is called By-path meadow. Christian said, If this meadow lies along our way, let's go into it. He went to the stile and a path ran beside the way on the other side of the fence. It is, as I hoped, easier going, Christian said. Come, good Hopeful, let us climb over.

HOPE. What if this path should lead us out of the way?

CHR. That is not likely. Look, it runs along the wayside.

So Hopeful, persuaded by Christian, followed him over the stile. When they entered the path, it was easy on their feet. Looking ahead, they saw a man walking. They called and asked him which way the path went. He answered, To the Celestial Gate. Look, said Christian, didn't I tell you? You see, we are right. So they followed him. But when night came, it grew very dark and they lost sight of the man that walked ahead.

The man walking ahead (Vain-Confidence by name) could not see the way. He fell into a deep pit and was dashed to pieces in the fall. The pit was placed there by the prince of those grounds, to catch vain-glorious fools (Is. 9:16).

Christian and his fellow heard him fall. They called to find out what happened. There was no answer, all they heard was groaning. Hopeful asked, Where are we now? Christian was silent, concerned that he had led him out of the way. Then it began to rain, thunder, and lightening in a most dreadful manner. The water quickly rose.

Hopeful groaned, Oh that I had kept in my way!

CHR. Who would have thought that this path would lead us out of the way?

HOPE. I was afraid from the first. I gave you a gentle caution. I would have spoken stronger, but you are older than I.

CHR. Good brother, do not be offended, I am sorry I have taken you out of the way and put you in imminent danger. Please, my brother, forgive me. I did not do this with evil intent.

HOPE. Be comforted, my brother, I forgive you. I believe that this will be for our good.

CHR. I am glad I have a merciful brother. We must not stand here. Let us try to go back.

HOPE. Good brother, let me lead.

CHR. No, let me go first. If there is any danger I will fall in. Because of me, we have both gone out of the way.

HOPE. You will not go first. Your troubled mind may again lead you out of the way. Then for their encouragement they heard a voice, "Set your heart toward the highway, the way in which you went" (Jer. 31:21). The waters had greatly risen and the way back was dangerous. (I thought it is easier to go out of the way when we are in it, than going back to it when we are out.) Yet they ventured back, but it was so dark and the water so high that they almost drowned nine or ten times.

They did not, despite their skill, reach the stile that night. Finally, stopping under a little shelter, they sat down and slept until dawn. Not far from the place where they slept was Doubting Castle, owned by Giant Despair. They were sleeping on his grounds. The giant got up early in the morning to walk his fields. He caught Christian and Hopeful asleep, with a grim and surly voice he woke them. He asked where they were from and what they were doing on his land. They said they were pilgrims who had lost their way.

The giant said, You have trespassed by trampling in and lying on my grounds. You must come with me. They were forced to go because he was stronger. There was little to say for they were at fault. The giant drove them ahead of him and put them into a dark, stinking, dungeon in his castle. There they lay from Wednesday morning until Saturday night, without one bit of bread, or drop of drink, or light, or anyone to ask how they were. They were in evil hands, far from loved ones, friends, and acquaintance (Ps. 88:18). Christian had double sorrow, it was his poor counsel that brought them into this distress.

When Giant Despair went to bed he told his wife, Diffidence, that he had taken a couple of prisoners and thrown them in the dungeon for trespassing. He asked her what he should do with them. She asked who they were, where they came from, and where they were going. He replied. She counseled that in the morning he should beat them without mercy. When he arose, he got a short, thick piece of wood from a tree and went down to the dungeon. He yelled at his prisoners as if they were dogs, although they never said a distasteful word to him. He dreadfully beat them. They were so helpless that they could not even turn over on the floor. He left them groaning and moaning.

The next night, she learned they were still alive. She advised her husband to tell the prisoners to kill themselves. In the morning the giant went to the dungeon, in a surly manner, and saw that they are hurting from the beating that he had given them the day before. He told them the only way they would ever come out of that place was to make an end of themselves with either a knife, a rope, or poison. Why, said he, would you choose to live, seeing it is accompanied with so much bitterness?

They wanted him to let them go. He turned ugly and rushed them. Doubtless, he would have killed them but he had a seizure (for sometimes in sunny weather he fell into seizures), and lost for a time the use of his hands. He left them to consider what to do. The prisoners talked between themselves whether it was best to take his counsel or not.

CHR. Brother, what can we do? The life that we now live is miserable. For my part, I do not know whether it is best to live like this, or to die by my hand. My soul chooses hanging and death; the grave is more easy for me than this dungeon (Job. 7:15). Will we be ruled by the giant?

HOPE. Our present condition is dreadful, and death would be far more welcome than staying here forever. Let us consider, the Lord of the country where we are going has said, "You shall not murder." We are forbidden to take his counsel and kill ourselves. Besides, he that kills another, can only kill his body, but one who kills himself, kills both body and soul. Moreover, my brother, you talk of ease in the grave. Have you forgotten hell where the murderers go? "No murderer has eternal life." Think again, the law is not in the hand of Giant Despair. Others, so far as I understand, have been captured by him and escaped. Who knows but God, who made the world, may cause Giant Despair to die. Or that at some time or other, he may forget to lock us in. Or he may, in a short time, have another seizure and lose the use of his limbs? If that happens again, for my part, I am resolved to be a man and try my utmost to escape. I was a fool not to try before. But, however, my brother, let us be patient and endure a while longer. The time may come when we will be given a happy release. Let us not be our own murderers. With these words Hopeful eased his brother's mind. They stayed together in the dark, in their sad and wretched condition.

Toward evening the giant came down to the dungeon to see if his prisoners had taken his counsel. When he arrived he found them alive, but that was about all. Between the shortage of food, water, and injuries from their beatings, they could barely breathe. But, I say, he found them alive and this threw him into a grievous rage. He told them that since they had disobeyed his counsel, it would be better if they had never been born.

They trembled and Christian fainted. When he revived, they renewed their conversation about the giant's counsel. Christian again seemed to favor doing it, but Hopeful replied:

HOPE. My brother, remember how valiant you have been! Apollyon could not crush you, nor could all that you heard, or saw, or felt, in the Valley of the Shadow of Death. What hardship, terror, and amazement you have already been through! Are you now nothing but fears? I am in the dungeon with you, a far weaker man by nature than you. This giant has wounded me as well as you. He has also cut off food and water from my mouth, and with you I mourn in the dark. But let us exercise a little more patience. Remember how you played the man at Vanity Fair. You were neither afraid of chain, cage, or a bloody death! Therefore, let us (at least to avoid the shame that does not become a Christian) bear with patience as best we can.

That night, the giant and his wife were in bed, and she asked if the prisoners had taken his counsel. They are sturdy rogues, he replied. They choose to bear all hardships rather than do away with themselves. She said, Take them into the castle yard tomorrow. Show them the bones and skulls of those you have already dispatched. Make them believe that before the week ends, you will tear them in pieces as you have done with other people.

In the morning, the giant took them into the castle yard and did as his wife instructed. These, said he, were once pilgrims, as you are. They trespassed on my grounds, as you have. I tore them to pieces. In ten days I will do the same to you. Get back to your dungeon. With that he beat them all the way down. Pathetic cases, they lay on the dungeon floor all day Saturday. At night, when Mrs. Diffidence and her husband the giant were in bed, they discussed their prisoners. The old giant wondered if his blows would kill them. His wife replied, I fear they live in hope that some will rescue them, or they have picklocks and hope to escape. If you say so, my dear, said the giant. I will search them in the morning.

Well, on Saturday about midnight, they began to pray and continued in prayer until daybreak.

A little before it was day, good Christian, as one half-amazed, broke into a passionate speech. What a fool I am to lie in a stinking dungeon when I may walk at liberty! I have a key, called Promise. It will, I am persuaded, open any lock in Doubting Castle. Hopeful said, This is good news, dear brother. Take it out and try it.

Christian pulled it out of his bosom and tried it in the dungeon door. The bolt, as he turned the key, came back. The door flew open with ease, and Christian and Hopeful came out. Then he went to the door that leads into the castle yard and with his key opened it. Then he went to the iron-gate; the lock was desperately hard but the key opened it. They rapidly pushed open the gate to escape. The gate made such a creaking noise that it woke Giant Despair. He started to pursue his prisoners, but his seizures took him again, his limbs failed and there was no way he could go after them. The Pilgrims hurried on and came to the King's highway. They were safe because they were now out of the giant's jurisdiction.

After they went over the stile, they thought about what they should do to prevent others from falling into the hands of Giant Despair. They decided to erect a pillar, and to engrave this sentence on it. "This stile is the way to Doubting Castle. It is kept by Giant Despair, who despises the King of the Celestial country and seeks to destroy his holy pilgrims." Many that followed read what was written and escaped the danger. This done, they sang:

> Out of the way we went, and then we found
> What it was to tread on forbidden ground:
> And let them that come after have a care,
> Lest heedlessness makes them as we to fare;
> Lest they, for trespassing, his prisoners are,
> Whose castle's Doubting, and whose name's Despair.

THE EIGHTH STAGE

They continued until they came to the Delectable Mountains that belongs to the Lord of that hill. We mentioned this before. They went up the mountains to see the gardens, orchards, vineyards, and water fountains. Here they drank, washed, and freely ate the fruit of the vineyards. On the tops of these mountains were shepherds, standing by the highway, feeding their flocks. The pilgrims went to them and, leaning on their staffs (this is common with weary pilgrims when they stand and talk with any by the way), they asked, Whose Delectable Mountains are these? Who owns the sheep that feed on them?

SHEP. These mountains are Emmanuel's land and are within sight of his city. The sheep are his. He has laid down his life for them (John 10:11, 15).

CHR. Is this the way to the Celestial City?

SHEP. You are just in your way.

CHR. How far is it?

SHEP. Too far for any except those who will get there.

CHR. Is the way safe or dangerous?

SHEP. Safe for those for whom it is to be safe. But transgressors will stumble (Hos. 14:9).

CHR. Is there any relief here for pilgrims that are weary and faint?

SHEP. The Lord of these mountains has given us a command, Do not forget to entertain strangers (Heb. 13:2). The best of this place is yours.

I also saw in my dream that when the shepherds noticed they were wayfaring men, they asked questions (to which they gave the same answers as in previous places). Where did you come from? How did you get in the way? How have you survived so far? Few pilgrims showed their faces on these mountains. When the shepherds heard their answers, they were pleased and looked lovingly on them. Welcome to the Delectable Mountains, they said.

The shepherds, whose names were Knowledge, Experience, Watchful, and Sincere, took them by the hand and led them to their tents. They ate food that had been prepared for them. We want you stay a while, become acquainted with us, and comfort yourselves with the good things of the Delectable Mountains. They replied that they would be pleased to stay. Then they went to sleep because it was very late.

I saw in my dream that in the morning the shepherds asked Christian and Hopeful to walk up the mountains with them. They did; it was a pleasant view on every side. The shepherds said to each other, Shall we show these pilgrims some wonders? They agreed. So they took them first to the top of a hill called Error. It was very steep on the farthest side; they asked them to look down. Christian and Hopeful looked and saw at the bottom several that were dashed to pieces by a fall from the top. Christian asked, What does this mean?

The shepherds answered, Have you heard about those that strayed concerning the faith of the resurrection of the body by listening to Hymenaeus and Philetus? (2 Tim. 2:17, 18). They answered, Yes. The shepherds replied, Those that you see dashed to pieces at the bottom of this mountain are those that strayed. They lie unburied, left as an example for others to take heed of how they climb, or how close to the brink of this mountain they come.

I saw that they took them to the top of another mountain, named Caution, and told them to look into the distance. When they did they saw several men walking among the tombs. They perceived the men were blind because they stumbled on the tombs and could not get away from them. Christian asked, What does this mean?

The shepherds answered, Did you see, a little below these mountains, a stile that led into a meadow on the left side of this way? They answered, Yes. The shepherds said, From that stile there is a path that leads directly to Doubting Castle, which is owned by Giant Despair. These men (pointing to them among the tombs) once were on a pilgrimage, as you are now. They came to that same stile and because the right way was rough in that place, they chose to leave it and go into that meadow. There they were captured by Giant Despair and thrown into Doubting Castle's dungeon. After they were there a while, the giant put out their eyes. Then he led them to those tombs where he has left them to wander so that the saying of the wise man might be fulfilled, "A man who wanders from the way of understanding will rest in the assembly of the dead" (Prov. 21:16). Christian and Hopeful looked at each other, tears gushed, but they said nothing to the shepherds.

Then I saw in my dream that the shepherds took them to where a door was on the side of a hill. They opened the door and asked them to look in. They did and saw that it was dark and smoky. They also thought that they heard a rumbling noise, like a fire, and a cry of someone tormented. They smelled brimstone. Christian asked, What does this mean? The shepherds replied, This is a by-way to hell, a way that hypocrites go. Those that sell their birthright, like Esau; those that sell their Master, like Judas; those that blaspheme the Gospel, like Alexander; those that lie and are hypocritical, like Ananias and his wife, Sapphira.

Hopeful said to the shepherds, I assume these appeared to be on a pilgrimage?

SHEP. Yes, and they kept up the appearance for a long time.

HOPE. How far did they go in their pilgrimage, since they were miserably cast away?

SHEP. Some beyond, and some not as far as these mountains.

The pilgrims said to each other, We need to cry to the Strong for strength.

SHEP. Yes, you will need it.

By this time the pilgrims wanted to move on and the shepherds agreed. They walked together toward the end of the mountains. Then the shepherds said, Let us show the pilgrims the gates of the Celestial City, provided they have the necessary skill to look through our perspective glass. The pilgrims lovingly accepted and went to the top of a high hill, called Clear. There, they gave them the glass to look.

They tried to look, but the memory of the last thing that the shepherds had shown them made their hands shake. Impeded they could not steadily look through the glass. Yet they thought they saw something like a gate and some of the glory of the place. They went away and sang,

> Thus by the shepherds secrets are revealed,
> Which from all other men are kept concealed:
> Come to the shepherds then, if you would see
> Things deep, things hid, and that mysterious be.

When they were about to leave, one of the shepherds gave them directions of the way. Another told them to be aware of the Flatterer. The third told them not to sleep on Enchanted Ground. The fourth wished them Godspeed. Then I awoke from my dream.

THE NINTH STAGE

I slept, and dreamed again, and saw the two pilgrims going down the mountain along the highway toward the city. Below these mountains, on the left, is the country of Conceit. Here they saw a little crooked lane and a lad walking briskly. His name was Ignorance. Christian asked where he was from and where he was going.

IGNOR. Sir, I was born in the country that lies over there, a little to the left. I am going to the Celestial City.

CHR. How do you expect to get in at the gate? You may find some difficulty there.

IGNOR. Like other good people do.

CHR. What do you have to show to open the gate?

IGNOR. I know my Lord's will. I live a good life. I pay every man what I owe. I pray, fast, tithe, give to charity, and have left my country to go to the Celestial City.

CHR. You did not come in at the gate. You came through that crooked lane. Regardless of what you think, when the reckoning day comes you will be charged as a thief and a robber and not admitted to the city.

IGNOR. Gentlemen, you are total strangers, I do not know you. Follow the religion of your country and I will follow the religion of mine. I hope all will be well. As for the gate, the world knows it is a great distance from our country. I do not think any man in our parts knows the way to it. Nor does it matter since we have, as you see, a fine, pleasant, green lane that runs from our country into the way.

When Christian saw the man was wise in his own conceit, he whispered to Hopeful, "There is more hope for a fool than for him (Prov. 26:12). When a fool walks along the way, he lacks wisdom, and he shows everyone that he is a fool (Eccl. 10:3). Shall we talk further, or leave him to think about what he has heard? We can talk with him later to see if we can do any good." Hopeful replied,

> Let Ignorance a little while now muse
> On what is said, and let him not refuse
> Good counsel to embrace, lest he remain
> Still ignorant of what is the chief gain.
> God said, those that no understanding have,
> (Although he made them), them he will not save.

HOPE. I do not think it wise to say too much at one time. Let us talk with him later, provided he can handle it.

So they passed Ignorance and continued on. After a short distance, they entered a dark lane. Here they saw a man that seven devils had bound with seven strong cords and were carrying him back to the door on the side of the hill (Matt. 12:45; Prov. 5:22). Good Christian and Hopeful began to tremble. As the devils led the man away, Christian looked to see if he knew him. He thought it might be Turn-away, from the town of Apostasy. He could not clearly see his face, for he hung his head like a thief that is caught. Hopeful saw on his back this inscription, "Wanton professor, and damnable apostate."

CHR. Now I remember what happened to a good man around here.

His name was Little-Faith. He lived in the town of Sincere. This was the problem. At the beginning of this passageway, there is a lane, Broadway-gate. It is called Dead-Man's lane, because many murders are committed there. It was there that Little-Faith, going on a pilgrimage, laid down and slept. Coming down the lane from Broadway-gate were three brothers, all rogues. Their names were Faint-Heart, Mistrust, and Guilt. They saw Little-Faith just as he was waking up. They approached him with threatening language. Little-Faith looked as white as a sheet; he did not have the power to fight or run. Faint-Heart said, Give us your purse. He did not hurry to do it (for he hated to lose his money). Mistrust ran up to him, put his hand in his pocket, and pulled out a bag of silver. Then he hollered, Thieves, thieves! Guilt, with a great club in his hand, struck Little-Faith on the head. The blow knocked him flat. He lay bleeding to death. All this time the thieves stood around. Then they heard someone on the road and feared it might be Great-Grace from the town of Good-Confidence. They ran and left this man alone. After a while, Little-Faith revived, got up, and scrambled on his way. This was the story.

HOPE. Did they take everything he had?

CHR. No. They missed his jewelry. The thieves got most of his spending money, but he was deeply afflicted by this loss. He did not have enough money to bring him to the journey's end. No (if I was not misinformed), he was forced to beg to stay alive for he could not sell his jewelry. He went, as we say, with a hungry belly the rest of the way (1 Pet. 4:18).

HOPE. It is a mystery why they did not get his certificate for admission to the Celestial Gate.

CHR. It is a mystery. They did not miss it through any plans of his. He was so surprised that he did not have the power or skill to hide anything. It was more good providence than his efforts that they missed the certificate (2 Tim. 1:12–14; 2 Pet. 2:9).

HOPE. It must be a comfort that they did not get his jewelry.

CHR. It might have been a greater comfort if he had used it as he should. Those that told me the story said he made little use of his jewelry the rest of the way. He was despondent over the loss of his money. Indeed, he forgot the jewelry for a great part of the journey. Anytime it came into his mind he began to be comforted. Then he thought of his money loss, and this would swallow it all up.

HOPE. Poor man, this could only be a great grief.

CHR. Grief? A grief indeed! It would have been so to any of us, if we had been used to it. It is a wonder that he did not die from the grief of being robbed and wounded in a strange place. I was told he traveled the rest of the way with nothing but doleful and bitter complaints. He told everyone where and how he was robbed, who did it, what he lost, how he was wounded, and how he barely escaped with his life.

HOPE. It is a wonder that hunger did not force him to sell or pawn some jewelry so that he might eat.

CHR. You talk like one whose head is a shell. What could he pawn them for? To whom could he sell them? In all that country where he was robbed, his jewelry was of no value. Nor did he want relief at the price of the jewelry. Besides, had his jewelry been missing at the gate of the Celestial City, he would (and this he knew) have been excluded from an inheritance there. That would have been worse than the appearance and villainy of ten thousand thieves.

HOPE. Why are you so harsh, my brother? Esau sold his birthright for a pot of pottage (Heb. 12:16). That birthright was his greatest jewel. If he did, why not Little-Faith?

CHR. Esau sold his birthright as many do; this excludes them from the chief blessing. But there is a difference between Esau and Little-Faith. Esau's birthright was typical; Little-Faith's jewelry was not. Esau's stomach was his god; Little-Faith's belly was not. Esau's wants came from his fleshy appetite; Little-Faith's did not. Esau could see no further than his lusts. "Look, I am about to die; so what is this birthright to me?" (Gen. 25:32).

Little-Faith thought it was his position to have only a little faith. This kept him from extravagances and made him value his jewelry so as not to sell it, like Esau with his birthright. You never read that Esau had even a little faith. Therefore, do no wonder where only the flesh is considered (as in that man where there is no faith to resist) if he sells his birthright and his soul to the devil of hell. A wild donkey used to the wilderness, that sniffs at the wind in her desire; in her time of mating, who can turn her away (Jer. 2:24)? When their minds are set on lusts, they will have it, whatever the cost.

Little-Faith was of a different temperament. His mind was on things divine. His livelihood was on spiritual things from above. Should he that is of such a temperament sell his jewelry (had there been anyone to buy it) to fill his mind with empty things? Will a man give a penny to fill his belly with hay? Can you persuade the turtledove to live on dead carcasses like a crow? Faithless ones can, for lusts of the flesh they will pawn, mortgage, or sell what they have, including themselves. Yet those with faith, saving faith, even just a little, cannot do it. This, my brother, is your mistake.

HOPE. I acknowledge it. Yet your severe reflection almost makes me angry.

CHR. Why? I just compared you to some of the brisk birds who run to and fro with a shell on their heads. But forget that, consider the subject under debate and all will be well between us.

HOPE. Christian, I am persuaded in my heart that these three fellows are a bunch of cowards. Otherwise they would never have run at the sound of someone on the road. Why didn't Little-Faith take great heart? I think that he might have stood one brush with them and yielded when only when there was no remedy.

CHR. Many have said that they are cowards, but few have found it so in the time of trial. As for a great heart, Little-Faith had none. My brother, I perceive that you would have stood one brush and then yielded. Since this is the height of your stomach now that they are at a distance, should they appear to you as they did to him, you might have second thoughts.

Think again, they are journeymen thieves. They serve under the king of the bottomless pit, who, if necessary, will come to their aid. He walks about like a roaring lion (1 Pet. 5:8). I myself have been where Little-Faith was. I found it a terrible thing. These three villains attacked me;

like a Christian, I began to resist. They just gave a call, and in came their master. I would, as the saying goes, not have given my life for a penny. But, as God would have it, I was clothed with the armor of proof. Even though I was so equipped, I found it hard work to be a man. Only those who have been in the battle can tell what they will do.

HOPE. Well, they ran, but suppose that Great-Grace was in the way.

CHR. True, they and their master have both fled when Great-Grace appeared. And no wonder, he is the King's champion. There is a difference, however, between Little-Faith and the King's champion. Not all the King's subjects are his champions. Nor can they, when tested, do his feats of war. Is it proper to think that a little child could fight Goliath like David? Or that a little wren would have the strength of an ox? Some are strong, some are weak, some have great faith, and some have little. This man was weak. Thus, he went to the wall.

HOPE. I wish it had been Great-Grace.

CHR. If it had, he would have had his hands full. I must tell you, Great-Grace is excellent with his weapons. As long as he keeps them at sword's point, he does well. But if Faint-Heart, Mistrust, or the others get close, it will go hard, for they will knock him down. When a man is down, what can he do?

Whoever looks closely at Great-Grace's face, will see scars and cuts that readily demonstrate what I say. Once I heard he said (when he was in combat), We despaired for our life. Those sturdy rogues and their fellows made David groan, mourn, and roar! Yes, Heman (Ps. 88), and Hezekiah too, though champions in their days, were forced to vigorous action when assaulted by them. Yet, they had their coats soundly brushed. Peter once tried, but even though some say he is the prince of the apostles, they handled him so that he was afraid of a little girl.

Their king responds to their whistle. He is never out of hearing. If at any time they get the worst of the fight, he, if possible, comes to help. It is said of him, "Though the sword reaches him, it cannot avail; nor does spear, dart, or javelin. He regards iron as straw, and bronze as rotten wood. The arrow cannot make him flee; sling-stones become like stubble to him. Darts are regarded as straw. He laughs at the threat of javelins" (Job 41:26–29).

What can a man do in this case? It is true, if a man could always have Job's horse, and the skill and courage to ride him, he might do able things. "Have you given the horse strength? Have you clothed his neck with thunder? Can you frighten him like a locust? His majestic snorting strikes terror. He paws in the valley, and rejoices in his strength; he gallops into the clash of arms. He mocks at fear, and is not frightened; nor does he turn back from the sword. The quiver rattles against him, the glittering spear and javelin. He devours the distance with fierceness and rage; nor does he come to a halt because the trumpet has sounded. At the blast of the trumpet he says, 'Aha!' He smells the battle from afar, the thunder of the captains and shouting" (Job 39:19–25).

But for footmen like you and me, let us never hope to meet an enemy, or boast that we could do better, when we hear of others who have been attacked. Let us not be fooled by thoughts of our own manhood. We would get the worst of it. Witness Peter, whom I mentioned before, he would swagger. Yes, he would. His conceited mind prompted him to say that he would do better for his Master than anyone. Yet who was so defeated and run down by villains as he?

When we hear of robberies on the King's highway, there are two things that we need to do.

1. Go equipped. Be sure to take a shield. It was not having a shield that made him who attacked the Leviathan yield. If we have no shield, he is not afraid of us. Therefore, he that has skill said, "Above all, taking the shield of faith with which you will be able to quench all the fiery darts of the wicked one" (Eph. 6:16).

2. It is also good to have the King's convoy. Yes, he will go with us himself. This made David rejoice in the Valley of the Shadow of Death. Moses would rather have died where he stood, than go one step without his God (Exod. 33:15).

111

Oh, my brother, if he will go with us, we will not be afraid of ten thousands of people who have set themselves against us (Ps. 3:5–8; 27:1–3). But without him, the proud helpers will fall among the slain (Is. 10:4).

I have been in the battle. Though (through the goodness of Him that is best) I am alive, I cannot boast of any manhood. Happy will I be if I meet no more violence, although I fear we are not beyond all danger. Since the lion and the bear, however, have not yet devoured me, I hope God will also deliver us from the next uncircumcised Philistine. Then Christian sang,

> Poor Little-Faith! has been among the thieves?
> Was robbed? Remember this, whoever believes,
> And get more faith; then shall you victors be
> Over ten thousand-else scarce over three.

They went on, and Ignorance followed. They eventually came to a place where they saw a way that put itself into their way. It seemed to be as straight as the way they should go. They did not know which of the two to take. They stopped to consider. As they were thinking, a black man wearing a white robe approached them. He asked why they stood there. They answered that they were going to the Celestial City, but did not know which way to take. "Follow me," said the man, "that is where I am going." They followed him. They came to a road that turned far from the city they desired. Soon, their faces were turned from it. Still they followed him. Before they knew what was happening, he led them into the center of a net. They became so tangled that they did not know what to do. The white robe fell off the black man's back. They were trapped. They lay crying because they could not get free.

CHR. Now I see my error. The shepherds warned us to beware of the Flatterer! As the wise man said, and we have found it this day, "A man who flatters his neighbor spreads a net for his feet" (Prov. 29:5).

HOPE. They gave us directions on how to find the way, but we forgot to read it. We have not kept ourselves from the paths of the destroyer. David was wiser than us, he said, "Concerning the works of men, by the word of Your lips, I have kept away from the paths of the destroyer" (Ps. 17:4). They lay fretting in the net.

At last they saw a Shining One coming toward them with a whip of small cords in his hand. When he arrived he asked where they came from and what they did there. They answered that they were poor pilgrims going to Zion. A black man, clothed in white, led them from their way. He told us to follow him for he was going to Zion. Then said he with the whip, It is Flatterer, a false apostle, that has transformed himself into an angel of light (Dan. 11:32; 2 Cor. 11:13, 14). He tore the net and let them out. Then he said, Follow me, I will set you in your way again. He led them back to the way they left to follow the Flatterer. Then he asked, Where did you sleep last night? They said, With the shepherds on the Delectable Mountains. He asked if they had the shepherds' directions. They answered, Yes. Did you not, said he, read your directions? They answered, No. He asked, Why? They said they forgot. He then asked, if the shepherds told them to beware of the Flatterer. They answered, Yes. But we did not imagine that this fine-spoken man was him (Rom. 16:17, 18).

I saw in my dream that he ordered them to lie down. When they did, he severely chastised them to teach where they should walk (Deut. 25:2; 2 Chr. 6:27). As he disciplined them, he said, "As many as I love, I rebuke and chasten; therefore be zealous and repent" (Rev. 3:19). This done, he ordered them on their way with instruction to pay strict attention to the shepherds' directions. They thanked him for all his kindness and went quietly along the right way, singing,

> Come here, you that walk along the way,
> See how the pilgrims fare that go astray:
> They are caught in an entangling net,
> Cause good counsel they lightly did forget:
> 'Tis true, they rescued were; but yet, you see,
> They're scourged to boot; let this your caution be.

After awhile, they saw in the distance one coming quietly and alone along the highway. Christian said, There is a man with his back toward Zion; he is coming to meet us.

HOPE. I see him. Let us pay attention, should he also prove a Flatterer. He came closer and closer and finally reached them. His name was Atheist. He asked where they were going.

CHR. We are going to Mount Zion.

Then Atheist fell into a great laughter.

CHR. Why are you laughing?

ATHEIST. You are ignorant. You take a tedious journey and have nothing but pains for your travel.

CHR. Man, do you think we will not be received?

ATHEIST. Received! There is not such a place as you dream of in all this world.

CHR. There is in the world to come.

ATHEIST. When I was in my own country, I heard what you now affirm. I have been seeking this city twenty years, but have found no more of it than I did the first day (Eccl. 10:15; Jer. 17:15).

CHR. We have heard and believe that there is such a place to be found.

ATHEIST. If I had not believed, I would not have come this far. Finding no city (and I should have, had been such a place, for I have gone farther than you to seek it), I am going back. I will try to refresh myself with the things that I threw away for hopes of that which is not.

CHR. Is what this man said true?

HOPE. Pay attention, he is one of the Flatterers. Remember what it has already cost for listening to his kind. What! No Mount Zion? Did we not see the gate of the city from the Delectable Mountains? Are we no longer going to walk by faith? (2 Cor. 5:7).

Let us continue, in case the man with the whip overtakes us. You should have taught me the lesson which I will sound in your ears, "Cease listening to instruction, my son, and you will stray from the words of knowledge" (Prov. 19:27). My brother, stop listening to him, and believe to the saving of the soul.

CHR. My brother, I did not put the question to you because I doubted the truth of our belief, but to prove and obtain a fruit of the honesty of your heart. I know the god of this world has blinded this man. Let you and me go on, knowing that we have the truth, for no lie is of the truth (1 John 5:21).

HOPE. Now I rejoice in hope of the glory of God. So they turned from the man. He laughed at them and went his way.

I saw in my dream that they went on until they came to a country whose air naturally tended to make strangers drowsy. Hopeful began to slow and grow sleepy. He said to Christian, I am so drowsy that I can scarcely hold my eyes open. Let us lie down here and take a nap.

CHR. No! If we sleep here, we many never wake.

HOPE. Why, my brother? Sleep is sweet to the working man. We will be refreshed if we take a nap.

CHR. Do you remember that one of the shepherds told us to be aware of the Enchanted Ground? He meant that we should not sleep here. "Therefore let us not sleep, as others do, but let us watch and be sober" (1 Thess. 5:6).

HOPE. I acknowledge my fault. Had I been alone, I would have run the danger of death by sleeping. What the wise man said is true, "Two are better than one" (Eccl. 4:9). Your company has been my mercy, and you will have a good reward for your labor.

CHR. Now, then, let's have a good discussion to keep from falling asleep.

HOPE. With all my heart.

CHR. Where will we begin?

HOPE. Where God began with us. You begin, if you please.

CHR. I will first sing you a song:

> When saints do sleepy grow, let them come hither,
> And hear how these two pilgrims talk together;
> Yea, let them learn of them in any wise,

Thus to keep open their drowsy, slumbering eyes.
Saints' fellowship, if it is managed well,
Keeps them awake, and that in spite of hell.

Christian said, I will ask you a question. When did you first think
of what you are doing now?

HOPE. Do you mean, how I first came to look after the good of
my soul?

CHR. Yes, that is my meaning.

HOPE. I continued for a long time to delight in things that were seen
and sold at our fair. Things that would have drowned me in perdition and
destruction.

CHR. What were they?

HOPE. I delighted in the treasures and riches of the world, rioting,
reveling, drinking, swearing, lying, uncleanness, Sabbath-breaking, and
what not. All the things that tend to destroy the soul. The end of these
things is death (Rom. 6:21–23). Because of these things the wrath of
God comes on the sons of disobedience (Eph. 5:6). I listened and considered things that are divine. Things I heard from you and beloved Faithful,
who was put to death for his faith and good living in Vanity Fair.

CHR. Did you fall under the power of this conviction?

HOPE. No, I was not willing to know the evil of sin, nor the
damnation that follows its commission. I endeavored, when my mind
first began to be shaken with the word, to shut my eyes against the light.

CHR. What caused the first workings of God's blessed Spirit on
you?

HOPE. The causes were, 1. I was ignorant that this was the work
of God in me. I never thought that by being aware of sin, God begins
the conversion of a sinner. 2. Sin was sweet to my flesh, and I hated to
leave it. 3. I did not know how to give up my old friends, their presence
and actions were what I wanted. 4. The hours of conviction were so
troublesome and terrifying that I could not stand the memory of them
on my heart.

CHR. It seems that at some point you got rid of your trouble?

HOPE. Yes, but it would come to mind again. Then I would be as bad, no, worse than I was before.

CHR. Why? What brought your sins to mind again?

HOPE. Many things:

1. If I met a good man in the streets; or,
2. If I heard any sins read in the Bible; or,
3. If I had a headache; or,
4. If I was told that some of my neighbors were sick; or,
5. If I heard the bell toll for someone that died; or,
6. If I thought of dying myself; or,
7. If I heard that sudden death happened to others.

8. But especially when I thought that I would quickly come to judgment.

CHR. Could you readily get rid of the guilt of sin when these thoughts came to you?

HOPE. No, when they got a grip on my conscience, if I thought about going back to sin (though my mind was turned against it), it was double torment.

CHR. How did you do it?

HOPE. I thought I must work to mend my life. Or else I was sure to be damned.

CHR. Did you endeavor to mend your life?

HOPE. Yes. I fled from not only my sins, but from sinful company. I took to religious duties, praying, reading, weeping for sin, speaking truth to my neighbors, etc. These things I did along with many other duties too numerous to mention.

CHR. Did you think well of yourself?

HOPE. Yes, for a while, but my trouble returned and I was up to my neck in reformations.

CHR. How did that happen, since you are now reformed?

HOPE. Several things brought it on me, especially sayings like, "All our righteousness are like filthy rags" (Isa. 64:6). "For by the works of the law no flesh shall be justified" (Gal. 2:16). "When you have done all those things which you are commanded, say, "We are unprofitable servants" (Luke 17:10).

Then I began to reason with myself. If all my righteousness is as filthy rags, if by the deeds of the law no man can be justified, and if, when we have done all, we are still unprofitable servants, then it is foolish to think we can obtain heaven by the law. If a man runs up a debt of one hundred pounds to a shopkeeper and then pays for everything he buys, his old debt stands in the book unpaid. The shopkeeper may sue and throw him in prison until he pays the debt.

CHR. How did you apply this?

HOPE. I thought that since my sins ran up a great debt in God's book, my reforming could not pay it off. Therefore I should still be reformed. But how will I be free from the danger of damnation that I brought by my former transgressions?

CHR. A good application, please go on.

HOPE. Another thing that has troubled me, if I look narrowly into the best of what I do now, I still see sin, new sin, mixing with the best of what I do. I am forced to conclude that despite my former fond conceits of myself and duties, I have committed sin enough in one day to send me to hell, even though my former life had been faultless.

CHR. What did you do?

HOPE. Do! I did not know what to do until I surrendered my mind to Faithful, for he and I were well acquainted. He told me that unless I could obtain the righteousness of a man who never sinned, neither my own, nor all the righteousness of the world, could save me.

CHR. Do you think he spoke the truth?

HOPE. Had he told me when I was pleased and satisfied with my life's changes, I would have called him a fool for his effort. Now, since I see my own infirmity and the sin that clings to my best performance, I am forced to agree with him.

CHR. Did you think, when he first suggested it, that there was such a man of whom it might justly be said, he never committed a sin?

HOPE. I must confess the words at first sounded strange. After spending more time talking with him, however, I had full conviction and believed it.

CHR. Did you ask him who that man was, and how you could be justified by him?

HOPE. Yes! He told me it was the Lord Jesus who sat down at the right hand of God (Heb. 10:12–21). He said, you must be justified by him, by trusting in what he has done himself when he was on earth and what he suffered when he hung on the tree (Rom. 4:5; Col. 1:14; 1 Pet. 1:19). I asked him how one man's righteousness could be sufficient to justify another before God. Faithful told me that he was the mighty God. He did what he did and died the death not for himself, but for me. His actions, and their worthiness, would be imputed, if I believed in him.

CHR. What did you do?

HOPE. I objected to believing. I thought he was not willing to save me.

CHR. What did Faithful say?

HOPE. He told me go to him and see. I said that was presumption. He said, No, I was invited to come (Matt. 11:28). Then he gave me a book of Jesus' writings, to encourage me to freely come. He said, concerning that book, heaven and earth will pass away, but My words will by no means pass away (Matt. 24:35). Then I asked him what I must do when I came. He told me to plead on my knees (Ps. 95:6; Dan. 6:10), with all my heart and soul (Jer. 29:12, 13), for the Father to reveal him to me. Then I asked how to make my requests. He said, Go, and you will find him on the mercy-seat, where he sits all year long to give pardon and forgiveness to those that come (Exod. 25:22; Lev. 16:2; Num. 7:89; Heb. 4:16). I told him that I did not know what to say. He told me to essentially say this, God be merciful to me a sinner. Make me to know and believe in Jesus Christ.

I see that if his righteousness had not been, or if I had no faith in that righteousness, I am utterly thrown away. Lord, I have heard that you are a merciful God, that you have ordained your Son Jesus Christ to be the Savior of the world, and that you are willing to offer him to such a poor sinner as I am—and I am a sinner indeed. Lord, take this opportunity and magnify your grace in the salvation of my soul, through your Son Jesus Christ. Amen.

CHR. Did you do as you were told?

HOPE. Yes, over, and over, and over.

CHR. Did the Father reveal the Son to you?

HOPE. Not at first, second, third, fourth, fifth, not the sixth time either.

CHR. What did you do?

HOPE. I did not know what to do.

CHR. Did you think about not praying?

HOPE. Yes, a hundred times twice over.

CHR. Why didn't you?

HOPE. I believed that the truth had been told me, that without the righteousness of this Christ all the world could not save me. Therefore, I thought if I stop praying, I would die, but I would rather die at the throne of grace. This came to my mind, "Though it tarries, wait for it; because it will surely come, it will not tarry" (Hab. 2:3). So I continued praying until the Father showed me his Son.

CHR. How was he revealed to you?

HOPE. I did not see him with my body's eyes, but with the eyes of my understanding (Eph. 1:18,19). One day I was very sad, I think sadder than at any time in my life. This sadness was through a fresh sight of the greatness and vileness of my sins. I was looking for nothing but hell and everlasting damnation for my soul. Suddenly, as I thought, I saw the Lord Jesus looking down from heaven on me and saying, "Believe on the Lord Jesus Christ, and you will be saved" (Acts 16:31).

I replied, Lord, I am a great, a very great sinner. He answered, "My grace is sufficient for you" (2 Cor. 12:9). Then I said, But, Lord, what is it to believe? Then I saw from that saying, "He who comes to me shall never hunger, and he who believes on me shall never thirst" (John 6:35). Believing and coming was one. He that came and ran in his heart and affections after salvation by Christ, he indeed believed in Christ. Then the water stood in my eyes and I asked, Lord, may such a great sinner as I, be accepted and saved by you? I heard him say, "The one who comes to me I will by no means cast out" (John 6:37).

I said, But how, Lord, must I consider you in coming to you that my faith may be placed on you? He said, "Christ Jesus came into the world to save sinners" (1 Tim. 1:15). He is the end of the law for righteousness to everyone who believes (Rom. 10:4, and chap. 4). He died for our sins, and rose again for our justification (Rom. 4:25). He loved us and washed us from our sins in his own blood (Rev. 1:5). He is the Mediator between God and us (1 Tim. 2:5). He ever lives to make intercession for us (Heb. 7:25).

From all this I gathered that I must look for righteousness in his person and satisfaction for my sins through his blood. What he did in obedience to his Father's law, and in submitting to the penalty of sin, was not for himself but for those who will thankfully accept it for salvation. Now my heart was full of joy, my eyes full of tears, and my affections running over with love for the name, people, and ways of Jesus Christ.

CHR. This was indeed a revelation of Christ to your soul. Tell me particularly what effect this had on your spirit.

HOPE. It made me see that the world, despite all its righteousness, is in a state of condemnation. It made me see that God the Father, though he is just, can justify the sinner who comes to him. It made me greatly ashamed of the vileness in my former life. It confounded me with the sense of my ignorance because there was never a thought in my heart that showed me the beauty of Jesus Christ. It made me love a holy life and long to do something for the honor and glory of the name of the Lord Jesus. I thought that if I now had a thousand gallons of blood in my body, I could spill it all for the sake of the Lord Jesus.

I saw in my dream that Hopeful looked back and saw Ignorance coming after them. Look, he said to Christian, how far back the youngster loiters.

CHR. Yes, yes, I see him, he does not care for our company.

HOPE. It would not hurt him to keep pace with us.

CHR. True, but I warrant he thinks otherwise.

HOPE. I think he does, but let us wait for him. (So they did.)

Then Christian said to him, Come, man, why do you stay so far behind?

IGNOR. I take pleasure in walking alone, much more than walking with company, unless I like them better.

Christian said to Hopeful (softly), I told you he did not care for our company. Come, let us talk away the time in this isolated place. Directing his speech to Ignorance, he said, How do you do? How does it stand between God and your soul?

IGNOR. I hope well. I am always full of good thoughts that come into my mind to comfort me as I walk.

CHR. What good thoughts? Please tell us.

IGNOR. I think of God and heaven.

CHR. So do the devils and damned souls.

IGNOR. But I think of them and desire them.

CHR. So do many that are never likely to come there. "The soul of the lazy man desires and has nothing" (Prov. 13:4).

IGNOR. But I think of them, and leave all for them.

CHR. I doubt that. To leave all is difficult, more difficult than many are aware of. Why are you persuaded that you have left all for God and heaven?

IGNOR. My heart tells me so.

CHR. The wise man says, "He who trusts in his own heart is a fool" (Prov. 28:26).

IGNOR. That is spoken about an evil heart. My heart is good.

CHR. Can you prove it?

IGNOR. It comforts me with hope of heaven.

CHR. Perhaps through its deceitfulness, a man's heart may minister comfort in the hope of that thing for which he has no basis to hope.

IGNOR. My heart and life agree. Therefore my hope is well grounded.

CHR. Who told you that your heart and life agree?

IGNOR. My heart tells me.

CHR. "Ask my friend if I am a thief." Your heart tells you so! Unless the word of God bears witness in this matter, other testimony is of no value.

IGNOR. Is it not a good heart that has good thoughts? Is not a good life lived according to God's commandments?

CHR. Yes, it is a good heart that has good thoughts. A good life is lived according to God's commandments. But it is one thing to have these, and another thing to think that you do.

IGNOR. Tell me, what do you consider good thoughts and a life according to God's commandments?

CHR. There are different kinds of good thoughts; some respecting ourselves, some God, some Christ, and some other things.

IGNOR. What is a good thought respecting ourselves?

CHR. Those that agree with the word of God.

IGNOR. When do thoughts of ourselves agree with the word of God?

CHR. When we pass the same judgment on ourselves that the word passes on us. Let me explain, the word of God says of people in a natural condition, "There is none righteous, no, not one. There is none that does good, no, not one." It also says, "Every intent of the thoughts of his heart was only evil continually" (Gen. 6:5; Rom. 3). And again, "The imagination of man's heart is evil from his youth" (Gen. 8:21). When we think this way about ourselves, are our thoughts good according to the word of God?

IGNOR. I will never believe that my heart is this bad.

CHR. Therefore you never had one good thought concerning yourself in your life. But let me continue. As the word passes judgment on our hearts, it also passes judgment on our ways. When the thoughts of our hearts and ways agree with the judgment that the word gives for both, then both are good because they are in agreement.

IGNOR. What do you mean?

CHR. The word of God says that man's ways are crooked, not good but perverse. It says they are naturally out of the good way and they do not know it (Ps. 125:5; Prov. 2:15; Rom. 3:12). Now, when a man thinks about his ways, when he sensibly and with heart-humiliation thinks, then he has good thoughts of his ways. Now, his thoughts agree with the judgment of the word of God.

IGNOR. What are good thoughts concerning God?

CHR. Even as I have said concerning ourselves, we have the right thoughts of God when we agree with what the word says about him; when we think of his being and attributes as the word teaches of which I cannot speak in general. We have the right thoughts of God when we speak of him with reference to us; when we think that he knows us better than we know ourselves; when we know he can see sin in us and we can see none in ourselves; when we think he knows our innermost thoughts; and our heart with all its depth is always open to his eyes; when we think that all our righteousness stinks in his nostrils and he cannot tolerate us to stand before him in any confidence, even in our best performances.

IGNOR. Do you think that I am a fool to think that God can see no further than I? Or I would come to God in the best of my performances?

CHR. What do you think?

IGNOR. Why, to be short, I think I believe in Christ for justification.

CHR. Why do you think you must believe in Christ when you see no need of him? You do not see either your original or actual infirmities. You have such an opinion of yourself, and what you do, that you never see the necessity of Christ's personal righteousness to justify you before God. How then can you say, I believe in Christ?

IGNOR. I believe well enough, for all that.

CHR. How do you believe?

IGNOR. I believe Christ died for sinners. I will be justified before God from the curse by his gracious acceptance of my obedience to his laws. Thus, Christ makes my religious duties acceptable to his Father by virtue of his merits. So will I be justified.

CHR. Let me give an answer to this confession of your faith.

1. You believe with a fantastical faith that is not described in the word.

2. You believe with a false faith that takes justification from the personal righteousness of Christ and applies it to you.

3. This faith does not make Christ a justifier of you, but your actions and yourself for your action's sake. This is false.

4. Therefore this faith is deceitful. It will leave you under wrath in the day of God Almighty. True justifying faith makes the soul, sensible of its lost condition by the law, fly for refuge to Christ's righteousness. (His righteousness is not an act of grace by which he makes, for justification, your obedience accepted with God. But his personal obedience to the law, in doing and suffering for us what that required at our hands.) This righteousness is accepted by true faith and under its skirt the soul is covered and presented spotless before God. It is accepted and exonerated from condemnation.

IGNOR. What! Would you have us trust in what Christ in his own person has done without us? This concept would loosen the reins of our lust and allow us to live as we wanted. What difference how we live, if we are justified by Christ's personal righteousness when we believe?

CHR. Ignorance is your name; as your name is so are you. Your answer demonstrates what I said. Ignorant you are of what justifying righteousness is. Ignorant you are of how to secure your soul, through faith, from the heavy wrath of God. Yes, you are ignorant of the true effects of saving faith in this righteousness of Christ. Christ's righteousness is to break and win the heart to God in Christ, to love his name, his word, ways, and people, and not as you ignorantly imagine.

HOPE. Ask him if ever he had Christ revealed to him from heaven.

IGNOR. What? You believe in revelations! I believe that what you and all the rest of you say about this subject is the fruit of a distracted brain.

HOPE. Why? Christ is so hidden in God from the natural contemplation of the flesh that he cannot be known, unless God the Father reveals him.

IGNOR. That is your faith, but it is not mine. I do not doubt that my faith is as good as yours, though I do not have so many whimsies as you in my head.

CHR. Let me say something. You should not speak so lightly. This I will boldly affirm, even as my good companion has done, no man can know Jesus Christ except by the revelation of the Father. Yes, and by faith the soul lays hold of Christ (if the soul is right), and is worked by the exceeding greatness of his mighty power (Matt. 11:27; 1 Cor. 12:3; Eph. 1:17–19). The working of faith, poor Ignorance, you are ignorant of. Wake up, see your wretchedness, and fly to the Lord Jesus. By his righteousness, which is the righteousness of God (for he himself is God), you will be delivered from condemnation.

IGNOR. You walk to fast. I cannot keep up. Go ahead, I must stay behind for a while.

Then they said,

> Well, Ignorance, will you yet foolish be,
> To slight good counsel, ten times given thee?
> And if thou yet refuse it, thou shalt know,
> Ere long, the evil of thy doing so.
> Remember, man, in time: stoop, do not fear:
> Good counsel, taken well, saves; therefore hear.
> But if thou yet shalt slight it, thou wilt be
> The loser, Ignorance, I'll warrant thee.

THE TENTH STAGE

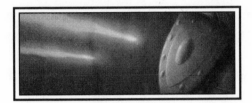

Then Christian said to his friend,

    CHR. Come, my good Hopeful, I perceive you and I must walk by ourselves again.

I saw in my dream that they went on and Ignorance came hobbling after. Christian said to his companion, I greatly pity this poor man. It will certainly go ill with him at the end.

    HOPE. There are many in our town in his condition, entire families, entire streets, and some are pilgrims too. If there is so many in our town, how many, do you think, must be in the place where he was born?

    CHR. The word said, "He has blinded their eyes, lest they should see (John 12:40).

Now that we are by ourselves, what do you think of such men? Have they ever been convicted of sin? Consequently do they not fear that their state is dangerous?

    HOPE. No, but answer that question yourself, for you are older.

    CHR. Sometimes (as I think) they may. Being naturally ignorant, they do not understand convictions are for their good. Thus, they desperately seek to stifle them and presumptuously continue to flatter themselves in the way of their own hearts.

HOPE. I do believe, as you say, fear does much for men's good. If it is proper fear, it makes them right at the beginning to go on their pilgrimage.

CHR. Without a doubt, the word says, "The fear of the Lord is the beginning of wisdom" (Job 28:28; Ps. 111:10; Prov. 1:7; 9:10).

HOPE. How would you describe proper fear?

CHR. True or proper fear is discovered by three things:

1. When it occurs, it is caused by saving convictions for sin.

2. It drives the soul to hold fast to Christ for salvation.

3. It develops and continues a great reverence of God, his word, and ways in the soul. It keeps the soul tender. It makes the soul afraid to turn to the right or to the left or to anything that would dishonor God, break its peace, grieve the Spirit, or cause the enemy to speak reproachfully.

HOPE. Well said. I believe you have spoken the truth. Are we almost past the Enchanted Ground?

CHR. Why? Are you weary of this conversation?

HOPE. No, I just want to know where we are.

CHR. We have about two miles to go. Let us return to our conversation. The ignorant do not know that conviction puts them in fear. This is for their good, but they try to stifle it.

HOPE. How do they stifle it?

CHR. 1. They think those fears are from the devil (though indeed they are God's work). Thinking this, they resist them as things that would directly overthrow them. 2. They also think that these fears tend to spoil their faith. When, alas for them, poor men that they are, they have no fears at all. Thus, they harden their hearts against them. 3. They presume they should not fear. Thus, they are presumptuously confident. 4. They see those fears tend to take away their pitiful old self-holiness. Thus, they resist them with all their might.

HOPE. I know something of this, before I knew myself it was so with me.

CHR. Well, for a while, we will leave our neighbor Ignorance by himself and discuss another profitable question.

HOPE. With all my heart. You begin.

CHR. Did you know, about ten years ago, one Temporary who lived in your parts? He was a forward man in religion then.

HOPE. Know him! Yes! He dwelt in Graceless, a town about two miles from Honesty. He lived next door to Turnback.

CHR. He actually lived under the same roof. Well, that man was much awakened once. I believe he had some sight of his sins and its wages.

HOPE. I agree, for (my house not being more than three miles from him) he would often come to me with many tears. I truly pitied the man. He was not altogether without hope, for it is not everyone that cries, "Lord, Lord!"

CHR. He told me that he resolved to go on a pilgrimage. Then, he met one Save-self and became a stranger.

HOPE. Since we are talking about him, let us discuss why he suddenly backslid.

CHR. It may be profitable.

HOPE. Well, in my judgment, there are four reasons.

1. Though the consciences of such men are awakened, their minds are not changed. When the power of guilt wears away, what made them religious ceases; then they naturally turn again to their own course. Just as a dog that is sick from what he has eaten, vomits and throws up. Not that he does this of a free mind (if we may say a dog has a mind), but because it troubles his stomach. When his sickness is over and his stomach has settled, he turns around and eats his vomit. It is truth that is written, "A dog returns to his own vomit" (2 Pet. 2:22). Thus, I say, being hot for heaven only because of the sense and fear of hell's torments will chill and cool as their desires for heaven and salvation cool. Then it comes to pass that when their guilt and fear is gone, their desires for heaven and happiness die and they return to their original course.

2. Another reason is they have slavish fears that master them. I speak of their fear of men; "The fear of man brings a snare" (Prov. 29:25). So then, though they seem to be hot for heaven so long as the flames of hell are about their ears, when that terror is over, they have second thoughts. Namely that it is good to be wise and not risk (they know not what) the hazard of losing all, or bringing themselves into unavoidable and unnecessary troubles. So they fall in with the world again.

3. The shame that comes with religion lies as a block in their way. They are proud and haughty; religion in their eye is low and contemptible. Thus, when they have lost their sense of hell and the wrath to come, they return again to the world.

4. Guilt, and meditating on terror, is grievous to them. They do not like to see misery before they come to it. Although the sight of it at first, if they love that sight, might make them fly to where the righteous fly and are safe. Because, as I hinted before, they shun the thoughts of guilt and terror, once they are rid of their awareness about the terrors and wrath of God, they gladly harden their hearts, and choose ways that will harden them more and more.

CHR. You are pretty close. The bottom is a lack of change in their mind and will. They are like the criminal that stands before the judge, quaking and trembling. He seems to heartily repent, but the bottom is fear of the hangman's noose. He does not detest his offence. This is evident, because if he is given liberty he will be a thief and rogue again. But, if his mind is changed, he will be different.

HOPE. Now that I have shown you why they are going back, will you show me how they go.

CHR. Willingly.

1. They no longer remember God, death, and the coming judgment.

2. They throw off by degrees their private duties, closet prayer, curbing their lusts, watching, sorrow for sin, and the like.

3. They shun the company of lively and warm Christians.

4. Then, they grow cold to public duty, hearing, reading, godly conference, and the like.

5. They begin to pick holes, as we say, in the coats of some of the godly. They devilishly have a seeming color to throw religion (for infirmities they have seen) behind their backs.

6. They begin to adhere to, and associate with, carnal, loose, and careless men.

7. They give way to carnal and careless secret discussions. They rejoice if they can see such things in any that are counted honest, so that they may more boldly do it through their example.

8. After this they begin to play with little sins openly.

9. Then, being hardened, they show themselves as they are, launched again into the gulf of misery. Unless a miracle of grace prevents it, they everlastingly perish in their deceit.

Now I saw in my dream that the pilgrims had passed the Enchanted Ground and were entering the country of Beulah. Here the air was sweet and pleasant (Isaiah 62:4-12; Song 2:10-12). Their way ran directly through Beulah, so they comforted themselves there for a season. They heard the bird constantly singing, saw the flowers appear in the earth, and heard the voice of the turtledove in the land. In this country the sun shines night and day because this was beyond the Valley of the Shadow of Death and out of the reach of Giant Despair. They could not see from this place the Doubting Castle. They were within sight of the city they were going to. Here, they also met some of the inhabitants, for in this land the Shining Ones commonly walked because it bordered heaven.

In this land the contract between the Bride and the Bridegroom was renewed. Yes, here, "as the bridegroom rejoices over the bride, so God rejoices over them." There was no shortage of corn and wine. They had abundance of everything they sought in their pilgrimage. They heard voices from the city, loud voices, saying, "Say to the daughter of Zion, Behold, your salvation comes! Behold, his reward is with him!" Here all the inhabitants of the country called them "the holy People, the redeemed of the Lord, sought out," etc.

Now, as they walked in this land, there was more rejoicing than in the remote parts of the kingdom. They had a perfect view of the city. It was built of pearls and precious stones. The streets were paved with gold. The natural glory of the city and the reflection of the sunbeams on it made Christian sick with desire. Hopeful had the same symptoms. They laid down for a while, crying out because of their desire, "If you see my Beloved, tell him that I am sick of love."

Being strengthened and better able to bear their sickness, they walked on and came closer. There were orchards, vineyards, and gardens; their gates opened to the highway. As they came to these places, the gardener stood in the way. The pilgrims asked, Who owns these fine vineyards and gardens? He answered, They are the King's, and are planted here for his delight and for the comfort of the pilgrims. The gardener invited them into the vineyards, told them to refresh themselves, and to eat their fill (Deut. 23:24). He also showed them the King's walks and arbors where he delights to be. Here they stopped and slept.

I saw in my dream that they talked more in their sleep than they did in their journey. They dreamed that the gardener said, It is the nature of the fruit of these vineyards that "the wine goes down smoothly for my beloved, moving gently the lips of sleepers" (Song 7:9).

I saw when they woke that they prepared to go up to the city. But, as I said, the reflection of the sun on the city (for the city was pure gold, Rev. 21:18), was so extremely glorious that they could only look at it through an instrument made for that purpose (2 Cor. 3:18). I saw as they went on that they met two men in garments that shined like gold, and their faces shined like light.

These men asked the pilgrims where they came from. They answered them. They asked them where they had lodged, what difficulties, dangers, comforts, and pleasures, they had met in the way. They told them. Then the men said, You have only two difficulties and you will be in the City, but you must obtain it by your own faith.

Christian and his companion asked the men to go with them. They agreed. I saw in my dream that they went together until they were in sight of the gate.

I further saw that between them and the gate was a deep river and no bridge. At the sight of this river the pilgrims were stunned. The men with them said, You must go through the river, or you cannot come in at the gate.

The pilgrims inquired if there was another way to the gate. They answered, Yes. But only two, Enoch and Elijah, walked that path since the foundation of the world, nor will any others until the last trumpet will sound. The pilgrims, especially Christian, began to despair. They looked but no way was found to escape the river. They asked the men if every part of the river was deep. They said, No, but they could not help them beyond saying that they would find it deeper or shallower as they believed in the King of the place.

They entered the water. Christian began to sink. He cried to his good friend Hopeful, I sink in deep waters. The billows go over my head. All his waves go over me. Selah.

Hopeful said, Be of good cheer, my brother, I feel the bottom. It is good. Christian said, Ah, my friend, the sorrows of death have surrounded me. I will not see the land that flows with milk and honey. Then a great darkness and horror fell on Christian. He could not see ahead. Here, in a great measure, he lost his senses. He could not remember or talk about any of the sweet refreshments he had in his pilgrimage. All his words tended to discover that he had horror of mind and heart fear that he would die in the river and never obtain entrance at the gate. They that stood by perceived he was greatly troubled by the thoughts of the sins he had committed, both before and during his pilgrimage. It was also observed that he was troubled with evil spirits, for he intimated as much.

Hopeful did everything he could do to keep his brother's head above water. Sometimes he would go down. Then, after a while, he would come up half dead. Hopeful tried to comfort him. Brother, I see the gate. The men are standing to receive us. Christian would answer, It is you, it is you they wait for. You have been hopeful ever since I knew you. So have you, he said to Christian. Ah, brother, Christian said, surely if I was right he would rise to help me. He has brought me to the snare and left me because of my sins. Hopeful said, My brother, you have forgotten the text where it said of the wicked, "There are no pangs in their death, but their strength is firm. They are not troubled as other men, nor are they plagued like other men" (Ps. 73:4, 5). These troubles and distresses that you go through in these waters are not a sign that God has forsaken you. They are sent to test you, to see if you will call to mind what you have received of his goodness and live on him in your distress.

Then I saw in my dream that Christian was thinking as Hopeful added these words, Be of good cheer, Jesus Christ makes you whole. With that Christian cried out in a loud voice, I see him again and he tells me, "When you pass through the waters, I will be with you; and through the rivers, they shall not overflow you" (Is. 43:2). Then they both took courage. After that the enemy was as still as a stone until they crossed over. Christian eventually found ground to stand on and the rest of the river was shallow. Thus they crossed over.

On the riverbank, waiting for them when they came out of the river, were the two shining men. They greeted them. We are ministering spirits, sent to minister to those that will be the heirs of salvation. They went toward the gate.

The city stood on a mighty hill. The pilgrims climbed that hill with ease because these two men lead them by the arms. They left their mortal garments in the river. Although they went in with them, they came out without them. Thus, they went with much agility and speed even though the foundation on which the city was built was higher than the clouds. They went up through the region of the air, sweetly talking, being comforted because they safely crossed the river and had glorious companions to help them.

The conversation with the Shining Ones was about the glory of the place. They were told that its beauty and glory was inexpressible. There, they said, is "Mount Zion, the heavenly Jerusalem, to an innumerable company of angels, and to the spirits of just men made perfect" (Heb. 12:22–24). You are going to the paradise of God. You will see the tree of life and eat of its never-fading fruits. You will be given white robes.

Every day your walk and talk will be with the King, even all the days of eternity (Rev. 2:7; 3:4, 5; 22:5).

You will never again see the things you saw in the lower region on earth. "There shall be no more death, nor sorrow, nor crying. There shall be no more pain, for the former things have passed away" (Rev. 21:4). You are going to Abraham, Isaac, Jacob, and the prophets, men that God has taken away from the evil to come. They are now "resting on their beds, each one walking in his righteousness."

The pilgrims asked, What will we do in the holy place? They answered, You will receive the comfort of all your work and have joy for all your sorrow. You will reap what you have sown, the fruit of all your prayers, tears, and sufferings for the King by the way (Gal. 6:7, 8). You will wear crowns of gold and enjoy the perpetual sight and vision of the Holy One, for "there you shall see Him as He is." (1 John 3:2).

There you will serve him whom you found difficult to serve in the world because of your flesh. There you will continually praise with shouting and thanksgiving. There your eyes will be delighted with seeing and your ears with hearing the pleasant voice of the Mighty One. There you will again enjoy your friends that came here before you. There you will with joy receive everyone that follows you into the holy place. There you will be clothed with glory and majesty and put into a carriage of state fit to ride with the King of Glory. When he shall come with trumpet sound in the clouds, as on the wings of the wind, you shall come with him. When he sits on the throne of judgment, you shall sit by him. Yes, and when he passes sentence on all the workers of iniquity, be they angels or men, you will have a voice in that judgment, because they were his and your enemies. When he shall again return to the city, you shall go too with the trumpet sound and be forever with him (1 Thess. 4:14–17; Jude 14, 15; Dan. 7:9, 10; 1 Cor. 6:2, 3).

While they were approaching the gate, a company of the heavenly host came out to meet them. The two Shining Ones said, These men loved our Lord when they were in the world. They left all for his holy name. He has sent us to go after them. We have brought them this far on their journey to go and look in their Redeemer's face with joy. Then the heavenly host gave a great shout, "Blessed are those who are called to the marriage supper of the Lamb" (Rev. 19:9). Several of the King's trumpeters, clothed in white and shining garments, made the heavens echo with their melodious sound. These trumpeters greeted Christian and his friend with ten thousand welcomes of shouts and trumpets.

This done, they surrounded them, some in front, some behind, some on the right, and some on the left (as it were to guard them through the upper regions). They continued their melodious sound in high notes. The sight was as if heaven itself had come down to meet them. They walked on together. As they walked, the trumpeters with joyful sound would mix their music with looks and gestures to signify to Christian and his brother how welcome they were.

Swallowed by the sight of angels and the sounds of their melodious notes, these two men were in heaven before they reached it. The city itself came into view. They thought they heard the bells ringing to welcome them. What tongue or pen can tell their glorious joyful thoughts of dwelling with this company forever and ever.

When they arrived at the gate, there was written over it, in letters of gold,

"BLESSED ARE THEY THAT DO HIS COMMANDMENTS, THAT THEY MAY HAVE RIGHT TO THE TREE OF LIFE, AND MAY ENTER IN THROUGH THE GATES INTO THE CITY."

Then, I saw in my dream, the shining men told them to call at the gate. This they did. Someone above looked over the gate; it was Enoch, Moses, and Elijah. It was said, These pilgrims have come from the City of Destruction because of the love they have for the King of this place. The pilgrims presented the certificate they received in the beginning of their journey. They were carried to the King, who read it and asked, Where are the men? It was answered, They are standing outside the gate. The King commanded, "Open the gates, that the righteous nation which keeps the truth may enter in" (Is. 26:2).

I saw in my dream the two men enter the gate. As they did, they were transfigured. They had garments that shined like gold. Harps and crowns were given them. The harps for praise and the crowns for honor. Then I heard in my dream all the bells in the city rang again for joy. It was said to them,

"ENTER INTO THE JOY OF YOUR LORD."

I also heard the men, they sang with a loud voice,

"BLESSING, AND HONOR, AND GLORY, AND POWER, BE TO HIM WHO SITS ON THE THRONE, AND TO THE LAMB, FOREVER AND EVER."

Just as the gates were opened to let the men in, I looked. The city was shining like the sun. The streets were paved with gold and many men walked on them. Crowns on their heads, palms in their hands, and golden harps, to sing praises.

There were those that had wings. They answered one another without intermission, Holy, holy, holy is the Lord. And after that they closed the gates. When I saw this, I wished I had been with them.

While I was gazing at all these things, I turned my head to look back. Ignorance had come to the river. He quickly crossed with half the difficulty the other two men had. It happened there was a ferryman, Vain-Hope, who with his boat helped him over. He climbed the hill to approach the gate. Only he was alone, no one met him. When he arrived at the gate, he looked at the writing above it and began to knock, thinking he would be quickly admitted. He was asked by the men at the top of the gate, Where did you come from? What do you want? He answered, I ate and drank in the presence of the King. He has taught in our streets. They asked for his certificate to show it to the King. He fumbled in his pocket and found none. They asked, Have you one? He never answered a word. They told the King, but he would not come down to see him. He commanded the two Shining Ones, that conducted Christian and Hopeful to the city, to go out and seize Ignorance, bind him hand and foot, and take him away. They carried him through the air to the door that I saw in the side of the hill and put him in there. I saw that it was a way to hell, even from the gate of heaven, as well as from the City of Destruction. Then I woke, and found it was a dream.

CONCLUSION

Now, reader, I have told my dream to thee,
See if thou can interpret it to me,
Or to thyself, or neighbor: but take heed
Of misinterpreting; for that, instead
Of doing good, will but thyself abuse:
By misinterpreting, evil ensues.
Take heed, also, that thou be not extreme
In playing with the outside of my dream;
Nor let my figure or similitude
Put thee into a laughter, or a feud.
Leave this for boys and fools; but as for thee,
Do thou the substance of my matter see.
Put by the curtains, look within my veil,
Turn up my metaphors, and do not fail.
There, if thou seek them, such things thou will find
As will be helpful to an honest mind.
What of my dross thou findest there, be bold
To throw away, but yet preserve the gold.
What if my gold be wrapped up in ore?
None throw away the apple for the core:
But if thou shalt cast all away as vain,
I know not but 't will make me dream again.

THE
PILGRIM'S
PROGRESS

PART II

THE
SETTING FORTH OF
CHRISTIAN'S WIFE AND CHILDREN

THE AUTHOR'S WAY OF SENDING FORTH
HIS SECOND PART OF THE PILGRIM

Go, now, my little Book, to every place
Where my first Pilgrim has but shown his face:
Call at their door: if any say, Who's there?
Then answer thou, Christiana is here.
If they bid thee come in, then enter thou,
With all thy boys; and then, as thou know'st how,
Tell who they are, also from whence they came;
Perhaps they'll know them by their looks, or name:
But if they should not, ask them yet again,
If formerly they did not entertain
One Christian, a Pilgrim? If they say
They did, and were delighted in his way;
Then let them know that these related were
Unto him; yea, his wife and children are.
Tell them, that they have left their house and home;
Are turned Pilgrims; seek a world to come;
That they have met with hardships in the way;
That they do meet with troubles night and day;
That they have trod on serpents; fought with devils;
Have also overcome a many evils;
Yea, tell them also of the next who have,
Of love to pilgrimage, been stout and brave
Defenders of that way; and how they still
Refuse this world to do their Father's will.
Go tell them also of those dainty things
That pilgrimage unto the Pilgrim brings.
Let them acquainted be, too, how they are
Beloved of their King, under his care;
What goodly mansions he for them provides;
Though they meet with rough winds and swelling tides,

How brave a calm they will enjoy at last,
Who to their Lord, and by his ways hold fast.
Perhaps with heart and hand they will embrace
Thee, as they did my firstling; and will grace
Thee and thy fellows with such cheer and fare,
As show well, they of Pilgrims lovers are.

OBJECTION I.
But how if they will not believe of me
That I am truly thine? 'cause some there be
That counterfeit the Pilgrim and his name,
Seek, by disguise, to seem the very same;
And by that means have wrought themselves into
The hands and houses of I know not who.

ANSWER.
'Tis true, some have, of late, to counterfeit
My Pilgrim, to their own my title set;
Yea, others half my name, and title too,
Have stitched to their books, to make them do.
But yet they, by their features, do declare
Themselves not mine to be, whose'er they are.
If such thou meet'st with, then thine only way
Before them all, is, to say out thy say
In thine own native language, which no man
Now useth, nor with ease dissemble can.
If, after all, they still of you shall doubt,
Thinking that you, like gypsies, go about,
In naughty wise the country to defile;
Or that you seek good people to beguile
With things unwarrantable; send for me,
And I will testify you pilgrims be;
Yea, I will testify that only you
My Pilgrims are, and that alone will do.

OBJECTION II.
But yet, perhaps, I may inquire for him
Of those who wish him damned life and limb.
What shall I do, when I at such a door
For Pilgrims ask, and they shall rage the more?

ANSWER.
Fright not thyself, my Book, for such bugbears
Are nothing else but groundless fears.
My Pilgrim's book has traveled sea and land,
Yet could I never come to understand
That it was slighted or turned out of door
By any Kingdom, were they rich or poor.
In France and Flanders, where men kill each other,
My Pilgrim is esteemed a friend, a brother.
In Holland, too, 'tis said, as I am told,
My Pilgrim is with some, worth more than gold.
Highlanders and wild Irish can agree
My Pilgrim should familiar with them be.
'Tis in New England under such advance,
Receives there so much loving countenance,
As to be trimm'd, newcloth'd, and deck'd with gems,
That it might show its features, and its limbs.
Yet more: so comely doth my Pilgrim walk,
That of him thousands daily sing and talk.
If you draw nearer home, it will appear
My Pilgrim knows no ground of shame or fear:
City and country will him entertain,
With Welcome, Pilgrim; yea, they can't refrain
From smiling, if my Pilgrim be but by,
Or shows his head in any company.
Brave gallants do my Pilgrim hug and love,
Esteem it much, yea, value it above
Things of greater bulk; yea, with delight

Say, my lark's leg is better than a kite.
Young ladies, and young gentlewomen too,
Do not small kindness to my Pilgrim show;
Their cabinets, their bosoms, and their hearts,
My Pilgrim has; 'cause he to them imparts
His pretty riddles in such wholesome strains,
As yield them profit double to their pains
Of reading; yea, I think I may be bold
To say some prize him far above their gold.
The very children that do walk the street,
If they do but my holy Pilgrim meet,
Salute him will; will wish him well, and say,
He is the only stripling of the day.
They that have never seen him, yet admire
What they have heard of him, and much desire
To have his company, and hear him tell
Those Pilgrim stories which he knows so well.
Yea, some that did not love him at first,
But call'd him fool and noddy, say they must,
Now they have seen and heard him, him commend
And to those whom they love they do him send.
Wherefore, my Second Part, thou need'st not be
Afraid to show thy head: none can hurt thee,
That wish but well to him that went before;
'Cause thou com'st after with a second store
Of things as good, as rich, as profitable,
For young, for old, for stagg'ring, and for stable.

OBJECTION III.
But some there be that say, He laughs too loud
And some do say, His Head is in a cloud.
Some say, His words and stories are so dark,
They know not how, by them, to find his mark.

ANSWER.

One may, I think, say, Both his laughs and cries
May well be guess'd at by his wat'ry eyes.
Some things are of that nature, as to make
One's fancy chuckle, while his heart doth ache:
When Jacob saw his Rachel with the sheep,
He did at the same time both kiss and weep.
Whereas some say, A cloud is in his head;
That doth but show his wisdom's covered
With its own mantles—and to stir the mind
To search well after what it fain would find,
Things that seem to be hid in words obscure
Do but the godly mind the more allure
To study what those sayings should contain,
That speak to us in such a cloudy strain.
I also know a dark similitude
Will on the curious fancy more intrude,
And will stick faster in the heart and head,
Than things from similes not borrowed.
Wherefore, my Book, let no discouragement
Hinder thy travels. Behold, thou art sent
To friends, not foes; to friends that will give place
To thee, thy pilgrims, and thy words embrace.
Besides, what my first Pilgrim left conceal'd,
Thou, my brave second Pilgrim, hast reveal'd;
What Christian left lock'd up, and went his way,
Sweet Christiana opens with her key.

OBJECTION IV.

But some love not the method of your first:
Romance they count it; throw't away as dust.
If I should meet with such, what should I say?
Must I slight them as they slight me, or nay?

ANSWER.

My Christiana, if with such thou meet,
By all means, in all loving wise them greet;
Render them not reviling for revile,
But, if they frown, I prithee on them smile:
Perhaps 'tis nature, or some ill report,
Has made them thus despise, or thus retort.
Some love no fish, some love no cheese, and some
Love not their friends, nor their own house or home;
Some start at pig, slight chicken, love not fowl
More than they love a cuckoo or an owl.
Leave such, my Christiana, to their choice,
And seek those who to find thee will rejoice;
By no means strive, but, in most humble wise,
Present thee to them in thy Pilgrim's guise.
Go then, my little Book, and show to all
That entertain and bid thee welcome shall,
What thou shalt keep close shut up from the rest;
And wish what thou shalt show them may be bless'd
To them for good, and make them choose to be
Pilgrims, by better far than thee or me.
Go, then, I say, tell all men who thou art:
Say, I am Christiana; and my part
Is now, with my four sons, to tell you what
It is for men to take a Pilgrim's lot.
Go, also, tell them who and what they be
That now do go on pilgrimage with thee;
Say, Here's my neighbor Mercy: she is one
That has long time with me a pilgrim gone:
Come, see her in her virgin face, and learn
'Twixt idle ones and pilgrims to discern.
Yea, let young damsels learn of her to prize
The world which is to come, in any wise.
When little tripping maidens follow God,

And leave old doting sinners to his rod,
'Tis like those days wherein the young ones cried
Hosanna! when the old ones did deride.
Next tell them of old Honest, whom you found
With his white hairs treading the Pilgrim's ground;
Yea, tell them how plain-hearted this man was;
How after his good Lord he bare the cross.
Perhaps with some gray head, this may prevail
With Christ to fall in love, and sin bewail.
Tell them also, how Master Fearing went
On pilgrimage, and how the time he spent
In solitariness, with fears and cries;
And how, at last, he won the joyful prize.
He was a good man, though much down in spirit;
He is a good man, and doth life inherit.
Tell them of Master Feeble-mind also,
Who not before, but still behind would go.
Show them also, how he had like been slain,
And how one Great-Heart did his life regain.
This man was true of heart; though weak in grace,
One might true godliness read in his face.
Then tell them of Master Ready-to-Halt,
A man with crutches, but much without fault.
Tell them how Master Feeble-mind and he
Did love, and in opinion much agree.
And let all know, though weakness was their chance,
Yet sometimes one could sing, the other dance.
Forget not Master Valiant-for-the-Truth,
That man of courage, though a very youth:
Tell every one his spirit was so stout,
No man could ever make him face about;
And how Great-Heart and he could not forbear,
But pull down Doubting-Castle, slay Despair!
Overlook not Master Despondency,

Nor Much-afraid, his daughter, though they lie
Under such mantles, as may make them look
(With some) as if their God had them forsook.
They softly went, but sure; and, at the end,
Found that the Lord of Pilgrims was their friend.
When thou hast told the world of all these things,
Then turn about, my Book, and touch these strings;
Which, if but touched, will such music make,
They'll make a cripple dance, a giant quake.
Those riddles that lie couched within thy breast,
Freely propound, expound; and for the rest
Of thy mysterious lines, let them remain
For those whose nimble fancies shall them gain.
Now may this little Book a blessing be
To those who love this little Book and me;
And may its buyer have no cause to say,
His money is but lost or thrown away.
Yea, may this second Pilgrim yield that fruit
As may with each good Pilgrim's fancy suit;
And may it some persuade, that go astray,
To turn their feet and heart to the right way,
Is the hearty prayer of

                        The Author,
                        JOHN BUNYAN

COURTEOUS COMPANIONS,

Telling you my dream about Christian, the pilgrim, and his dangerous journey to the Celestial country, was enjoyable for me and good for you. I told you about his wife and children, and their unwillingness to go with him. So he was forced to go on his progress without them. He dared not risk the destruction he feared would come to the City of Destruction, so he left them and departed.

The pressure of business hindered me from traveling there. So I did not, until now, have an opportunity to inquire about the family Christian left behind. Recently, I became more concerned and went there. I took my lodging in woods about a mile from the place. As I slept, I again dreamed.

In my dream, an old gentleman came to where I slept. Because he was going my way, I got up and went with him. We walked and as travelers usually do, we fell into a conversation. Our talk centered on Christian and his travels. This is what I said to the old man.

Sir, what town is that below, on the left side of our way?

Mr. Sagacity (for that was his name) replied, It is the City of Destruction, a populous place, occupied by an ill-conditioned and idle people.

I thought that was that city, I said. I once went through that town so I know your comments are true.

SAG. Too true! I wish I could speak truth in speaking better of them that live there.

Well, sir, I said, I perceive you are a well-meaning man who takes pleasure in hearing and telling what is good. Tell me, did you hear what happened to a man from this town (whose name was Christian), who went on a pilgrimage toward the higher regions?

SAG. Hear of him! Yes. I also heard of the disturbances, trouble, wars, captivities, cries, groans, frights, and fears that he had on his journey. Our country rings with his name. There are few that have not heard of him; most have the records of his pilgrimage. His hazardous journey has many that wish him well. Though when he was here, he was fool in every man's mouth. Now that he is gone, he is highly commended by all. It is said that he lives well where he is. Many are resolved to never run his danger, but their mouths water at his gains.

They are correct if they think that he lives well. He now lives in the fountain of life. What he has is without effort and sorrow; there is no grief mixed in. Tell me, what do the people say about him?

SAG. People talk strangely about him. Some say that he now walks in white (Rev. 3:4); that he has a chain of gold about his neck; that he has a crown of gold, inlaid with pearls, on his head. Others say that the shining ones, who sometimes revealed themselves to him in his journey, are his companions. That he is as familiar with them where he is, as one neighbor is with another here. It is confidently affirmed that the King of the place has granted him a rich and pleasant dwelling at court. That every day he eats, drinks, walks and talks with him. That he receives the smiles and favors of him that is Judge of all (Zech. 3:7; Luke 14:14, 15). Moreover, it is expected by some that his Prince, the Lord of that country, will come here and want to know the reason, if they can give any, why his neighbors thought so little of him. Why they held him in such great disdain when he became a pilgrim (Jude 14, 15).

They say he is so close to his Prince that his Sovereign is greatly concerned about the indignity put on Christian when he became a pilgrim. He will look on all this as if it was done to him (Luke 10:16). No wonder, it was Christian's love for his Prince that made him undertake the journey.

I am glad for the poor man's sake that he now has rest from his labor. He reaps the benefit of his tears with joy. He is beyond the gun shot range of his enemies. He is out of the reach of those that hate him (Rev. 14:13; Ps. 126:5, 6). I also am pleased that a rumor of these things is spread around this country. Who knows, it may work some good on those that are left behind? Tell me, sir, while it is fresh on my mind, do you hear anything about his wife and children? Poor hearts! I wonder in my mind how they are doing.

SAG. Christiana and her sons? They are likely to do as well as Christian. They all played the fool at first and would not be persuaded by Christian's tears and pleas. Yet second thoughts have worked wonders on them. They packed up and followed him.

What! Wife, children, and all?

SAG. It is true. I can give you an account. I was there when it happened and was thoroughly acquainted with the whole affair.

Then, I said, you may report it for a truth.

SAG. You need not fear to affirm it. I mean they are all gone on a pilgrimage, both the good woman and her four boys. Since, as I perceive, we are going a distance together, I will tell you the entire story.

Christiana (for that was her name from the day she and her children became pilgrims), after her husband had gone over the river and she heard no more of him, began to think. First, she had lost her husband. The loving bond of that relation was totally broken. You know, he said to me, nature can do no less than entertain the living with heavy contemplation in remembering the loss of loving relations. This loss of her husband cost many a tear, but this was not all.

Christiana began to realize that her behavior toward her husband was the one reason she saw him no more. Her unkind, unnatural, and ungodly conduct to her dear friend swarmed into her mind, clogged her conscience, and loaded her with guilt. She was broken remembering his restless groans and salty tears. She had hardened her heart against all his pleas and loving attempts to persuade her and the boys to go with him. Everything that Christian said or did while the burden was on his back, returned to her like a flash of lightning. It tore her heart in pieces, especially his bitter cry, "What must I do to be saved?"

She said to her children, Sons, we are finished. I have sinned away your father and he is gone. He wanted us with him, but I would not go. I also have hindered your life. The boys fell into tears and cried to go after their father. Oh, said Christiana, if only we had gone with him! We would have fared better. I foolishly imagined, concerning your father's troubles, that they proceeded from a foolish fancy, or that he was overrun with melancholy. Yet now, I can not get it out of my mind that the troubles sprang from another cause; the light of life was given him

(James 1:23–25; John 8:12). With this help, I perceive that he has escaped the snares of death (Prov. 14:27). Then they all wept again!

The next night Christiana had a dream. She saw a parchment open, in it all her ways were recorded. Her crimes looked very black. She cried out in her sleep, "God, be merciful to me a sinner!" (Luke 18:13). Her little children heard her.

After this she thought she saw two ill-favored ones standing by her bed. They said, What can we do with this woman? She cries for mercy, waking and sleeping. If she continues, we will lose her as we have lost her husband. We must, one way or another, take her thoughts. Or else she will become a pilgrim.

She awoke trembling in a great sweat. After a while she again fell asleep. She thought she saw Christian, her husband, in a place of bliss among many immortals. He was standing, playing a harp, before One that sat on a throne with a rainbow around his head. She saw that he bowed his head to the paved work that was under his Prince's feet and said, "I heartily thank my Lord and King for bringing me to this place." Then a company that stood around shouted and played on their harps. No living man could tell what they said.

Next morning, she prayed to God and then talked with her children. A hard knock was heard at the door. She said, "If you come in God's name, come in." He said, "Amen," opened the door and greeted her, "Peace be to this house. Christiana, do you know where I am from?" She blushed and trembled. Her heart warmed with desire to know where he was from and his errand. He said, "My name is Secret. I dwell with those that are on high. It is talked of where I live that you have a desire to go there. There is also a report that you are aware of the evil you have done to your husband. You hardened your heart against his way and kept these babies in their ignorance. Christiana, the Merciful One has sent me to tell you that he is a God ready to forgive; that he takes delight to multiply the pardon of offences. He would have you know that he invites you to come into his presence and to his table. There he will feed you with the fat of his house and with the heritage of Jacob your father.

"Christian, who was your husband, and many companions always see the face that ministers life to the viewers. They will rejoice when they hear the sound of your footsteps on your Father's threshold."

Christiana was ashamed and bowed her head to the ground. The visitor continued, "Christiana, here is a letter that I brought from your husband's King." She opened it. The fragrance was like the finest perfume (Song 1:3). It was written in letters of gold. This was its contents. The King would have her do what Christian, her husband, did. This is the way to come to his city and to dwell in his presence with joy forever. The good woman was overcome. She cried to her visitor, Sir, will you carry me and my children with you that we may go and worship the King?

The visitor replied, Christiana, bitter comes before sweet. You must go through troubles, as those that have already gone, before you enter this Celestial City. I advise you to do as Christian, your husband, did. Go to the Narrow gate across the plain. It stands at the beginning of the way you must go. I wish you good speed. Put this letter in your bosom, read it to yourself and your children until you have it memorized. It is one of the songs that you must sing while you are in the house of your pilgrimage (Ps. 119:54). It must be delivered at the distant gate.

I saw in my dream that as this old gentleman told me the story, he seemed greatly affected. Christiana called her sons together, and said, "My sons, I have, as you may perceive, been greatly concerned in my soul about your father's death. Not that I doubt he is happy, for I am now satisfied that he is well. I have also been deeply affected with the thoughts of my state and yours. My attitude to your father in his distress is a great burden on my conscience. I hardened my heart and yours against him. I refused to go on his pilgrimage.

The thoughts of these things would now kill me, except that I had a dream last night and encouragement from a stranger this morning. Come, my children, let us pack, and be off to the gate that leads to the Celestial country. There we will see your father and his companions in peace, according to the laws of that land.

Her children burst into tears of joy. Their visitor bid them farewell. They began to prepare for the journey.

When they were almost ready to go, two women neighbors came to her house and knocked at the door. She said as before, If you come in God's name, come in. The women were stunned. They were not use to hearing these words from her lips. Yet they came in and found the good woman preparing to be leave.

They began, Neighbor, what is the meaning by this?

Christiana answered the oldest woman, Mrs. Timorous, I am preparing for a journey.

Mrs. Timorous was daughter of the man that met Christian on the Hill of Difficulty and wanted him to go back because of the lions.

TIM. What journey?

CHR. To go after my good husband, she wept.

TIM. I hope not, good neighbor. Think, for your poor children's sake, do not so unwomanly throw yourself away.

CHR. My children will go with me. Not one of them is willing to stay behind.

TIM. I wonder what or who has brought you to this conclusion!

CHR. Neighbor, if you knew as much as I do, you would go with me.

TIM. Tell me, what new knowledge do you have that works in your mind and tempts you to go who knows where?

CHR. I have been seriously afflicted since my husband's departure. Especially since he went over the river. What troubles me the most, however, is my crude attitude when he was under distress. Now, I am as he was, nothing will satisfy but going on a pilgrimage. I dreamed last night that I saw him. Oh that my soul was with him! He dwells in the presence of the King of the country. He sits and eats with him at his table. He is a companion of immortals. He has a house; compared to his house the best palace on earth seems a garbage heap (2 Cor. 5:1–4). The Prince of the place has sent for me. There is a promise of entertainment if I come. His messenger brought a letter that invites me. She pulled out her letter and read it. What do you say to this?

TIM. Madness has possessed you and your husband! I am sure you heard what your husband met with at his first step on the way. Our neighbor, Obstinate, can testify; he went with him. Pliable too, until like wise men they were afraid to go any further. We heard, over and above this, how he met with the lions, Apollyon, the Shadow of Death, and the danger at Vanity Fair. You should forget none of this! If a man was this hard put, what can you, a poor woman, do? Consider your four sweet children, your own flesh and blood. Although you may be rash enough to throw yourself away, for the sake of your children, stay home.

Christiana said, Do not tempt me, neighbor. I would be a fool of the greatest size if I did not have the heart to strike with this opportunity. From what you tell me of all the troubles that I am likely to meet in the way, it is far from discouraging. They show I am in the right. The bitter must come before the sweet and that will make the sweet all the sweeter. Since you did not come to my house in God's name, I ask you to leave and not disturb me any further.

Timorous reviled her and said, Come, neighbor Mercy, let us leave her in her own hands, since she scorns our counsel and company.

Mercy, however, was undecided and could not readily comply with her neighbor for two reasons. 1. Her heart pained over Christiana. She said to herself, if my neighbor is going, I will go a little way with her and help. 2. Her heart pained over her own soul. What Christiana had said took hold on her mind. She said to herself, I will talk more with Christiana. If I find truth and life in what she says, I will go with her. Mercy replied to her neighbor, Timorous:

MER. Neighbor, I did come with you to see Christiana this morning. Since she is taking her farewell of the country, I will walk with her a little on this sunny morning and help her on her way. She kept the second reason to herself.

TIM. I see you have a mind to go a fooling. Take heed and be wise. When we are out of danger, we are out of danger. When we are in danger, we are in danger.

Mrs. Timorous returned to her house and sent for some of her neighbors, Mrs. Bat's-Eyes, Mrs. Inconsiderate, Mrs. Light-Mind, and Mrs. Know-Nothing. When they came she told them the story of Christiana and her intended journey.

TIM. Neighbors, having little to do this morning, I visited Christiana. When I knocked at her door she answered, If you come in God's name, come in. So in I went thinking all was well. But I found her and the children preparing to leave town. I asked what she was doing. She told me, in short, that she was of a mind to go on a pilgrimage, like her husband. She also told me about a dream that she had. The King of the country where her husband was had sent an invitation to her to come there.

Mrs. Know-Nothing asked, Do you think she will go?

TIM. Go she will, whatever happens. I know because my great argument to persuade her to stay home (considering the troubles she was likely to meet on the way), only sent her forward. She told me in so many words, The bitter goes before the sweet and since it does it makes the sweet all the sweeter.

MRS. BAT'S-EYES. Oh, this blind and foolish woman! She would not take a warning from her husband's afflictions. For my part, if he was here again he would be content and never run so many hazards for nothing.

Mrs. Inconsiderate replied, Away with fanatical fools, good riddance. She should stay where she lives and keep her mind. Who could live next to her? She will either be stupid, not neighborly, or talk about things until no one can stand her. I will never be sorry if she leaves. Let her go. Let better come to her house. It was never a good world since these whimsical fools lived here.

Mrs. Light-Mind added, Come, put this kind of talk away. I was at Madam Wanton's yesterday, we were as merry as maids. Who do you think was there? Mrs. Love-the-Flesh, Mrs. Lechery, Mrs. Filth, and three or four others. There was music, dancing, and everything to fill up on pleasure. I dare say, my lady herself is an admirable well-bred gentlewoman, and Mr. Lechery is her equal.

THE FIRST STAGE

By this time Christiana and her children were on their way. Mercy went with her. Mercy, said Christiana, for you to accompany us part of the way is an unexpected favor.

MER. Young Mercy said (for she was young), If I thought I could go all the way with you, I would never go near this town again.

CHR. Mercy, throw your lot in with me. I well know what the end of our pilgrimage will be. My husband would rather be where he is than have all the gold in the Spanish mines. You will not be rejected, even though you come on my invitation. The King, who sent for us, is one that delights in mercy. If you wish, I will hire you to go with me as my servant. We will have all things in common between you and me. Please come.

MER. How can I be certain that I will be accepted? If I had hope of being helped by Him that can help, even though the way was ever so tedious, I would go.

CHR. Loving Mercy, I will tell you what to do. Come with me to the Narrow gate. There I will inquire for you. If you receive no encouragement, I will be content for you to return. I will also pay for the kindness you have shown my children and me in accompanying us in the way.

MER. I will go there and take whatever happens. May the Lord grant that the King of heaven will have his heart set on me.

Christiana heart was glad, not because she had a companion, but that she had prevailed on this poor girl to fall in love with her own salvation. Mercy began to weep. Christiana asked, Why are you weeping my sister?

MER. I can only weep when considering the condition of my poor relatives who remain in our sinful town. What makes my grief so heavy is that they have no instructor, or anyone to tell them what is to come.

CHR. Pity becomes pilgrims. You weep for your friends as my good Christian did for me. He mourned because I would not listen. But his Lord and ours caught his tears and put them into his bottle. Now you, my sweet children, and I are reaping the fruit and benefit. I hope, Mercy, that your tears will not be lost. The truth says, "Those who sow in tears shall reap in joy. He who continually goes forth weeping, bearing seed for sowing, shall doubtless come again with rejoicing, bringing his sheaves with him" (Ps. 126:5, 6).

Mercy replied,

> Let the Most Blessed be my guide,
> If it be his blessed will,
> Unto his gate, into his fold,
> Up to his holy hill.
> And let him never suffer me
> To swerve, or turn aside
> From his free-grace and holy ways,
> Whatever shall me betide.
> And let him gather them of mine
> That I have left behind;

Lord, make them pray they may be thine,
With all their heart and mind.

When Christiana stopped at the Swamp of Despond she said, This is the place where my dear husband almost suffocated with mud. She also perceived, despite the King's command to make this place solid for pilgrims, it was worse than it had been. I asked if that was true. Yes, said the old gentleman, too true. Many pretended to be the King's laborers. They said they were repairing the King's highways but they brought dirt and slime instead of stones, marring rather than repairing the way. Christiana and her boys did not move. Mercy said, Come, let us walk and not be weary. They paid close attention to their steps as they moved across the swamp.

Christiana almost fell in more than once or twice. They had no sooner crossed than they heard, "Blessed is she who believed, for there will be a fulfillment of those things which were told her from the Lord" (Luke 1:45).

Mercy said, Christiana, if I had as good a hope for a loving reception at the Narrow gate as you, no Swamp of Despond could discourage me.

You know your problems and I know mine. We will have enough evil before we reach our journey's end. Can it be imagined that the people who desire excellent glories, and are envied that happiness, will meet all the fears, snares, troubles, and afflictions that those who hate us can possibly assault us with?

Mr. Sagacity then left me to dream my dream. I thought I saw Christiana, Mercy, and the boys, go up to the gate. After a short debate about how to manage calling at the gate, and what should be said to him that opened it, they reached this conclusion. Christiana, being the oldest, would knock and speak for the rest. She began to knock as her poor husband did. She knocked and knocked again. Instead of an answer, all they heard was a dog barking. It was a big dog and this made the women and children afraid. She stopped knocking for fear the mastiff would attack. Their minds tumbled up and down. They did not know what to do. They dared not knock for fear of the dog. They dared not go back for fear the keeper of the gate would be offended if he saw them leave. Finally, they knocked more vehemently. The gatekeeper said, Who is there? The dog stopped barking, and the keeper opened the gate.

Christiana made a low bow and said, Let our Lord not be offended that we have knocked at his princely gate. The keeper asked, Where did you come from? What do you want?

Christiana answered, We come where Christian came from and on the same errand. If it pleases you, graciously admit us at this gate to the way that leads to the Celestial City. I, my Lord, am Christiana; once the wife of Christian who is now above.

The keeper of the gate marveled, Is she now a pilgrim that a while ago abhorred that life? Christiana bowed her head and said, Yes, and so are these my sweet children.

He took her by the hand, led her in, and said, Let the little children come to me. He shut the gate and called a trumpeter that was over the gate to entertain Christiana with shouting and the sound of a joyful trumpet. The trumpeter obeyed and filled the air with melodious notes.

All this time poor Mercy was standing outside, trembling and crying from fear of being rejected. Once Christiana was admitted, she made intercession for Mercy.

CHR. My Lord, I have a companion standing outside. She has come for the same reason as me. She is greatly dejected; she thinks she comes without being sent for. Where as I was sent for by my husband's King.

Mercy became impatient; each minute seemed like an hour. She prevented Christiana from a fuller interceding by knocking at the gate. She knocked so loud that Christiana jumped. The keeper of the gate asked, Who is there? Christiana replied, It is my friend.

He opened the gate and looked, but Mercy had fainted and fallen down. She fainted because she was afraid that the gate would not be opened for her.

He took her by the hand and said, Woman, arise.

Sir, she said, I am faint. There is hardly any life left in me. He answered that one once said, "When my soul fainted within me, I remembered the Lord; and my prayer went up to You, into Your holy temple" (Jonah 2:7). Fear not, stand on your feet, and tell me where you came from.

MER. I came uninvited. My invitation was from Christiana, my friend. The King invited her. I do not want to presume.

KEEP. Did she want you to come with her to this place?

MER. Yes, as you can see, I am here. If there is any grace and forgiveness of sins to spare, I ask that your poor maidservant may partake of it.

He took her again by the hand and led her gently in. He said, I pray for all that believe on me, by whatever means they come to me. He said to those that stood by, Bring something to smell and give it to Mercy to keep her from fainting. They brought her a bundle of myrrh, and after awhile she revived.

The Lord, at the beginning of the way, received Christiana, her boys, and Mercy. He spoke kindly to them. They said, We are sorry for our sins and beg our Lord's pardon. They asked for additional information on what to do.

I grant pardon, he said, by word and deed. By word in the promise of forgiveness, by deed in the way I obtained it. Take the first from my lips with a kiss and the other will be revealed (Song 1:2; John 20:20).

I saw in my dream that he spoke many good words to them and they were greatly gladdened. He took them up to the top of the gate and showed them how they were saved. He said they would see it again, to their comfort, as they went along the way.

He left them in a summer parlor below where Christiana said, O how glad I am that we are here.

MER. You may well be, but I am the one who has the greatest reason to leap for joy.

CHR. At one time, as I stood at the gate, I thought because no one answered all our labor had been lost. Especially when that ugly dog barked so loud.

MER. My worst fear came after you were taken inside and I was left behind. I thought what is written is now fulfilled, "Two women will be grinding at the mill: one will be taken and the other left" (Matt.

24:41). It took much effort to keep from crying. I was afraid to knock anymore. When I looked and saw what was written over the gate, I took courage. I knew that I would knock again, or die. I knocked, but I cannot tell you how. My spirit struggled between life and death.

CHR. Your knocks were so intent that the sound made me jump. I never heard such knocking in all my life. I thought you would come in by a violent hand, or take the kingdom by storm (Matt. 11:12).

MER. Who could have knocked? You saw the door was shut. There was a vicious dog. I was so faint-hearted that I could not have knocked with all my might. Tell me, what did my Lord say about my rudeness? Was he angry?

CHR. When he heard your lumbering noise, he gave a wonderful innocent smile. I believe you pleased him; he showed no sign to the contrary. I wonder in my heart why he keeps such a dog. If I had known that, I would not have ventured out. But now we are in, we are in, and I am glad with all my heart.

MER. I will ask him why he keeps such a filthy dog in his yard. I hope he will not take it wrong.

Do so, said the children, and persuade him to hang the dog. We are afraid he will bite us.

At last he came down, and Mercy fell to the ground on her face and worshiped him. She said, "Let my Lord accept the sacrifice of praise that I now offer him with my lips."

He said to her, Peace be to you. Stand up. But she stayed on her face and said, "Righteous are You, O Lord, when I plead with you; yet let me talk with You about Your judgments" (Jer. 12:1). Why do you keep such a mean dog in your yard? The sight of him makes women and children run from your gate in fear.

He answered, That dog is not mine. He belongs to the castle that you see in the distance, but he comes up to the walls of this place. My pilgrims hear him bark. He frightens many from worse to better with the great voice of his roaring. His owner does not keep him because of goodwill toward me or mine. His sole purpose is to keep pilgrims from knocking at this gate. Sometimes he has broken loose and has worried some that I loved. But I am patient, I give my pilgrims timely help to keep them from being delivered to his power, which is what his dog nature wants. But my purchased one, if you had known before hand, would you have been afraid of the dog? The beggars that go from door to door, rather than lose a handout, will run the risk of a bawling, barking, and biting dog. Can a barking dog in another man's yard, keep any pilgrim from coming to me? I deliver them from the lions and from the power of the dog (Ps. 22:21, 22).

MER. I confess my ignorance. I said what I did not understand. I acknowledge that you do all things well.

Christiana began to talk about their journey and inquire about the way. He fed them, washed their feet, and set them in the way of his steps, just as he had dealt with her husband.

THE SECOND STAGE

S o I saw in my dream that they walked on their way. The weather
was comfortable.

Christiana began to sing,

> Blessed be the day that I began
> A pilgrim for to be;
> And blessed also be the man
> That thereto moved me.
> 'Tis true, 't was long ere I began
> To seek to live for ever;
> But now I run fast as I can:
> 'Tis better late than never.
> Our tears to joy, our fears to faith,
> Are turned, as we see;
> Thus our beginning (as one saith)
> Shows what our end will be.

On the other side of the wall that fenced the way Christiana and her companions were traveling was a garden that belonged to the barking dog's owner. Some of the branches of the fruit trees that grew in that garden extended over the wall. Many found the fruit ripe, picked it, and ate so much that they hurt. Christiana's boys, as boys are apt to do, picked some fruit that hung from the tree and began to eat it. Their mother chided them but they continued to eat it.

Well, she said, my sons, you transgress. That fruit is not ours. She did not know that it belonged to the enemy. I guarantee you that had she known, she would have been ready to die from fear. When they were about two bow shots from the place that led them into the way, they saw two ill-favored ones coming down to meet them. Christiana and Mercy, her friend, covered themselves with their veils and kept on the journey. The children went ahead. At last they all met. The two ill-favored ones came up to the women as if to embrace them. Christiana said, Stand back, or go peaceably. The men ignored her words. They laid hands on them. Christiana became angry and kicked with her feet. Mercy also tried to move them. Christiana said, Stand back, and be gone. Being pilgrims, we have no money to lose and will not live on the charity of our friends.

ILL-FAV. We do not assault you for money. We have come to tell you that if you grant one small request, we will make women of you forever.

CHR. Christiana, imagining what they might mean, answered, We will not listen, regard, or yield to what you ask. We are in a hurry and cannot stay. Our business is life and death. They tried again to get past. The two men stepped in their way.

ILL-FAV. We do not intend to hurt you. There is something else we want.

CHR. You would have us body and soul. I know why you are here. We would rather die on the spot than allow ourselves to be brought into a snare that will risk our well-being hereafter. With that they shrieked, Murder! murder! and put themselves under the law that is provided to protect women (Deut. 22:25–27). The men still approached them with plans to prevail. They cried out again.

Not being far from the gate, their voices were heard. Some of the house came out, recognized Christiana's voice, and hurried to help her. The women were in a great scuffle. The children stood crying. He that came to their relief called to the ruffians, What are you doing? Would you make my Lord's people transgress? He attempted to capture them, but they escaped over the wall into the garden of the man who owned the great dog. So the dog became their protector. The Reliever asked how they were? They answered, We thank your Prince, pretty well, but we have been frightened. We thank you for coming to our help, otherwise we would have been overcome.

RELIEVER. I wondered when you were entertained at the gate why you did not petition the Lord for a guard, seeing you are weak women. This might have avoided these troubles and dangers.

CHR. We were so taken with our present blessing that future dangers were forgotten. Besides, who would have thought that such evil ones would lurk so close to the King's palace? Indeed, it would have been well had we asked our Lord for a guard. Yet, since our Lord knew it would be for our benefit, I wonder why he did not send one.

REL. It is unnecessary to grant things not requested. By doing this they could become things of little esteem. When the need for something is felt in the eyes of him that wants, it is properly due and consequently it will be given. Had my Lord granted you a guard, you would not have regretted your oversight in not asking for one. So all things work for good and tend to make you more alert.

CHR. Shall we go back to my Lord, confess our folly, and ask for a guard?

REL. You do not have to go back. The confession of your folly I will present to him. In all the places you go, you will find no want. In my Lord's lodgings, that he has prepared for his pilgrims, there is sufficient to equip them. As I said, He will inquire to do this for them (Ezek. 36:37). It is a poor thing that is not worth asking for. After he finished speaking, he went back to his place and the pilgrims went on their way.

MER. What a sudden void! I thought that we were past all danger and would never see sorrow again.

CHR. Your innocence, my sister, may excuse you. My fault is much greater. I saw this danger before I left home, yet I did not provide for it when provision was available. I am to be greatly blamed.

MER. How did you know this before you left home? Please explain this riddle.

CHR. I will tell you. One night as I lay in my bed I had a dream about this. I saw two men, just like these. They stood at the foot of my bed, plotting to prevent my salvation. I will tell you their very words. They said (it was when I was in my troubles), What will we do with this woman? Waking and sleeping she cries for forgiveness. If she is permitted to go on, we will lose her as we have lost her husband. This should have made me pay attention and secure protection when it was available.

MER. Well, we had an opportunity to see our imperfections. Our Lord has taken this occasion to show us the riches of his grace. As we have seen, he has followed us with unasked for kindness, delivering us from hands that were stronger than ours by his good pleasure.

After they talked a little more they approached a house (the house of the Interpreter) that was built for the relief of pilgrims. You will find it fully explained in the first part of the records of the Pilgrim's Progress. When they came to the door they heard much talking. They listened and thought Christiana was mentioned by name. You must know that talk of her and the children going on a pilgrimage proceeded them. This was most pleasing because they heard that she was Christian's wife, the woman who was unwilling to go on the pilgrimage. They stood quietly and listened to the good people inside commending her. They had no idea that she was at the door. At last Christiana knocked. A young girl came to the door, opened it, looked, and there were two women there.

DAM. With whom would you speak?

CHR. We understand this is a privileged place for pilgrims. We request to partake of the privileges. The day, as you can see, is far spent and we do not want to go any further tonight.

DAM. What is your name that I may tell my Lord?

CHR. My name is Christiana. I was the wife of a pilgrim that some years ago traveled this way. These are his four children. This girl is also my companion, she is going on the pilgrimage too.

INNOCENT. Innocent (for that was her name) ran inside. Who do you think is at the door? It is Christiana, her children, and her companion, waiting to be entertained. They leaped for joy and told their Master. He came to the door, looked at her, and said, Are you Christiana whom Christian the good man left behind when he became a pilgrim.

CHR. I am the woman who was so hard-hearted as to ignore my husband's troubles and force him to go alone on his journey. These are his four children. Now I have come, for I am convinced that no way is right but this.

INTER. Then is fulfilled what is written of the man who said to his son, "Go, work today in my vineyard. He answered and said, I will not, but afterward he regretted it and went" (Matt. 21:29).

CHR. So be it. Amen. God made it a true saying. Grant that I may be found by him in peace, without spot, and blameless.

INTER. Why are you standing at the door? Come in, daughter of Abraham. We were just talking about you. The news had come to us that you are a pilgrim. Come, children, come maid, come in. So he took all of them into the house.

Inside, they were invited to sit and rest. Then those that attended the pilgrims in the house came into the room to see them. One smiled, another smiled, and they all smiled for joy that Christiana was a pilgrim. They looked at the boys and stroked them on their faces as a token of their kind reception. They lovingly extended hospitality to Mercy and welcomed all into their Master's house.

Before supper, the Interpreter took them into his Significant Rooms. He showed them what Christian had seen. They saw the man in a cage, the man and his dream, the man that cut his way through his enemies, the picture of the biggest of them all, together with the rest of the things that were so profitable to Christian.

This done, and after those things had been somewhat understood by Christiana and her company, the Interpreter took them into a room where there was a man that could only look down. He had a muck rake in his hand. Standing over his head with a celestial crown in his hand was one that offered the crown for the muck rake. The man did not look up or acknowledge his presence. He continued to rake straw, small sticks, and dust from the floor.

Christiana said, I think I know a little of this meaning. This is a figure of a man of this world. Is it not, good sir?

INTER. You are right. His muck rake shows his carnal mind. He pays full attention to raking up straw, sticks, and dust from the floor. He ignores the call from the one with the celestial crown in his hand. This shows that heaven is only a fable to some, and only material things are counted as substantial. Since you saw the man could only look down, this lets you know that earthly things, when they are on men's minds, carries their hearts away from God.

CHR. Deliver me from this muck rake (Prov. 30:8).

INTER. That prayer has been so little used that it is almost rusty. "Give me no riches," is scarcely the prayer of one in ten thousand. Straw, sticks, and dust are the great things most people look after.

With that Christiana and Mercy wept. They said, It is unfortunately all too true.

When the Interpreter had shown them this, he took them to a large room. He asked them to look around and see if they could find anything profitable. They looked but there was nothing to be seen except a great spider on the wall and they missed it.

MER. Sir, I see nothing. Christiana held her peace.

INTER. Look again. She looked and said, There is not a thing here except an ugly spider that hangs by her hands on the wall. He asked, Is there only one spider in all this spacious room? Then water stood in

Christiana's eyes, for she was a woman of quick apprehension. She responded, Yes, Lord, more than one. There are spiders here whose venom is far more destructive than that which is in her. The Interpreter looked pleasantly at her and said, You have told the truth. This made Mercy blush and the boys covered their faces. They all began to understand the riddle.

The Interpreter said, "The spider skillfully grasps with its hands, and it is in kings' palaces" (Prov. 30:28). This is written to show that regardless of how full of sin's venom you may be, by the hand of Faith, you may dwell in the best room of the King's house above.

CHR. I thought it was something like this. I could not imagine it all. I thought we were like spiders, that we looked like ugly creatures, in whatever fine room we were in. From this spider, a venomous and ill-favored creature, we learned faith. That did not enter my mind. Yet, this spider has grasped with its hands and dwells in the best room in the house. God has made nothing useless.

They all seemed to be happy, but water stood in their eyes. They looked at each other and bowed before the Interpreter.

He took them into a room where there was a hen and her chickens. He told them to observe. One of the chickens went to the trough to drink. She drank and lifted her head and her eyes to heaven. See, said he, what this little chick does. Learn from her, acknowledge where your mercies come from and receive them by looking up. Observe and look again. They did and perceived that the hen walked with a fourfold purpose toward her chickens. 1. She had a common call all day long. 2. She sometimes had a special call. 3. She had a brooding note (Matt. 23:37). 4. She had an outcry.

Now, said he, compare this hen to your King, and these chickens to his obedient ones. He has his methods when he walks toward his people. With his common call, he gives nothing. With his special call, he always has something to give. He has a brooding voice for those that are under his wing. He has an outcry to give an alarm when he sees the enemy. I choose, my darlings, to take you into the room where these things are, because you are women and it is easy for you to understand.

CHR. Sir, please let us see some more. So he took them into the slaughterhouse where a butcher was killing a sheep. The sheep was quiet and took her death patiently. Then said the Interpreter, You must learn from this sheep to suffer and put up with wrongs without murmuring or complaining. See how quietly she takes her death. Without objecting, she allows her skin to be pulled over her ears. Your King calls you his sheep.

Then he took them into his garden where there was a great variety of flowers. He said, Do you see all these? Christiana answered, Yes. Then he said, Notice that the flowers are diverse in height, quality, color, fragrance, and uprightness. Some are better than others. Where the gardener plants them, there they stand. They do not quarrel with one another.

He took them to his field that was planted with wheat and corn. They saw the tops were cut off and only straw remained. He said, This ground was dug, plowed, and sown, but what will we do with the crop? Christiana said, Burn some and make muck of the rest. The Interpreter replied, Fruit is what you look for. When there is no fruit, you condemn it to the fire, or to be trodden under foot. Beware that in all this, you do not condemn yourself.

As they were returning to the house, they saw a little robin with a large spider in his mouth. The Interpreter said, Look! Mercy wondered, but Christiana said, What a detraction to such a pretty little bird as the robin-red-breast. He is a bird that loves to be sociable with men! I thought they lived on bread crumbs or other harmless things. I don't like him as much as I did.

The Interpreter replied, This robin is a fine emblem of some professors. To look at them, they are like this robin, pretty of note, color, and bearing. They seem to have a great love for sincere believers and a desire to associate with them. It is as if they could live on the good man's crumbs. They pretend to frequent the house of the godly and the appointments of the Lord. Yet when they are by themselves, like the robin, they catch and gobble spiders. They change their diet, drink iniquity, and swallow sin like water.

Supper was not ready when they returned to the house, so Christiana asked the Interpreter to show or tell them other things that are profitable.

The Interpreter began, The fatter the sow, the more she desires the mud. The fatter the ox, the more quickly he goes to the slaughter. The healthier the lust, the more the man is prone to evil. There is a desire in women to be neat; it is a good thing to wear what in God's sight is of great value. It is easier watching for a night or two, than to sit up for a whole year. It is easier for one to begin to profess well, than to hold on to the end. Every shipmaster, in a storm, will willingly throw overboard items of small value. Who will throw the best item away first? Those who do not fear God. One leak will sink a ship. One sin will destroy a sinner. He that forgets his friend is ungrateful. He that forgets his Savior is unmerciful to himself. He that lives in sin and looks for happiness after, is like him that plants shells and expects to fill his barn with wheat or barley. If a man would live well, let him remember his last day and always make it his company keeper. Whispering and change of thoughts prove that sin is in the world. If this world is counted value by men, what is heaven that God commends? If this life with all its troubles is so difficult to let go of, what is the life above? Everybody will talk about the goodness of men, but who is affected by the goodness of God? We seldom sit down to eat meat, but we still eat and leave. So there is in Jesus Christ more merit and righteousness than the entire world needs.

When the Interpreter finished, he took them into his garden again. They looked at a tree whose inside was rotten. Still it grew and had leaves. Then Mercy said, What does it mean? This tree's outside is fair, said he, but its inside is rotten. Many in the garden of God may be compared to it. Their mouths speak high in behalf of God, but they do nothing for him. Their leaves are beautiful, but their heart is only good to be fuel for the devil's wood box.

Supper was ready, the table was spread, and all things were set on it. They sat down and ate after one had given thanks. The Interpreter usually entertained those that lodged there with music during the meals. So the minstrels played and one, who had a very fine voice, sung:

> The Lord is only my support,
> And he that does me feed;
> How can I then want any thing
> Whereof I stand in need?

When the song and music ended, the Interpreter asked Christiana what it was that first made her become a pilgrim. She answered, First, the loss of my husband which greatly grieved me. But that was natural affection. Then my husband's troubles and pilgrimage, and how like a boor I added to it. Guilt took hold of my mind and would have drawn me into the pond to drown. But I had a dream about the well being of my husband. Then I received a letter from the King of that country where my husband lives to come there. The dream and the letter worked on my mind and forced me to come this way.

INTER. Did you have any no opposition before you started the journey?

CHR. Yes, Mrs. Timorous, a neighbor. She was related to him that tried to persuade my husband to go back because of the lions. She also fooled me. She called it, my intended desperate adventure. She tried to discourage me by talking of the hardships and troubles that my husband met in the way. I got over all this pretty well. Then I had a dream of two ill-looking ones that plotted to interrupt my journey. This greatly troubled me. It still makes me afraid of everyone I meet, afraid that they would do mischief and turn me out of my way. I tell my Lord this, though I would not tell everyone. Between here and the gate we were severely assaulted and forced to cry out murder. The two that assaulted us were like the two that I saw in my dream.

INTER. Your beginning is good. Your end will be better. Then he addressed Mercy, What made you come here, sweet heart?

MER. Mercy blushed, trembled, and for a while was silent.

INTER. Do not be afraid. Just believe and speak your mind.

MER. Truly, sir, my lack of experience is what makes me silent. It also fills me with fear of shortcomings. I had no visions and dreams as my friend Christiana. Nor do I know what it is to mourn for refusing good counsel.

INTER. What was it, dear heart, that prevailed with you to do what you have done?

MER. When our friend was packing to leave town, another lady and I accidentally went to see her. We knocked at the door and went in. When we saw what she was doing, we asked her the meaning of it. She said that she was invited to go to her husband. Then she told us how she had seen him in a dream. He was dwelling in a curious place, among immortals, wearing a crown, playing a harp, eating and drinking at his Prince's table, and singing praises to him for bringing him there. While she was telling us, my heart burned within me. I said in my heart, If this is true, I will leave my father, my mother, and the land of my birth to go with Christiana. I asked her more about the truth of these things and if she would take me with her. I now saw that every dwelling in our town was in danger of ruin. Yet I left with a heavy heart. Not that I was unwilling to come, but that so many of my relatives were left behind. I have come with all the desire of my heart, and if I may, I will go with Christiana to her husband and his King.

INTER. Your beginning is good. You have given credit to the truth. You are a Ruth, who for her love for Naomi and her God, left father, mother, and the land of her birth, to go with a people she did not know. "The Lord repay your work, and a full reward be given you by the Lord God of Israel, under whose wings you have come for refuge" (Ruth 2:11, 12).

Supper was ended; preparation was made for bed. The women slept alone, and the boys by themselves. When Mercy was in bed, she could not sleep for joy. Her doubts of missing the prize were removed more than ever. So she blessed and praised God who granted her such favor.

In the morning they rose with the sun and prepared to leave. The Interpreter wanted them to linger. He said, You must go orderly from here. Then he ordered the girl that opened the door for them, Take them into the garden for a bath. Wash and clean them from the dirt of the journey. Then Innocent, the girl, led them into the garden to the bath. She told them that they must wash and be clean. Her Master would have all the women on a pilgrimage who called at his house do that. They went in and washed, even the boys. They came out of the bath, not only sweet and clean, but refreshed and strengthened. When they returned to the house, they looked better than when they went out to bathe.

The Interpreter looked at them and said, "Fair as the moon." Then he called for the seal to prove that they had been washed in his bath. The seal was brought and he put his mark on them so they would be known in the places where they were going. The seal was the contents and sum of the passover that the children of Israel ate (Exod. 13:8–10) when they left the land of Egypt. The mark was placed between their eyes and added to their beauty for it was an ornament to their faces. It also added to their seriousness and made their appearance more like angels.

The Interpreter said to the girl, Go into the vestry and bring clothing for these people. She returned with white garments and laid them down before him. He commanded them to put them on. It was fine linen, white and clean. When the women were dressed, they seemed to be in terror of each other; they could not see their own glory. They began to esteem each other better than themselves. You are fairer than I, said one. You are more beautiful than I, said the other. The children were amazed at the changes in the women.

THE THIRD STAGE

The Interpreter called for a man-servant, Great-heart. He told him to take a sword, helmet, and shield and conduct his daughters to the house called Beautiful, where they will next rest. He took the weapons and walked ahead of them. The Interpreter said, Godspeed. Those that belonged to the family he sent away with good wishes. They left singing,

> This place hath been our second stage:
> Here we have heard, and seen
> Those good things, that from age to age
> To others hid have been.
> The dunghill-raker, spider, hen,
> The chicken, too, to me
> Have taught a lesson: let me then
> Conformed to it be.
> The butcher, garden, and the field,

The robin and his bait,
Also the rotten tree, does yield
Me argument of weight,
To move me for to watch and pray,
To strive to be sincere;
To take my cross up day by day,
And serve the Lord with fear.

Now I saw in my dream that they went with Great-Heart. They came to the place where Christian's burden fell off his back and tumbled into a sepulchre. Here they paused and blessed God. Now, said Christiana, it comes to my mind what was said at the gate. We have pardon by word and deed. Word is the promise. Deed is the way it is obtained. I know something of what the promise is. But what is it to be pardoned by the way it was obtained? Mr. Great-Heart, I suppose you know. Would you please tell us?

GREAT. Pardon by the deed done, is pardon obtained by someone for another that needs it. Not by the person pardoned, but in the way it is obtained. To speak to the question, the pardon that Mercy, the boys, and you attained, was obtained by another. Namely, him that let you in at the gate. He obtained it in this double way. He performed righteousness to cover you and shed his blood to wash you in.

CHR. If he gives his righteousness to us, what will he have for himself?

GREAT. He has more righteousness than you need, or than he needs himself.

CHR. Please make that appear.

GREAT. First I must make a premise. He of whom we are about to speak, is one that does not have an equal. He has two natures in one person, plain to be distinguished, impossible to be divided. Each of these natures has righteousness and each is essential to that nature. One may as easily cause that nature to be extinct, as to separate it from justice or righteousness.

Besides these, there is a righteousness this person has, as these two natures are joined in one. This is not the righteousness of the Godhead, as distinguished from the manhood; nor the righteousness of the manhood, as distinguished from the Godhead. It is a righteousness that stands in the union of both natures. It may properly be called the righteousness that is essential to his being entrusted by God to be our mediator. If he parts with his first righteousness, he parts with his Godhead. If he parts with his second righteousness, he parts with the purity of his manhood. If he parts with his third righteousness, he parts with the perfection that capacitates him to the office of mediation.

He has another righteousness that stands in performance, or obedience to a revealed will, and that is what he puts on sinners. That is how their sins are covered. Thus he said, "As by one man's disobedience many were made sinners, so also by one Man's obedience many will be made righteous" (Rom. 5:19).

CHR. Is all other righteousness useless?

GREAT. Yes, though they are essential to his natures and office, and cannot be communicated to another, it is by virtue of them that the righteousness that justifies is effectual. The righteousness of his Godhead gives virtue to his obedience. The righteousness of his manhood gives capability to his obedience to justify. The righteousness that stands in the union of these two natures to his office, gives authority to that righteousness to do the work for which it was ordained.

So here is a righteousness that Christ, as God, does not need. He is God without it. Here is a righteousness that Christ, as man, does not need to make him so. He is perfect man without it. Here is a righteousness that Christ, as God-man, has no need off. He is perfect without it. Here then is a righteousness that Christ, as God, and as God-man, has no need of, with reference to himself. Thus he can spare it. A justifying righteousness, that he for himself does not want, and therefore he gives it away. Thus, it is called the gift of righteousness.

This righteousness, since Christ Jesus the Lord has made himself under the law, must be given away. The law not only binds him that is under it to be just, but to use love (Rom. 5:17). Thus, he must or ought to under the law, if he has two coats give one to him that has none. Now, our Lord indeed has two coats, one for himself, and one to spare. So he freely gives one to those that have none.

Christiana, Mercy, and the rest of you that are here, your pardon comes by deed, or by the work of another man. Your Lord Christ is he that works. He has given away what he works for, to the next poor beggar he meets.

Again, in order to pardon by deed, something must be paid to God as a price, as well as something prepared to cover us. Sin has delivered us to the curse of a righteous law. Now from this curse we must be justified by way of redemption, a price being paid for the harm we have done. This is by the blood of your Lord, who came and stood in your place and died your death for your transgressions. He has ransomed you from your transgressions by blood and covered your polluted and deformed souls with righteousness (Rom. 8:34). For his sake, God passes by you and will not hurt you when he comes to judge the world (Gal. 3:13).

CHR. This is brave! Now I see that there was something to be learned by our being pardoned by word and deed. Good Mercy, let us work to keep this in mind. My children, you also must remember it. Sir, was it this that made my good Christian's burden fall from his shoulder and made him take three leaps for joy?

GREAT. Yes, it was this belief that cut those strings that could not be cut. It was to give him proof of the virtue of this that he was permitted to carry his burden to the cross.

CHR. I thought so. My heart was light and joyous before, now it is ten times lighter and more joyous. I am persuaded by what I have felt, though I have felt but little as yet, that if the most burdened man in the world was here, and could see and believe as I now do, it would make his heart merrier and more buoyant.

GREAT. There is not only comfort and ease of a burden brought to us by the sight and consideration of this, but an endeared affection is placed in us. Who can, if he once thinks that pardon comes not only by promise but by this, be affected with the way and means of his redemption and with the man that has worked it for him?

CHR. True. It makes my heart bleed to think that he bled for me. Oh, loving One, blessed One, you deserve me for you bought me. You deserve me for you paid ten thousand times more than I am worth. No wonder this made the tears stand in my husband's eyes and made him trudge so adroitly on. I am persuaded he wanted me with him, but vile wretch that I was, I let him come alone. Oh, Mercy, that your father and mother were here. Yes, and Mrs. Timorous too. I wish with all my heart that Madam Wanton was here. Surely, surely, their hearts would be affected. Nor would the fear of one, or the powerful lusts of the other, prevail with them to go home and refuse to become good pilgrims.

GREAT. You speak now in the warmth of your affections. Will it always be this way with you? Besides, this is not communicated to everyone, or to everyone that saw your Jesus bleed. Many watched the blood run from the heart to the ground and were far off the mark. Instead of becoming his disciples, they hardened their hearts against him. All that you have, my daughters, you have by a special impression made by divine contemplation on what I have said. Remember, what was told you by the hen; her common call gives no food to her chickens. This you have by special grace.

Now I saw in my dream that they went on until they came to the place where Simple, Sloth, and Presumption slept when Christian went by on his pilgrimage. They were hanging in irons a little way off on the other side.

MER. Who are these three men? Why are they hanging there?

GREAT. These three men are of bad qualities. They had no mind to be pilgrims. They hindered whomever they could. They were sloth and folly themselves. Whoever they could persuade they taught them to presume that they would do well at last. They were asleep when Christian went by. Now as you go by, they are hanged.

MER. Did they persuade any to their opinion?

GREAT. Yes, they turned several out of the way. There was Slow-pace, they persuaded him. They also prevailed with Short-wind, with

No-heart, with Linger-after-Lust, with Sleepy-head, and with a young woman, named Dull. They gave a false report about your Lord. They persuaded others that he was a hard taskmaster. They brought an evil report of the good Land, saying it was not half so good as some pretended it was. They began to vilify his servants and to count the best of them meddlesome, troublesome busybodies. Further, they would call the bread of God husks, the comforts of his children fancies, and the travel and labor of pilgrims things of no purpose.

CHR. No, I will not mourn them. They have what they deserve. I think it is well they hang near the highway so that others may see and take warning. Would it not be well to have their crimes engraved on a plate of iron or brass and left as a caution to others?

GREAT. This has been done, as you will see if you will go closer to the wall.

MER. No, no, let them hang, let their names rot, and let their crimes live forever against them. I think it is a great favor that they were hanged before we came here. Who knows what they might have done to poor women like us? Then she turned it into a song,

> Now then you three hang there, and be a sign
> To all that shall against the truth combine.
> And let him that comes after, fear this end,
> If unto pilgrims he is not a friend.
> And thou, my soul, of all such men beware,
> That unto holiness opposers are.

They went on until they arrived at the foot of the hill Difficulty. Here, good Mr. Great-Heart told what happened when Christian went by. He took them to the spring. This, said he, is the spring that Christian drank from before he climbed this hill. Then it was clear and good. Now it is dirty from the feet of some that do not want pilgrims to quench their thirst (Ezek. 34:18, 19), but it will do. Mercy asked, How? The guide answered, If the water is put into a vessel that is sweet and good, the dirt will sink to the bottom and the water will be clear. This they were force to do, then they drank.

Next he showed them the two by-ways at the foot of the hill, where Formality and Hypocrisy were lost. He said, These are dangerous paths. Two were lost here when Christian came by. As you can see, these ways are now blocked with chains, posts, and a ditch. Still, there are those that will choose to travel here rather than go up this hill.

CHR. "The way of the unfaithful is hard" (Prov. 13:15). It is a wonder that they can get into these ways without breaking their necks.

GREAT. They will try. If any of the King's servants see them, they tell them that they are in the wrong way and warn them of the danger. But they rail against them, "As for the word that you have spoken to us in the name of the Lord, we will not listen to you! But we will certainly do whatever has gone out of our own mouths" (Jer. 44:16, 17). If you look a little further, you will see that these ways are made safe enough, not only by the posts, chains, and ditch, but also by being fenced. Still they will choose to go there.

CHR. They are lazy. They will not make any effort. The up-hill way is unpleasant to them. So it is fulfilled, "The way of the lazy man is like a hedge of thorns" (Prov. 15:19). Yes, they would rather walk on a snare than go up this hill to the city.

They started up the hill. Before they got to the top, Christiana began to breathe hard. She said, This is a breathing hill. No wonder they who love their ease more than their souls choose a smoother way.

Mercy said, I must sit down. The children began to cry. Come, come, said Great-Heart, do not sit here. A little above is the Prince's arbor. Then he took the little boy by the hand and led him there.

When they reached the arbor, they were willing to sit down. They were in a pelting heat. Mercy said, "How sweet is rest to them that labor" (Matt. 11:28). How good is the Prince of pilgrims to provide this resting place! I have heard much about this arbor, but I never saw it before. Let us beware of sleeping here, for it cost poor Christian dearly.

Mr. Great-Heart said to the little ones, Come, boys, how do you do? What do you now think of going on a pilgrimage? Sir, said the smallest, I was almost beat out of heart. I thank you for lending me a hand. I remember what my mother told me, the way to heaven is a ladder, and the way to hell is down a hill. I would rather go up the ladder to life, than down the hill to death.

Mercy said, The proverb is, "To go down the hill is easy." But James said (for that was his name), The day is coming when, in my opinion, going down the hill will be the hardest of all. You are a good boy, said his master, you have given the right answer. Mercy smiled, the little boy blushed.

CHR. Come, said Christiana, will you eat a bit to sweeten your mouths while you sit and rest your legs? I have a piece of pomegranate Mr. Interpreter gave me when I came out of his door. He also gave me a piece of honeycomb and a little bottle of spirits. I thought he gave you something, said Mercy, because he called you aside. Yes, he did, said Christiana. It will still be as I said it would be, when we first left home. You will share in all the good that I have because you so willingly became my companion. Then she gave the sweets to them and Mercy and the boys ate. Christiana said to Mr. Great-Heart, Sir, will you join us? He answered, You are going on a pilgrimage and what you eat may do you much good. Presently I will return home and eat regularly every day.

THE FOURTH STAGE

N ow when they had eaten, drank, and chatted a little longer, their guide said, The day wears away. Let us prepare to be going. They got up and left, the little boys went ahead. Christiana forgot her bottle of spirits, so she sent her little boy back to get it. Mercy said, I think this is a losing place. This is where Christian lost his roll, and Christiana left her bottle. Sir, what is the reason? Their guide answered, The reason is sleep, or forgetfulness. Some sleep when they should keep awake and some forget when they should remember. This is why, at the resting-places, some pilgrims are losers. Pilgrims should watch and remember what they have already received for their greatest enjoyment. For lack of watching, rejoicing often ends in tears and sunshine in clouds. Witness the story of Christian.

When they arrived at the place where Mistrust and Timorous met Christian, to persuade him to go back for fear of the lions, they perceived a stage. In front of it, toward the road, was a broad plate with a copy of verses written on it. Underneath was the reason why the stage was built there. The verses read,

> Let him that sees this stage, take heed
> Unto his heart and tongue;
> Lest, if he do not, here he speed
> As some have long agone.

The words under the verses were, "This stage was built to punish those who, through fearfulness or mistrust, were afraid to go further on their pilgrimage. On this stage Mistrust and Timorous were burned through the tongue with a hot iron for attempting to hinder Christian on his journey."

Mercy said, This is like the saying of the Beloved: "What shall be given unto thee, or what shall be done unto thee, thou false tongue? Sharp arrows of the mighty, with coals of juniper (Ps. 120:3, 4).

They continued until they were within sight of the lions. Mr. Great-Heart was a strong man, so he was not afraid of a lion. When they came to the place where the lions were, the boys were afraid. They stepped back and cringed. Their guide smiled and said, How now, my boys? You love to go ahead when there is no danger and you love to be behind when the lions appear.

As they went on, Mr. Great-Heart drew his sword to make a way for the pilgrims in spite of the lions. Then one appeared that, it seems, had backed the lions. He said to the pilgrims' guide, What is the reason you have come here? Now the name of the man was Grim, or Bloody-man, because of his slaying the pilgrims. He was from the race of giants.

GREAT. These women and children are going on a pilgrimage. This is the way they must go. And go it they will in spite of you and the lions.

GRIM. This is not their way. They will not go this way. I am here to prevent it. To that end, I will back the lions.

Now, to tell the truth, because of the fierceness of the lions and the grim carriage of him that backed them, this way had lately been unoccupied. It was almost grown over with grass.

CHR. Though the highways have been deserted and travelers forced to walk the byways, it must not be so now that I have arisen, arisen a mother in Israel (Judges 5:6, 7).

Then he swore by the lions that they would not pass. He ordered them to turn aside.

Great-Heart their guide made the first approach. He hit Grim so hard with his sword that he forced him to retreat.

GRIM. Will you slay me on my own ground?

GREAT. This is the King's highway. You have placed lions in this way. These women and children, though weak, will pass in spite of your lions. He gave him another blow that brought him to his knees and broke his helmet. Another slash and he cut off an arm. The giant roared so hideously that his voice frightened the women, but they were glad to see him sprawling on the ground. The lions were chained and could do nothing. Old Grim, who intended to back them, was dead. Mr. Great-Heart said to the pilgrims, Come, follow me, and the lions will not harm you. They went on. The women trembled as they passed the lions and the boys looked as if they would die. But they all got by without any harm.

When they were within sight of the Porter's lodge, they hurried because traveling is dangerous there at night. When they arrived at the gate, the guide knocked and the Porter answered, Who is there? As soon as the guide said, It is I, he knew his voice for the guide had often been a conductor of pilgrims. He opened the gate and saw the guide standing in front of it (he did not see the women, for they were behind him). He said, How now, Mr. Great-Heart, what is your business here this late at night? I have brought, said he, some pilgrims. By my Lord's commandment they must lodge here. I would have been here some time ago had the giant that backed the lions not opposed me. But after a long and tedious combat, I cut him off and brought the pilgrims here in safety.

POR. Will you come in and stay until morning?

GREAT. No, I will return to my Lord tonight.

CHR. Sir, I do not know how to allow you to leave us in our pilgrimage. You have been so faithful and loving, you have fought so strongly, you have been so hearty in counseling that I will never forget your favor.

MER. Oh that we might have your company to our journey's end! How can poor women hold out in a way so full of trouble, without a friend and defender?

JAMES. James, the youngest of the boys, said, Please, sir, come with us and help us. We are weak and the way is dangerous.

GREAT. I am at my Lord's command. If he will allow me to be your guide, I will willingly wait on you. But here you failed. When he ordered me come this far, you should have begged him to let me go through with you. He would have granted your request. At present, however, I must withdraw. So, good Christiana, Mercy, and my brave children, adieu.

The Porter, Mr. Watchful, asked Christiana about her country and her relatives. She responded, I came from the city of Destruction. I am a widow, my husband is dead, his name was Christian, the pilgrim. He was your husband? said the Porter. Yes, said she, and these are his children. Then pointing to Mercy she added, This is one of my town's women. Then the Porter rang his bell and a girl came to the door whose name was Humble-Mind. The Porter said to her, Go tell that Christiana, the wife of Christian, and her children are here on a pilgrimage. She went in and told them, and great gladness was in the lodge.

They hurried out to the Porter, for Christiana was still at the door. Then some of the most solemn ladies said, Come in, Christiana, come in, wife of that good man. Come in, blessed woman, come in, and everyone who is with you. So she went in and her companion and children followed. Inside they entered a large room where they were seated. The heads of the house were called to welcome the guests. They came in and greeted one another with a kiss and said, Welcome, you vessels of the grace of God. Welcome friends.

The pilgrims were weary from their journey, weak from watching the fight and the terrible lions. It was late and the pilgrims wanted to rest as soon possible. No, said the family, refresh yourselves first with some meat. They had prepared a lamb with the typical sauces (Ex. 12:21; John 1:29). The Porter had earlier heard of their coming. After they dined and ended their prayer with a psalm, they wanted to rest.

Christiana said, If we may be so bold as to choose a bedroom, let it be the room that was my husband's when he was here. They took them up there and when they were in bed, Christiana and Mercy had a conversation.

CHR. Little did I think, when my husband went on a pilgrimage, that I would follow him.

MER. Little did you think that you would lie in his bed to rest.

CHR. Much less did I ever think of seeing his face and worshiping the Lord the King with him. Yet I now believe I will.

MER. Do you hear a noise?

CHR. Yes. I believe it is joyful music because we are here.

MER. Wonderful! Music in the house, music in the heart, music in heaven for joy that we are here! They talked awhile and then fell asleep.

When they woke in the morning, Christiana said to Mercy, Why did you laugh in your sleep? Did you have a dream?

MER. Yes, a sweet dream it was. Are you sure I laughed?

CHR. Yes, you laughed heartily. Mercy, tell me your dream.

MER. I was dreaming that I sat alone in a solitary place, lamenting the hardness of my heart. I had not sat there long but many came to see me and to hear what I said. They listened and I went on lamenting the hardness of my heart. At this, some of them laughed, some called me a fool, and some began to throw me around.

I looked up and saw one coming toward me with wings. He came directly to me and said, Mercy, what troubles you? When he heard my complaint, he said, Peace to you. He wiped my eyes with his handkerchief and dressed me in silver and gold (Ezek. 16:8–11). He put a chain around my neck, ear rings in my ears, and a beautiful crown on my head. Then he took me by the hand and said, Mercy, come after me. So he went up and I followed until we came to a gate of gold. He knocked. When they opened the gate, the man went in, and I followed him up to a throne on which one sat. He said, Welcome, daughter. The place was bright and twinkling like the stars, or rather like the sun. I thought I saw your husband. Then I woke from my dream. But did I laugh?

CHR. Laugh! Yes, and well you might to see yourself there. You must allow me to tell you that was a good dream. Just as you have begun to find the first part true, so you will find the second. "God may speak in one way or in another, yet man does not perceive it. In a dream, in a vision of the night, when deep sleep falls on men, while slumbering on their beds" (Job 33:14, 15). We need not, when in bed, lie awake to talk with God. He can visit us while we sleep, and make us hear his voice. Our heart often wakes when we sleep, and God can speak to it either by words, proverbs, signs or the like, as well as if one was awake.

MER. Well, I am glad of my dream. I hope before long to see it fulfilled. Then I will laugh again.

CHR. I think it is high time to rise and find out what we must do.

MER. Please, if they invite us to stay, let us accept. I am willing to stay and grow better acquainted with the ladies. I think Prudence, Piety, and Charity, have attractive and serious appearances.

CHR. We will see what they will do.

They got up and were ready. When they came down, they asked one another about their rest. Was it comfortable?.

MER. It was one of the best night's lodging I ever had in my life.

Prudence and Piety said, If you can be persuaded to stay, you will have the best of the house.

CHAR. Yes and with good will, said Charity. So they agreed and stayed there a month or more. It was profitable for all. Prudence could see how Christiana raised her children, and she asked permission to question them. It was freely given. She began with the youngest, James.

PRUD. Come, James, can you tell me who made you?

JAMES. God the Father, God the Son, and God the Holy Ghost.

PRUD. Good boy. Can you tell who saved you?

JAMES. God the Father, God the Son, and God the Holy Ghost.

PRUD. Good boy again. How does God the Father save you?

JAMES. By his grace.

PRUD. How does God the Son save you?

JAMES. By his righteousness, death, blood, and life.

PRUD. And how does God the Holy Ghost save you?

JAMES. By his illumination, by his renovation, and by his preservation.

Prudence said to Christiana, You are to be commended for the way you have raised your children. I suppose I do not need to ask the rest of these questions, since the youngest has answered them so well. I will apply myself to the next youngest.

PRUD. Come, Joseph (for his name was Joseph), will you let me query you?

JOSEPH. With all my heart.

PRUD. What is man?

JOSEPH. A reasonable creature, made by God, as my brother said.

PRUD. What is the definition of this word, saved?

JOSEPH. Man, by sin, has brought himself into a state of captivity and misery.

PRUD. What is meant by his being saved by the Trinity?

JOSEPH. Sin is so great and mighty a tyrant that none can pull us out of its clutches except God. And God is so good and loving to man, as to pull him indeed out of this miserable state.

PRUD. What is God's plan in saving poor men?

JOSEPH. Glorifying his name, his grace, and justice, etc., and the everlasting happiness of his creature.

PRUD. Who will be saved?

JOSEPH. Those that accept his salvation.

PRUD. Good boy, Joseph, your mother has taught you well. You have listened to what she has told you.

Then Prudence said to Samuel, who was the second oldest,

PRUD. Samuel, are you willing for me to interrogate you?

SAM. Yes, if you please.

PRUD. What is heaven?

SAM. A place and state most blessed, because God dwells there.

PRUD. What is hell?

SAM. A place and state most awful, because it is the dwelling place of sin, the devil, and death.

PRUD. Why do you want to go to heaven?

SAM. To see God and serve him without weariness. To see Christ and love him everlastingly. To have the fullness of the Holy Spirit in me which I can by no means enjoy here.

PRUD. A very good boy and one that has learned well.

Then she addressed the oldest, whose name was Matthew. Come, Matthew, may I also question you?

MATT. With a very good will.

PRUD. I ask then, if there was ever anything that had a being antecedent to or before God?

MATT. No, for God is eternal, nor is there anything, excepting himself, that had a being until the beginning of the first day. For in six days the Lord made heaven and earth, the sea, and all that is in them.

PRUD. What do you think of the Bible?

MATT. It is the holy word of God.

PRUD. Is there anything written in it that you do not understand?

MATT. Yes, a great deal.

PRUD. What do you do when you find places that you do not understand?

MATT. I think God is wiser than I. I pray that he will be pleased to let me know all that he knows for my good.

PRUD. What do you believe about the resurrection of the dead?

MATT. I believe they shall rise that were buried, the same in nature, though not in corruption. I believe this on a double account. First, because God has promised it. Second, because he is able to perform it.

Prudence said to the boys, You must continue to listen to your mother. She can teach you more. You must diligently listen to good conversation from others, for your sake may they speak good things. Carefully observe what the heavens and the earth teach. Especially meditate in the book that caused your father to become a pilgrim. I, for my part, will teach you what I can while you are here and will be pleased if you ask me questions that will godly edify.

The pilgrims had been there a week when Mercy had a visitor. His name was Mr. Brisk, a man of some breeding. He pretended to be religious but stuck close to the world. He came twice or more to see Mercy and offer love. Mercy was attractive and alluring.

Mercy was always busy. When she had nothing to do for herself, she would make clothing and give it to the needy. Mr. Brisk did not know what she did with the clothes she made. He seemed to be greatly impressed, for he never found her idle. I warrant her a good housewife, he said to himself.

Mercy asked the other ladies of the house about Mr. Brisk, for they knew him. They said that he was a busy young man who pretended to be religious. They feared he was a stranger to the power of what is good.

No, said Mercy, I will not look on him. I purposed never to have an obstruction in my soul.

Prudence replied there was no need to discourage him. If Mercy continued to make clothing for the poor, it would quickly cool his courage.

The next time he visited, he found her making things for the poor. He said, What, always at it? Yes, said she, either for myself or for others. He asked, What do you earn a day? I do these things, said she, that I may be rich in good works, laying up stores for a good foundation against the time to come, that I may lay hold on eternal life (1 Tim. 6:17–19). Why, he asked, what do you do with them? Clothe the naked, said she. With that his appearance fell. He never visited her again. When asked the reason, he said, Mercy is a pretty lass but troubled with ill conditions.

After he left, Prudence said, I told you Mr. Brisk would soon forsake you? Yes, he will give a poor report of you. Despite his pretence of religion, and his seeming love for Mercy, he and Mercy are such different personalities that I believe they will never come together.

MER. I might have had a husband before now, but they did not like my personality. Though none ever found fault with my person. We just could not agree.

PRUD. Mercy in our days there is little set by your conditions.

MER. Well, if nobody will have me I will die unmarried, or my conditions will be my husband. I cannot change my nature. I will never have one who is at cross-purposes with me. I had a sister, Bountiful, she was married to one of these brutes. They could never agree. My sister was resolved to show kindness to the poor. Her husband first tried to stop her, then he turned her out of his house.

PRUD. Yet he was a professor, I warrant?

MER. Yes, such a one as he was. The world is now full of them but I am for none of them.

Matthew, the eldest son of Christiana, became ill. His sickness was heavy. He was in great pain. At times it seemed both ends of his body was being pulled apart. Living close by was Mr. Skill, an ancient and approved physician. After he entered the room and observed the boy, he diagnosed that he was sick with the colic. He said to his mother, What has Matthew been eating? Eating, Christiana said, nothing but wholesome food. The physician answered, This boy has eaten something that lies undigested in his stomach. He must be purged, or else he will die.

SAM. Mother, what did my brother pick and eat after we came through the gate at the beginning of the way? You know there was an orchard on the left and some tree branches hung over the wall. My brother picked and ate some of the fruit.

CHR. True, my child, he did. He was a naughty boy, I chided him but he continued to eat.

SKILL. I knew he had eaten something that was not wholesome. It is the fruit of Beelzebub's orchard. I wonder why no one warned you, it is the most harmful fruit of all. Many have died from it.

CHR. Christiana began to cry. Oh, naughty boy! Oh, careless mother! What will I do for my son?

SKILL. Come, do not be too dejected, the boy may do well again. But he must be purged and vomit.

CHR. Please, sir, try your utmost skill on him, whatever it costs.

SKILL. I hope I will be reasonable. He made a purge from the blood of a goat, the ashes of a heifer, and juice of a hyssop (Heb. 9:13, 19;

10:1–4), but it was too weak. When Mr. Skill saw this, he made one that would do the job. It was ex carne et sanguine Christi (John 6:54–57; Heb. 9:14); (you know physicians give strange medicines to their patients). It was made into pills, with a promise or two, and a proportionate quantity of salt (Mark 9:49). He was to fast and take the pills three times a day in half a quarter of a pint of the tears of repentance (Zech. 12:10).

When this potion was prepared and brought to the boy, he did not want to take it. Come, come, said the physician, you must take it. It goes against my stomach, said the boy. I must have you take it, said his mother. I shall vomit it up again, said the boy. Please, sir, Christiana said to Mr. Skill, how does it taste? It has no bad taste, said the doctor. She touched one of the pills with the tip of her tongue. Oh, Matthew, this potion is sweeter than honey. If you love your mother, if you love your brothers, if you love Mercy, if you love your life, take it. So, with much ado, after a short prayer for the blessing of God, he took the pill. It worked well. He purged, slept, and rested quietly. It put him into a fine heated sweat. It cured his illness. In a little while he got up, walked around with a cane, went from room to room talking to Prudence, Piety, and Charity, about his illness and how he was healed.

When the boy was cured, Christiana asked Mr. Skill, Sir, what is your fee for the care of my child? He said, You must pay the master of the College of Physicians (Heb. 13:11–15), according to the rules.

CHR. Sir, what else is this pill good for?

SKILL. It is a universal pill. Good against all diseases afflicting pilgrims. When it is well prepared, it will keep, regardless of time.

CHR. Please, sir, make up twelve boxes for me. If I can get these, I will never take another medicine.

SKILL. These pills prevent diseases and cure the sick. Yes, I dare say and stand by it, if a man will use this physic as he should, he will live forever (John 6:51). Good Christiana, you must only give these pills the way I have prescribed, otherwise, they will do no good. The he gave Christiana a physic for herself, the boys, and Mercy. He told Matthew not to eat any more green plums, kissed them, and went his way.

It was told you before that Prudence invited the boys to ask her questions that might be helpful to them.

MATT. Matthew, who had been sick, asked why for the most part a physic was bitter to taste.

PRUD. It shows how unwelcome the word of God and its effects are to a carnal heart.

MATT. Why does a physic, if it does good, make you vomit?

PRUD. It shows that the word, when it works effectively, cleans the heart and mind. What one does for the body, the other does for the soul.

MATT. What do we learn by watching the flame of our fire go up, and by seeing the beams and sweet influences of the sun strike down?

PRUD. The rising flames teach us to ascend heaven by fervent and hot desires. The sun sending his heat, beams, and sweet influences down, teaches the Savior of the world, though high, reaches down with grace and love to us.

MATT. Where do the clouds get their water?

PRUD. Out of the sea.

MATT. What may we learn from that?

PRUD. Ministers should obtain their doctrine from God.

MATT. Why are they emptied on earth?

PRUD. To show that ministers should give what they know of God to the world.

MATT. Why is the rainbow created by the sun?

PRUD. To show that the covenant of God's grace is confirmed to us in Christ.

MATT. Why do the springs come from the sea through the earth?

PRUD. To show that the grace of God comes through the body of Christ.

MATT. Why do some of the springs rise out of the tops of high hills?

PRUD. To show that the Spirit of grace will spring up in some that are great and mighty, as well as in many that are poor and low.

MATT. Why does the fire fasten to the candle wick?

PRUD. To show that unless grace kindles the heart, there is no true light of life in us.

MATT. Why are the wick, tallow, and all, spent to maintain the candle's light?

PRUD. To show that body, soul, and all, should spend themselves to maintain the grace of God that is in us.

MATT. Why does the pelican pierce her breast with her bill?

PRUD. To nourish her young with her blood. This shows that Christ, the blessed, so loved his young (his people) as to save them from death by his blood.

MATT. What may one learn by hearing the cock crow?

PRUD. Remember Peter's sin and repentance. The cock's crowing also shows that day is dawning. Let the crowing of the cock remind you of that last and terrible day of judgment.

About this time their month was up. They told the people of the house that they would be leaving. Joseph said to his mother, Do not forget to send a message to Mr. Interpreter's house, to ask if Mr. Great-Heart may be our conductor the rest of the way. Good boy, said she, I almost forgot. So she wrote a petition and asked Mr. Watchful, the porter, to send it to her good friend, Mr. Interpreter. When he read the petition, he said to the messenger, Tell them that I will send him.

When the family saw that Christiana was going to leave, they called the entire house together to give thanks to their King for sending such wonderful guests. They said to Christiana, We will show you something to think about when you are on the way. They took Christiana, her children, and Mercy, into a closet and showed them an apple that Eve had bitten into and one that she gave her husband. Eating these apples turned both of them out of paradise. They asked what she thought it was. Christiana said, It is food or poison, I do not know which. She held up her hands and wondered (Gen. 3:6; Rom. 7:24).

Then they took her to a place and showed her Jacob's ladder (Gen. 28:12). At that time there were some angels ascending it. Christiana, and the rest of the group, watched the angels. As they prepared to go to another place to see something else, James said to his mother, Ask them if we may stay a little longer for this is a curious sight. They then turned and watched.

After this, they went to where a golden anchor was hung. They asked Christiana to take it down. You shall have the anchor. It is absolutely necessary that you lay hold of it within the veil (Heb. 6:19). This will keep you steadfast in turbulent weather (Joel 3:16). They were glad.

They took them to the mount where Abraham offered Isaac his son, and showed them the altar, the wood, the fire, and the knife. They may be seen there to this day (Gen. 22:9). After they had seen it, they held up their hands, blessed themselves, and said, Oh, what a man was Abraham to love his Master and deny himself!

After they had seen all these things, Prudence took them into a dining room where there was a pair of superb spinets. She played them and sung an excellent song about what she had shown them.

> Eve's apple we have showed you;
> Of that be you aware:
> You have seen Jacob's ladder too,
> Upon which angels are.
> An anchor you received have;
> But let not these suffice,
> Until with Abra'm you have gave
> Your best, a sacrifice.

About this time there was a knock at the door. The Porter opened it and Mr. Great-Heart was there. When he came in, there was great joy! They remembered how he had slain old Grim Bloody-man the giant, and had delivered them from the lions.

Mr. Great-Heart said to Christiana and Mercy, My Lord sent each of you a bottle of wine, some parched corn, and a couple of pomegranates. He sent the boys some figs and raisins to refresh you on your way.

They made ready for their journey. Prudence and Piety went along with them. When they reached the gate, Christiana asked the Porter if any one had recently passed. He said, No, but sometime ago I learned that a great robbery had been committed on the King's highway. The thieves have been captured and will shortly be tried for their lives. Christiana and Mercy were afraid. Matthew said, Mother, do not fear as long as Mr. Great-Heart is our conductor.

Christiana said to the Porter, Sir, I am much obliged to you for the kindness that you have shown me since I arrived. You have also been kind and loving to my children. I do not know how to repay your kindness. Please, as a token of my respect, accept this small gift. She put a gold angel in his hand.

He bowed low and said, "Let your garments always be white, and let your head lack no oil" (Eccl. 9:8). "Let Mercy live and not die, nor let her works be few" (Deut. 33:6). To the boys he said, "Flee youthful lust; but pursue righteousness, faith, love, peace with those who call on the Lord out of a pure heart (2 Tim. 2:22). Then you will put gladness into your mother's heart and obtain praise from all that are soberminded. They thanked the Porter and departed.

THE FIFTH STAGE

Now I saw in my dream that they went forward until they came to the crest of the Hill. There Piety cried out, I forgot what I intended to give Christiana and her companions. I will go back and get it. While she was gone, Christiana thought she heard, in a grove a little way off on the right hand, a curious melodious note with words much like these:

> Through all my life thy favor is
> So frankly shown to me,
> That in thy House for evermore
> My dwelling place shall be.

Continuing to listen, she thought she heard someone answer.

> For why? The Lord our God is good;
> His mercy is forever sure;
> His truth at all times firmly stood,
> And shall from age to age endure.

Christiana asked Prudence who made those melodious notes (Song 2:11, 12). They are, she answered, our country birds. They seldom sing these notes, except in the spring when the flowers appear and the sun shines warm. Then you may hear them all day long. I often go out to listen. We have some caged in our house; they are fine company when we are melancholy. They also make the woods, groves, and solitary places desirable.

Piety returned and said to Christiana, Look here, I have brought you a plan of all the things that you have seen at our house. You may look when you forget and again recall those things that edify and comfort.

They began to go down to the Valley of Humiliation. It was a steep hill and the way was slippery. They were careful and got down without incident. When they reached the valley, Piety said to Christiana, This is the place where Christian, your husband, met that foul fiend Apollyon and had that dreadful fight. Be of good courage, with Mr. Great-Heart for your guide and conductor, you will be fine. After Prudence and Piety committed the pilgrims to the protection of their guide, he went forward and they followed.

GREAT. We need not fear this valley. There is nothing here to hurt us, unless we do it ourselves. It is true that Christian met Apollyon here and they fought, but that fight was caused by a mis-step. They that slip there, must expect combat here. This is how the valley got so hard a name. The common people, when they hear that some frightful things happened here, are of the opinion that this place is haunted with some foul fiend or evil spirit. Alas, it is their doings that is the frightful thing. This Valley of Humiliation is as fruitful a place as the crow flies over. I am persuaded that we might find someone here to give us an account of why Christian was attacked in this place.

James said to his mother, Over there is a pillar. It looks as if something is written on it. Let's go and see what it is. They found this written, "Let Christian's mis-steps, before he came here, and the battles that he met in this place, be a warning to those that follow." Did I not tell you, said their guide, that there was something here that would tell why Christian was so hard pressed in this place? Turning to Christiana, he said, No aspersion on Christian more than any other in similar circumstances. It is easier going up this hill than down and that can be said of few hills in these parts of the world. He is at rest, we will leave the good man. He had a brave victory over the enemy. Let Him who dwells above grant that we fare no worse than he when we are tested.

We will come again to this Valley of Humiliation. It is the best and most fruitful ground in all these parts, rich with beautiful meadows. If a man came here in the summer, as we do now, he would see that it is delightful. See how green this valley is and how the lilies make it more beautiful (Song 2:1). I have known many working men that received fine estates in this Valley of Humiliation because God resists the proud, but gives grace to the humble (James 4:6; 1 Pet. 5:5). The soil is fruitful; it produces an abundant harvest. Some wish that this was next to their Father's house, then there would be no more trouble with hills or mountains. But the way is the way and there is an end.

They were walking when they saw a boy feeding his father's sheep. The boy was poorly dressed but he was happy. He sat by himself and sung. Listen, said Mr. Great-Heart, to what the shepherd boy is singing,

> He that is down, needs fear no fall;
> He that is low, no pride:
> He that is humble, ever shall
> Have God to be his guide.
> I am content with what I have,
> Little be it or much;
> And, Lord, contentment still I crave,
> Because thou saves such.
> Fullness to such, a burden is,
> That go on pilgrimage;
> Here little, and hereafter bliss,
> Is best from Age to Age.

The guide said, Do you hear him? I dare say this boy lives a happier life and wears more of that herb called heart's-ease than he that is dressed in silk and velvet. We will continue our discussion.

In this valley our Lord use to have his country house. He loved to walk these meadows in the pleasant air. Here a man is free from noise and the hurrying of this life. All states are full of noise and confusion; only the Valley of Humiliation is empty and solitary. Unlike other places, a man here will not be hindered in contemplation. This is a valley that nobody walks except those that love a pilgrim's life. Though Christian had the hard task of encountering Apollyon, I must tell you that in former times men have met angels here (Hos. 12:4, 5), found pearls (Matt. 13:46), and found the words of life (Prov. 8:36).

Did I tell you that our Lord had his country house here and loved to walk in the meadows? In this place, to the people that love and walked these grounds, he left a yearly revenue to be faithfully paid for maintenance and encouragement in their pilgrimage.

SAM. As they traveled, Samuel said to Mr. Great-Heart, Sir, I understand that in this valley my father and Apollyon had their battle. Where was the fight?

GREAT. Your father had the battle with Apollyon ahead of us, in a narrow passage, just beyond Forgetful Green. That place is the most dangerous in these parts. If the pilgrims meet opposition, it is when they forget the favors they have received and how unworthy they are of them. This is also the place where others have been hard pressed. But more of that when we arrive there. I am persuaded that to this day there remains either some sign of the battle, or some monument to testify that such a battle was fought there.

MER. I think I am happier in this valley than anywhere else on our journey. This place suits my spirit. I love to be in a place like this; there is no rattling of coaches and no rumbling of wheels. Here one may, without interruption, think of whom he is, where he came from, what he has done, and his calling. Here one may think, break his heart, and melt one's spirit until his eyes are like the pools in Heshbon (Song 7:4). They that pass through the Valley of Baca, they make it a spring; the rain also covers it with pools. This valley is where the King will give her the vineyards, and the valley as a door of hope and she shall sing there, as Christian did when he met Apollyon (Ps. 84:5–7; Hos. 2:15).

GREAT. It's true, said their guide, I have gone through this valley many times and never felt better. I have also guided several pilgrims and they said the same thing. "On this one I will look:" said the King, "on him who is poor and of a contrite spirit, and who trembles at My word" (Is. 66:2).

They came to the place where the battle was fought. The guide said, On this ground Christian stood and Apollyon came against him. Look! Did I not tell you? Here, to this day, is some of your husband's blood on these stones. Look here and there and you can find pieces of Apollyon's broken darts. Notice how they trampled the ground as they fought. Some of their blows split the stones in pieces. Here Christian played the man and proved himself as brave as Hercules. When Apollyon was defeated, he retreated to the next valley, the Valley of the Shadow of Death, to which we will soon come. There is a monument engraved with this battle and the fame of Christian's victory. Because it stood on the way, they stepped up to it and read the engraving:

> Hard by here was a battle fought,
> Most strange, and yet most true;
> Christian and Apollyon fought
> Each other to subdue.
> The man so bravely play'd the man,
> He made the fiend to fly;
> Of which a monument I stand,
> The same to testify.

When they passed this place, they came to the borders of the Shadow of Death. This Valley was longer than the other. It was a place strangely haunted with evil things, as many can testify. But these women and children went easily through it because they had daylight and Mr. Great-Heart was their conductor.

When they were entering this valley, they thought they heard groaning, great groaning, like men dying. They also thought that they heard lamentations, spoken as if one was in extreme torment. These things made the boys shake, the women look pale, but their guide told them to be of good comfort.

They went a little further. The ground began to shake under them, like it was hollow. They heard hissing, like serpents, but nothing appeared. The boys said, Are we at the end of this mournful place? The guide told them be brave, watch their step, or they would be caught in a snare.

James began to be sick. I think the cause was fear. His mother gave him some spirits and three pills that Mr. Skill had prepared. The boy started to revive. They went on to the middle of the valley. Christiana said, I see something on the road ahead, a thing with a shape that I have never seen. Joseph said, Mother, what is it? An ugly thing, child, an ugly thing. Mother, what is it like? I cannot tell, she said, it is still a way off. Then she said, It is close.

Well, said Mr. Great-Heart, if you are afraid, keep close to me. The fiend came on, the conductor met it, and it vanished from their sights. Then they remembered what had been said, "Resist the devil and he will flee from you" (James 4:7).

They went on, refreshed. They had not gone far when Mercy looked behind her and thought she saw a lion. It came at a great padding pace. It had a hollow roaring voice. Every roar made the valley echo and their hearts, except the heart of their guide, ache. The lion came. Mr. Great-Heart went behind the pilgrims. The lion kept coming and Mr. Great-Heart prepared for battle (1 Pet. 5:8, 9). When the lion saw that there would be resistance, he stopped and came no further.

They continued on, their conductor leading, until they came to a pit the width of the way. Before they could pass, fog and darkness fell on them. They could not see. The pilgrims said, What can we do? The guide answered, Fear not, stand still. They thought they heard the noise and rushing of their enemies. The fire and smoke from the pit was now easier to see. Christiana said to Mercy, I know what my poor husband went through. Poor man! He came here alone, at night. These fiends were busy around him, as if they would tear him to pieces. I have heard much about this place but I have never been here. Many have spoken about it but none can tell what the Valley of the Shadow of Death means until they come to it themselves. The heart knows its own bitterness, and a stranger does not share its joy (Prov. 14:10). It is frightening to be here.

GREAT. This is like being in great waters in the heart of the sea, or going down into the depths and being at the bottom of the mountains. It seems as if the earth, with its bars, surrounded us. Who walks in darkness and has no light? Let him trust in the name of the Lord and rely upon his God (Is. 50:10). For my part, as I have already told you, I have frequently gone through this valley with greater difficulties than now. Yet you see I am alive. I would not boast. I am not my own savior. I trust we will be delivered. Come, let us pray for light to Him that can lighten our darkness and can rebuke not only these but all the Satans in hell.

They cried, prayed, and God sent light and deliverance. The pit did not stop them. They went on and met a great stench and loathsome smells that greatly annoyed them. Mercy said to Christiana, It is not as pleasant being here as at the gate, the Interpreter's, or the last house where we stayed.

O, said one of the boys, it would be terrible to live here but it is not so bad to walk through. One reason we must go this way is so the home prepared for us will be sweeter.

Well said, Samuel, you have spoken like a man, the guide responded. If I ever get out of here, said the boy, I will value light and good ways better than I ever did. The guide said, We will soon be out.

They went on. Joseph said, Can we see the end of the valley? The guide said, Watch your step, we will soon be among the snares. They went on, but the thoughts of the snares troubled them. When they reached the snares, they saw a man who had been thrown into the ditch on the left. His flesh was ripped and torn. The guide said, That is Heedless. He was going this way. He has been there a great while. Take-Heed was with him when he was captured and slain, but he escaped. You cannot imagine how many are killed here. Yet men are so foolishly venturous as to set out on a pilgrimage without a guide. Poor

Christian! It was a wonder he escaped. He was loved by God, he had a good heart or else he could never have done it.

Now as they drew close to where Christian had seen the cave, out came Maul, a giant. Maul spoiled young pilgrims with foolish arguments. He called Great-Heart by name and said, How many times have you been forbidden to do these things? Mr. Great-Heart said, What things? What things, said the giant, you know what things. I will put an end to your trade.

But, Mr. Great-Heart said, before we fall to it, let us understand why we must fight. The women and children stood trembling, not knowing what to do. The giant replied, You rob the country, rob it with the worst of thefts. These are vague generalities, said Mr. Great-Heart. Give me the particulars.

The giant said, You are a kidnapper of women and children. You carry them into a strange country. This weakens my master's kingdom. Great-Heart replied, I am a servant of the God of heaven. My business is to persuade sinners to repent. I am commanded to turn men, women, and children, from darkness to light and from the power of Satan to God. If this is the basis of your quarrel, let us fight as soon as you like.

The giant came up. Mr. Great-Heart went to meet him with drawn sword. The giant had a club. They fell to it. The giant with his first blow struck Mr. Great-Heart, knocking him to one knee. The women and children cried out. Mr. Great-Heart recovered and with great enthusiasm gave the giant a wound in his arm. They fought for an hour. The breath came out of the giant's nostrils like steam from a boiling cauldron.

Then they sat down to rest but Mr. Great-Heart prayed. The women and children did nothing but sigh and cry.

After they rested, they both fell to it again. Mr. Great-Heart with a blow drove the giant to the ground. Stop, let me recover, he said. Mr. Great-Heart let him up. They went at it again and the giant almost broke Mr. Great-Heart's skull with his club.

Mr. Great-Heart runs at him in the full heat of his spirit and pierced him under the fifth rib. The giant began to faint and could no longer hold his club. Mr. Great-Heart gave a second blow and removed the head of the giant from his shoulders. The women and children rejoiced and Mr. Great-Heart praised God for their victory.

When this was done, they erected a pillar and put the giant's head on it. They wrote under it so that other might read,

> He that did wear this head was one
> That pilgrims did misuse;
> He stopped their way, he spared none,
> But did them all abuse;
> Until that I Great-Heart arose,
> The pilgrims guide to be;
> Until that I did him oppose
> That was their enemy.

THE SIXTH STAGE

N ow I saw that they went up the ascent that the pilgrims use to see the land ahead. This was where Christian first met Faithful, his brother. They sat, rested, ate, drank, and were happy for their deliverance from this dangerous enemy. Christiana asked the guide if he had been hurt in the battle. Mr. Great-Heart said, No, except for a little flesh. It is not detrimental, it is proof of my love for my master and you. It will be a means, by grace, to increase my reward.

CHR. Were you afraid, good sir, when you saw him coming with his club?

GREAT. It is my duty to mistrust my own ability in order to rely on Him who is stronger than all.

CHR. What did you think when the first blow knocked you down?

GREAT. I thought my Master himself was hit like that and he conquered (2 Cor. 4:10, 11; Rom. 8:37).

MATT. Think what you please, God has been wonderfully good to us. Both in bringing us out of this valley and delivering us out of the enemy's hand. For my part, I see no reason not to trust our God since he has given us this testimony of his love. Then they all got up and went on.

A little ahead stood an oak. Under it they found an old pilgrim sound asleep. They knew that he was a pilgrim by his clothes, staff, and belt.

The guide, Mr. Great-Heart, woke him. The old gentleman, as he opened his eyes, cried out, What's the matter? Who are you? What is your business?

GREAT. Do not be so hostile. We are friends. The old man gets up, keeps his guard, and wants to know who they are. My name is Great-Heart. I am the guide for these pilgrims going to the Celestial country.

HON. Mr. Honest said, I cry you mercy. I feared that you were some of those that robbed Little-Faith of his money. Now that I look at you, I see you are honest.

GREAT. What could you have done to have helped yourself if we had been robbers?

HON. I would have fought as long as I had breath. If I had done so, I am sure you could never have given me the worst of it. A Christian can never be overcome, unless he quits.

GREAT. Well said, you are the right kind. You have spoken the truth.

HON. I know that you know what a true pilgrim is. Others think that we are easily overcome.

GREAT. Now that we have happily met, what is your name and where are you from?

HON. I cannot tell you my name, but I came from the town of Stupidity, about four degrees beyond the city of Destruction.

GREAT. Are you that countryman? Then I have half a guess. Your name is Old Honesty, isn't it?

HON. The old gentleman blushed. Not honesty in the abstract, but Honest is my name. I wish my nature agreed with what I am called. How could you guess, since I came from such a place?

GREAT. I heard of you before. My Master knows all things that are done on the earth. I have often wondered that any would come from your town; it is worse than the city of Destruction.

HON. Yes, we are further from the sun and are colder and senseless. Even if you were a man in a mountain of ice, if the Sun of righteousness rises on you, your frozen heart will be thawed. It is this way with me.

GREAT. I believe it, father Honest, I believe it. I know the thing is true.

Then the old gentleman greeted the pilgrims with a holy kiss of love. He asked their names and how they had fared since starting their pilgrimage.

CHR. I suppose you have heard my name. Good Christian was my husband; these are his four children. Can you imagine what the old gentleman did when she told him who she was? He skipped, he smiled, and he blessed them with a thousand good wishes,

HON. I have heard much of your husband, his travels, and wars. Let this be your comfort, your husband's name rings all over these parts. His faith, his courage, his endurance, and his sincerity have made his name famous. He turned to the boys and asked their names. They told him. Then he said, Matthew, be like Matthew the publican, not in vice, but in virtue (Matt. 10:3). Samuel, be like Samuel the prophet, a man of faith and prayer (Ps. 99:6). Joseph, be like Joseph in Potiphar's house, pure, one that flees temptation (Gen. 39). James, be like James the just, and like James the brother of our Lord (Acts 1:13). Then they told him about Mercy, how she left her town and her relatives to come with Christiana and her sons. The old honest man said, Mercy is your name. By mercy you will be sustained and carried through the difficulties that will assault you, until you come to where you will see the face of the Fountain of mercy. All this time the guide, Mr. Great-Heart, was well pleased and smiled on his companions.

As they walked along, the guide asked the old gentleman if he knew Mr. Fearing from his town.

HON. Yes, very well, he was a man that had the root of the subject in him. Yet he was one of the most troublesome pilgrims I ever met.

GREAT. You knew him! You have accurately described his character.

HON. Knew him! I was a great companion of his! I was with him when he first began to think what would happen to us.

GREAT. I was his guide from my Master's house to the gates of the Celestial City.

HON. Then you knew him to be trouble.

GREAT. I did, but I could handle it. Men of my calling are often trusted with guiding his kind.

HON. Well then, tell us a little about him. How did he manage himself under your conduct?

GREAT. He was always afraid that he would fall short of where he wanted to go. Everything frightened him if it had the least appearance of opposition. I heard that he stayed near the Swamp of Despond for over a month, afraid to move. He saw several cross it. Many offered to lend him a hand but he would not move. Nor would he go back! The Celestial City—he said he would die if he could not reach it. Every difficulty dejected him. He stumbled over every straw that anyone put in his way. After he stayed at the Swamp of Despond for a great while, one sunny morning, I do not know how, he got across. When he was over, he could scarce believe it. He had, I think, a Swamp of Despond in his mind, a swamp that he carried everywhere.

He arrived at the gate that stands at the head of this way. There he stood a long time before he dared to knock. When the gate was opened, he would step back, give his place to others, and say that he was not worthy. The poor man would stand there shaking and shrinking. I dare say that it would have pitied one's heart to watch him. Nor would he go back again. Finally, he took the hammer that hangs on the gate and gave a small rap or two. One opened the gate but he again stepped back. He that opened it stepped out and said, Trembling one, what do you want? With that he fell to the ground.

The one who opened the gate said, Peace. I have set before you an open door. Come in, you are blessed. With that he got up, went in and was ashamed to show his face.

After he had been entertained for a while, you know how it is, he was told to go on his way. He was also told the way to take. He went on until he came to our house, but he acted at the Interpreter's door just like he did at the gate. He laid in the cold for a long time before he called. Still, he would not go back. The nights were long and cold. He had a note for my master to receive him, to grant him the comfort of his house, and to give him a strong and valiant conductor.

He was so chicken-hearted that he was afraid to call at the door. So he lay outside until he almost starved. His dejection was great, though he saw several others knocking to get in, he was afraid to try it. I looked out of the window and saw a man around the door. I went out and asked what he wanted. The poor man, water stood in his eyes. I perceived what he wanted, went in, and told the Master of the house. He sent me out to plead with him to come in. I dare say that it was hard work. Finally, he came in.

Let me say this for my Lord, he wonderfully loved him. There were only a few good bites on the table, but more was brought. Then he presented the note to my Lord, who said that his desires should be granted. When he had been there a good while, he seemed to take heart and was a little more comfortable. My Master, you must know, is very tender hearted, especially to those that are afraid. Well, when he had seen all the things of the place and was ready to continue his journey, my Lord gave him a bottle of spirits and some good things to eat. We started, I led the way, but he was a man of few words. All he would do was sigh.

When we came to where the three men were hanged, he said he doubted that would be his end. He seemed glad when he saw the cross and the sepulchre; he wanted to stay there longer. Then he seemed for a while to be a little cheerful. When he came to the hill Difficulty it did not trouble him, nor did he fear the lions. His troubles were not about things like this; his fear was about being accepted.

I got him in at the house Beautiful, I think before he was ready. I made him acquainted with the ladies of the place. He was ashamed to be in their company; he very much wanted to be alone. Yet he always loved good conversation and would often listen behind the screen. He loved and pondered ancient things. He later told me that he loved to be in the houses at the gate and at the Interpreter's. But he would never be so bold as to ask.

When we went from the house Beautiful, down to the Valley of Humiliation, he went as well as any man. He did not care, so long as he could finally be happy. Yes, there was sympathy between that Valley and him. He was never better on his pilgrimage than when he was in that Valley.

Here he would lie down, embrace the ground, and kiss the flowers (Lam. 3:27–29). He would be up at day break, walking back and forth in the valley.

When he reached the entrance of the Valley of the Shadow of Death, I thought I lost him. Not that he had any inclination to go back; he always abhorred that. But he was ready to die from fear. The ghosts will have me! The ghosts will have me! he cried. I could not beat it out of him. He made such a noise and outcry that if anyone heard him, it was enough to encourage them to attack us.

I noticed this, the valley was as quiet when we went through it as ever I knew it to be. I suppose our enemies were held in check by our Lord and commanded not to interfere until Mr. Fearing had passed through.

It would be too tedious to tell you everything. I will only mention a passage or two. When he came to Vanity Fair, I thought he would fight all the men in the fair. I feared we would both be knocked on the head. At the Enchanted Ground he was wide-awake. Yet when we reached the river without a bridge, he was a heavy case. Now, now, he said, I will be drowned forever. I will never see that face I have come so many miles to look at.

I took notice of what was very remarkable; the water of that river was lower than I had ever seen it. When he finally crossed, the water wasn't much higher than his shoe tops. Going up to the gate, I started to leave him. I wished him a good reception above. He said, I will, I will. Then we parted and I never saw him again.

HON. Then it seems he was finally well?

GREAT. Yes, yes, I never had doubt. He was a man of a choice spirit, except he was always depressed and that made his life burdensome to himself and troublesome to others (Ps. 88). He was, above many, aware of sin. He was so afraid of injuring others that he would often deny himself for fear he would offend (Rom. 14:21; 1 Cor. 8:13).

HON. Why would such a good man would spend all his days in the dark?

GREAT. There are two sorts of reasons. One is, the wise God will have it so, some must play and some must weep (Matt. 11:16). Mr. Fearing played the bass, his companions played the trombone. Their notes were more melancholy than any other music. Some say, the bass is music's bottom. For my part, I do not care for any profession that causes heaviness of mind. The first string the musician usually touches is the bass when he intends to tune the other instruments. God plays this string first when he tunes the soul to himself. Mr. Fearing's imperfection was that he could play no other music.

[I speak metaphorically to ripen the minds of young readers. And because, in the book of Revelation, the saved are compared to musicians that play trumpets, harps, and sing before the throne (Rev. 5:8; 14:2, 3).]

HON. He was a zealous man, as one may see from your description. Difficulties, lions, Vanity Fair, he did not fear. Only sin, death, and hell were a terror to him for he had doubts about his claim to that celestial country.

GREAT. You are right. Those were the things that troubled him. As you well observed, they arose from the weakness of his mind and not from the weakness of his spirit. I believe, as the proverb says, he could have bitten a firebrand if it stood in his way. Yet the things that oppressed him, no man could easily shake off.

CHR. This story about Mr. Fearing has been good for me. I thought nobody was like me, but I see a resemblance between this good man and me. We differed in only two things. His troubles were so great that he could not keep them to himself, mine I kept within. His were so hard that they stopped him from knocking at the houses provided for his entertainment. My trouble was that it made me knock all the louder.

MER. If I may say what is on my heart, something of him dwells in me. I was more afraid of the lake and the loss of a place in paradise, than the loss of other things. O, thought I, may I have the happiness to live there! It is enough, though I part with all the world to win it.

MATT. Fear was one thing that made me think I was far from having what accompanies salvation. If it was so with such a good man, why won't it go well with me?

JAMES. No fear, no grace. Although there is not always grace where there is a fear of hell. Yet, to be sure, there is no grace where there is no fear of God.

GREAT. Well said, James, you hit the mark. The fear of God is the beginning of wisdom. They that want the beginning have neither the middle nor the end. We will conclude our conversation about Mr. Fearing, after we send him this farewell.

> Well, Master Fearing, thou did fear
> Thy God, and was afraid
> Of doing any thing, while here,
> That would have thee betrayed.
> And did thou fear the lake and pit?
> Would others do so too!
> For, as for them that want thy wit,
> They do themselves undo.

They continued talking after Mr. Great-Heart finished the story of Mr. Fearing. Mr. Honest began to tell them of another, Mr. Self-will. He pretended to be a pilgrim, but I was persuaded that he never came through the gate at the beginning of the way.

GREAT. Did you talk with him about it?

HON. Yes, more than once or twice, but he was always self-willed. He did not care for man, argument, or example. What his mind prompted him to, he would do. But nothing else.

GREAT. What principles did he hold?

HON. A man might follow the vices as well as the virtues of the pilgrims. And if he did both, he would certainly be saved.

GREAT. How? If he had said, it is possible for the best to be guilty of the vices, as well as to partake of the pilgrims' virtues, he could not have been blamed. Indeed we are exempted from no vice absolutely, but on condition that we watch and strive. But this I perceive, is not the thing. If I correctly understand you, your meaning is that he was of the opinion that it was allowable to do so.

HON. Yes, that is what I mean. He believed and practiced it.

GREAT. What grounds did he have for saying this?

HON. He said that he had the Scripture.

GREAT. Mr. Honest, give us some particulars.

HON. I will. He said that David, God's beloved, practiced having other men's wives. Therefore he could do it. To have more than one woman was a thing Solomon practiced. Therefore he could do it. Sarah and the godly midwives of Egypt lied, as did Rahab. Therefore he could do it. The disciples went at their Master's order and took the owner's donkey. Therefore he could do it. Jacob got his father's inheritance through deception. Therefore he could do it.

GREAT. Are you sure this was his opinion?

HON. I heard him give Scripture for it and then argue it.

GREAT. This opinion is not worth any allowance!

HON. You must correctly understand me. He did not say anyone could do this, only those that had the virtues of these things.

GREAT. What a false conclusion! This says that if good men have sinned, he is entitled to sin. If the wind blows a child down, or if a child stumbles on a stone and falls into the mud, he can willingly lie down and wallow in it like a pig. Who would have thought that anyone could be so blinded by the power of lust? What is written is true. "They stumble being disobedient to the word, to which they also were appointed" (1 Peter 2:8).

His assumption that men may have the virtue of the godly, but be addicted to their vices, is a strong delusion. To eat the sin of God's people (Hos. 4:8), as a dog licks vomit, is not a sign that one is possessed with their virtues. I can't believe that anyone of this viewpoint has faith or love in him. I know you have strongly objected to this. What can he say?

HON. Why, he says, to do this seems abundantly more honest than to hold a contrary opinion.

GREAT. A wicked answer, to let go of lusts' bridle, while our opinions are against such things, is bad. Yet to sin and then plead for toleration is worse. One causes the beholder to accidentally stumble. The other leads them into the snare.

HON. There are many like this man but they do not have his mouth. This makes their going on a pilgrimage of little value.

GREAT. You have said the truth and it is to be lamented. He that fears the King of paradise will be ahead of them all.

CHR. There are strange opinions in the world. I know one who said that it was time enough to repent when we are dying.

GREAT. They are not really wise. The man who would not run twenty miles in his life, should not defer his journey to the last hour of that week.

HON. You are right. Yet the generality of those that count themselves pilgrims, do indeed do this. I am, as you see, an old man and have been a traveler on this road for many a day. I have taken notice of many things.

I have seen some start as if they would drive the world before them. Yet, in a few days, they died in the wilderness and never got sight of the promised land. I have seen some pilgrims that promised nothing, and one would have thought they could not last a day. Yet, they proved to be good pilgrims. I have seen some run rapidly forward and after a little time run back just as fast. I have seen some speak well of a pilgrim's life at first, then after a while they speak against it. I have heard some, when they first started for paradise, say positively, there is such a place. Yet when they were almost there, have come back and said there is no such place. I have heard some brag about what they would do if opposed. Yet, at even a false alarm, they flee faith and the pilgrim's way.

Now, as they were on their way, one came running to meet them.

He said, Gentlemen, and you of the weaker sort, if you love life, move quickly, robbers are coming.

GREAT. They are the three that attacked Little-Faith. We are ready for them. They went on their way and looked for them at every turn. Whether they heard of Mr. Great-Heart, or whether they had another game, they did not approach the pilgrims.

Christiana wanted to stop at an inn because they were weary. She said to Mr. Honest, There is an inn, a little ahead, where an honorable disciple, Gaius, lives (Rom. 16:23). They agreed to turn in there because the old gentleman gave a good report about it. When they came to the door they did not knock, for folks do not knock at inn doors. They called for the master of the house and asked if they might spend the night there.

GAIUS. Yes, if you are true pilgrims. My house is only for pilgrims. Christiana, Mercy, and the boys were happy because the innkeeper loved pilgrims. He showed them a room for Christiana, her children, and Mercy. Then another room for Mr. Great-Heart and the old gentleman.

GREAT. Good Gaius, what do you have for supper? These pilgrims have come far today and are weary.

GAIUS. It is late. We cannot conveniently go out to get food. But what we have you are welcome to, if that will make you content.

GREAT. We will be content with what you have. As many times as I have been here, you are never destitute of good food and drink.

He went down and spoke to the cook, Taste-that-which-is-good, to prepare supper for the pilgrims. This done, he said, Come, my good friends, you are welcome. I am glad that I have a house to entertain you. While supper is being prepared, let us entertain one another with good conversation.

GAIUS. Whose wife is this elderly lady? Whose daughter is this young girl?

GREAT. This woman is the wife of Christian, a former pilgrim. These are his four children. The girl is an acquaintance she persuaded to come on a pilgrimage. The boys all take after their father and want to walk in his steps. If they see any place where the old pilgrim has slept, or any print of his foot, it brings joy to their hearts. They want to lie or walk in the same place.

GAIUS. Is this Christian's wife? Are these Christian's children? I knew your husband's father, and also his father's father. They are of good stock. Their ancestors lived in Antioch (Acts 11:26). Christian's forefathers (I suppose you heard your husband talk about them) were worthy men. They have, above any I know, proven to be men of great virtue and courage for the Lord of the pilgrims, for his ways, and for those that love him. Your husband's relations have stood all trials for the sake of the truth. Stephen, one of the first of the family from where your husband sprang, was stoned (Acts 7:59, 60). James, another of that generation, was slain with the sword (Acts 12:2). To say nothing of Paul and Peter, who were men of your husband's family. Then there was Ignatius, he was thrown to the lions. Romanus, whose flesh was cut by pieces from his bones. Polycarp, he played the man in the fire. There was one hanged in a basket in the sun for the wasps to eat. Another was put into a sack and thrown into the sea. It would be impossible to count all from that family who have suffered injuries and death for the love of a pilgrim's life. I am pleased to see that your husband has left four such boys. I hope they will carry their father's name, walk in his steps, and come to their father's end.

GREAT. Indeed, sir, they seem to heartily choose their father's ways.

GAIUS. That is what I said. If Christian's family is likely to spread across the ground and be numerous on the face of the earth, let Christiana look for girls for her sons to marry. So the name of their father, and the house of his forefathers, will never be forgotten in this world.

HON. It would be a pity should his family become extinct.

GAIUS. Extinct it cannot be, diminished it may be. Christiana take my advice, this is the way to uphold it. Christiana, said this innkeeper, I am glad to see you and your friend Mercy together. Now, if I may give you some advice, take Mercy into your family. If she is willing, let her be given to Matthew, your oldest son. It is the way to preserve your future generations on earth. So this match was concluded, and in process of time they were married, but more about that later.

Gaius said, I will speak on behalf of all women to remove their reproach. For as death and the curse came into the world by a woman (Gen. 3), so also did life and health. God sent his Son, born of a woman (Gal. 4:4). Happy was the woman who might be the mother of the Savior of the world. I will say it again, when the Savior came women rejoiced in him before man or angel (Luke 1:42–46). I never read that any man gave Christ so much as one penny, but the women followed him and ministered to him from their substance (Luke 8:2, 3). It was a woman that washed his feet with tears (Luke 7:37–50). It was a woman that anointed his body for burial (John 11:2; 12:3). It was women that wept when he was going to the cross (Luke 23:27). It was women that followed him from the cross (Matt. 27:55, 56; Luke 23:55) and sat near his sepulchre when he was buried (Matt. 27:61). It was women that were first with him on his resurrection morning (Luke 24:1). It was women that first brought the news to his disciples that he was risen from the dead (Luke 24:22, 23). Thus, women are highly favored and are sharers with us in the grace of life.

The cook signified that supper was almost ready. He had someone put the tablecloth on the table and then the bread and salt.

Matthew said, The sight of this cloth is the forerunner of supper. I have a greater appetite for food than I ever had.

GAIUS. Let all the ministering doctrines in this life create a greater desire in us to sit at the supper of the great King in his kingdom. All preaching, books, and ordinances are just preparing the table when compared with the feast that our Lord will prepare when we come to his house.

Supper came up. First a heave-shoulder and a wave-breast were set on the table to show they must begin their meal with prayer and praise to God. The heave-shoulder David lifted his heart to God with. The wave-breast, where his heart lay, he used to lean on his harp when he played (Lev. 7:32–34; 10:14, 15; Psalm 25:1; Heb. 13:15). These two dishes were fresh and good. All ate heartily.

Next, they brought up a bottle of wine, red as blood (Deut. 32:14; Judges 9:13; John 15:5). Gaius said, Drink freely. This is the true juice of the vine. It makes the heart of God and man glad. So they drank and were merry.

Next was a dish of pure milk. Gaius said, Let the boys have that so they may grow (1 Pet. 2:1, 2).

Then they brought a dish of butter and honey. Gaius said, Eat freely, this is good to cheer and strengthen your judgments and understandings. This was our Lord's dish when he was a child. "Curds and honey He shall eat, that He may know to refuse the evil and choose the good" (Isa. 7:15).

Then they brought a dish of apples that tasted good. Matthew said, May we eat apples, since it was with these that the serpent beguiled our first mother?

Gaius said,

> Apples were they with which we were beguil'd,
> Yet sin, not apples, hath our souls defil'd:
> Apples forbid, if ate, corrupt the blood;
> To eat such, when commanded, does us good:
> Drink of his flagons then, thou church, his dove,
> And eat his apples, who art sick of love.

Matthew said, Because eating fruit made me sick, I decided not to eat it again.

GAIUS. Forbidden fruit will make you sick. But not what our Lord has allowed.

While they were talking, they were presented with a dish of nuts (Song 6:11). Someone at the table said, Nuts spoil tender teeth, especially children's teeth. When Gaius heard this, he said,

> Hard texts are nuts (I will not call them cheaters),
> Whose shells do keep the kernel from the eaters:
> Open the shells, and you shall have the meat;
> They here are brought for you to crack and eat.

They were happy and sat talking at the table for a long time. Then the old gentleman said, My good landlord, while we are cracking nuts, if you please, reveal this riddle:

> A man there was, though some did count him mad,
> The more he cast away, the more he had.

They paid strict attention to what Gaius would say. He sat a while before he replied:

> He who bestows his goods upon the poor,
> Shall have as much again, and ten times more.

Joseph said, I dare say, sir, I did not think you could have solved it.

Oh, Gaius said, I have been trained in this a long time; nothing teaches like experience. I have learned from my Lord to be kind, and by experience have gained kindness. There is one who scatters, yet increases more; there is one who withholds more than is right, but it leads to poverty. There is one who makes himself rich, yet has nothing; and one who makes himself poor, yet has great riches (Prov. 11:24; 13:7).

Samuel whispered to his mother, Mother, this is a good man's house. Let us stay awhile. Let my brother Matthew be married to Mercy here. Gaius the host overheard this and said, Agreed, my child.

They stayed more than a month. Mercy married Matthew.

Mercy, as was her custom, continued to make coats and clothing for the poor. This brought a good report about the pilgrims.

But to return to our story: After supper the lads wanted to go to bed, for they were weary from traveling. Gaius started to show them to their rooms. Mercy said, I will put them to bed, and she did. They slept well but the rest of the pilgrims sat up all night because Gaius was such great company that they could not leave. After much talk of their Lord, themselves, and their journey, old Mr. Honest began to nod. Great-Heart said, Sir, you are drowsy. Come, wake up, here is a riddle for you. Mr. Honest said, Let us hear it.

He that would kill, must first be overcome:
Who live abroad would, first must die at home.

Ha, said Mr. Honest, it is difficult, hard to expound, and harder to practice. Come, landlord, I will, if you please, leave my part to you. Expound it and I will listen to what you say.

No, said Gaius, it was put to you. It is expected that you answer it. The old gentleman said,

He first by grace must conquered be,
That sin would mortify;
Who that he lives would convince me,
Unto himself must die.

Correct, said Gaius, good doctrine and experience teach this. Until grace first displays itself, and overcomes the soul with its glory, it is totally unable to oppose sin. Beside, if sin is Satan's cords that tie the soul, how can it resist before it is loosened? Second, anyone that knows reason or grace, does not believe that such a man can be a living monument of grace if he is a slave to corruption.

This comes to mind, I will tell you a story worth hearing. There were two men on a pilgrimage. One started when he was young, the other when he was old. The young man had strong corruption to grapple with. The old man's were weak from the decay of nature. The young man walked in the steps of the old one and was equally in the light. Now, which one had their graces shining clearest, since both seemed to be alike?

HON. Doubtless, the young man, the one that makes progress against the greatest opposition best demonstrates that he is the strongest. Especially when it keeps pace with that which does not meet half as much opposition. I have observed that old men have blessed themselves with this mistake, they take the decay of nature for a gracious conquest over corruption. They fool themselves. Gracious old men are best able to give advice to the young because they have seen the emptiness of things. Yet, when an old and a young man start together, the young has the advantage of discovering a work of grace, even though the old man's corruption is naturally the weakest. They talked until day break.

When the family got up, Christiana told her son, James, to read a chapter from the Bible. He read the 53rd of Isaiah. When he finished, Mr. Honest asked why it said that the Savior would come "as a tender plant, and as a root out of dry ground. He has no form or comeliness."

GREAT. My answer to the first question is because the church of the Jews, from which Christ came, lost almost all the sap and spirit of their religion. Unbelievers asked the second question. They lacked eyes to see our Prince's heart and so judged him by his appearance. Like those who find precious stones covered with a homely crust, they throw them away because they do not know what they have found.

Gaius said, Since Mr. Great-Heart is good with his weapons, after we have refreshed ourselves, we will walk to the fields to see if we can do any good. About a mile from here is Slay-good, a giant. He does much to annoy the King's highway. I know where he lives. He is master of a number of thieves. It would be well if we could rid these parts of him. They agreed to go. Mr. Great-Heart took his sword, helmet, and shield. The rest of the company took spears and staffs.

When they came to the place of the giant, they found his servants had captured Feeble-mind. The giant was in the process of robbing him; then he would pick his bones, for the giant was a cannibal.

When the giant saw Mr. Great-Heart and his friends armed, he demanded to know what they wanted.

GREAT. We want you. We have come to revenge the many pilgrims you have slain when you dragged them from the King's highway. Come out of your cave. The giant armed himself and came out. They fought for more than an hour. Then they stopped to catch their breath.

SLAY. Why are you here on my ground?

GREAT. I told you, to revenge the blood of pilgrims. They went at it again. The giant forced Mr. Great-Heart back. Then he counter attacked and in the greatness of his mind he let fly and hit the giant's head and side. Slay-good's weapon fell from his hand. He struck him again, killed him, and cut off his head. Mr. Great-Heart took the head back to the inn. He also took Feeble-mind, the pilgrim, and brought him to their lodgings. When they arrived, they showed the giant's head to the family, and placed it as they had done before. This was a warning to those that would attempt to harm the pilgrims.

They asked Mr. Feeble-Mind how he was captured.

FEEBLE. I am a sick man. Death usually knocks at my door once a day. I knew I would never be well at home, so I became a pilgrim. I traveled here from the town of Uncertain, where I was born. There is no strength at all in my body or mind. Though I can only crawl, I would spend my life in the pilgrim's way. When I arrived at the gate at the start of the way, the Lord of that place freely entertained me. He did not object to my weakness, or my feeble mind. He gave me things that were necessary for my journey and offered hope to the end.

When I came to the house of the Interpreter, I received much kindness. Because the hill of Difficulty was judged too hard for me to climb, I was carried up by one of his servants. Indeed, I have found much help from pilgrims, although none were willing to go so slowly as I am forced to. Still, as they passed, they told me to be of good cheer. They said that it was the Lord's will for comfort to be given the feeble-minded (1 Thess. 5:14). Then they went on at their own pace.

When I reached Assault-lane, this giant met me and ordered me to prepare for a fight. Feeble as I was, I had more need of refreshments than battle. So he came up and took me. I did not think he would kill me. When he got me in his cave, since I did not go willingly, I believed I would come out alive. I have heard that any pilgrim captured by violent hands, if he keeps heart toward his Master will, by the laws of providence, not die by the hand of the enemy. I expected to be robbed, and robbed I was. But I have, as you see, escaped with my life, for which I thank my King.

I look for more violence. Yet I have resolved to run when I can, to walk when I cannot run, and to crawl when I cannot walk. I thank him that loved me. I am determined. My way is before me. My mind is beyond the river that has no bridge even though, as you see, I have a feeble mind.

HON. Were you, sometime ago, acquainted with Mr. Fearing, a pilgrim?

FEEBLE. Acquainted with him? Yes, he came from the town of Stupidity that lies four degrees north of the city of Destruction. We were well acquainted. He was my uncle, my father's brother. He and I had similar personalities. He was a little shorter than me, but our appearance was similar.

HON. I thought you knew him and I believed that you were related. You have his pale color, similar eyes, and your speech is similar.

FEEBLE. Those who knew us said the same thing. Besides, what I have seen in him, I have for the most part found in myself.

GAIUS. Come, sir, be of good cheer. You are most welcome. What you have a mind for, ask freely. What you would have my servants do for you, they will do with a willing mind.

FEEBLE. This is an unexpected favor, like the sun shining through a dark cloud. Did giant Slay-good intend this favor when he stopped me? Did he intend after he had rifled my pockets that I should go to Gaius my host? Yet it is so.

As Mr. Feeble-mind and Gaius were talking, someone came running to the door. He said that about a mile and a half back a pilgrim, Mr. Not-right, was struck dead by a thunderbolt.

FEEBLE. Was he slain? He overtook me some days ago and wanted my company. He was with me when Slay-good, the giant, captured me. But he was nimble of heels and escaped. Yet it seems he escaped to die, and I was taken to live.

> What one would think doth seek to slay outright,
> Ofttimes delivers from the saddest plight.
> That very Providence whose face is death,
> Doth ofttimes to the lowly life bequeath.
> I taken was, he did escape and flee;
> Hands cross'd gave death to him and life to me.

About this time Matthew and Mercy were married. Gaius gave his daughter Phebe to James, Matthew's brother, for a wife. They stayed about ten days at Gaius' house, spending their time as pilgrims.

When they were ready to depart, Gaius prepared a feast. They ate, drank, and were merry. When the time came to leave, Mr. Great-Heart called for the bill. Gaius told him that at his house, it was not the custom for pilgrims to pay for their entertainment. He boarded them by the year but looked for his pay from the Good Samaritan. This man had promised, upon his return that whatever charges they had would faithfully be repaid (Luke 10:34, 35).

GREAT. Beloved, do faithfully whatever you do for the brethren and for strangers who have borne witness of your love before the church. If you send them forward on their journey in a manner worthy of God, you will do well (3 John 5, 6). Gaius said farewell to them all, his children, and particularly Mr. Feeble-mind. He also gave him something to drink on the way.

Mr. Feeble-mind, when they were going out of the door, lingered. Mr. Great-Heart saw this and said, Come, Mr. Feeble-mind, come along with us. I will be your conductor and you will fare like the rest.

FEEBLE. I want a suitable companion. You are all healthy and strong, but I am weak. I choose to come behind, less my many infirmities be a burden to you and me. I am a man with a weak and feeble mind, offended and made weak at what others can do. I do not like laughing. I do not like bright attire. I do not like unprofitable questions. I am so weak a man as to be offended by the liberty of others. I do not yet know all the truth. I am an ignorant Christian man. Sometimes, if I hear some rejoice in the Lord, it troubles me because I cannot rejoice. I do not know what to do. It is with me as it is with the weak among the strong, or with the sick among the healthy, or a lamp despised. "A lamp is despised in the thought of one who is at ease; it is made ready for those whose feet slip" (Job 12:5).

GREAT. Brother, I have it in my commission to comfort the feeble-minded and to support the weak. You must come with us. We will wait for you. We will lend you our help. We will deny ourselves of some things, both opinionative and practical, for your sake. We will not enter into doubtful disputes in front of you. We will be all things to you, rather than leave you behind (1 Thess. 5:14; Rom. 14; 1 Cor. 8:9–13; 9:22).

Now, while they were talking at Gaius' door, Mr. Ready-to-halt came with his crutches. He also was going on a pilgrimage.

FEEBLE. Man, how did you come here? I was just complaining that I did not have a suitable companion. You are what I want. Welcome, welcome, good Mr. Ready-to-halt, I hope you and I may be of some help.

READY. I will be pleased with your company, good Mr. Feeble-mind. Since we have happily met, I will loan you one of my crutches.

FEEBLE. No, though I thank you for your good will. I am not inclined to limp before I am lame. When the occasion arises, however, it may help me against a dog.

READY. If either me or my crutches can do you pleasure, we are both at your command, good Mr. Feeble-mind.

Thus, they went on. Mr. Great-Heart and Mr. Honest ahead, Christiana and her children next, then Mr. Feeble-mind and Mr. Ready-to-halt with his crutches.

HON. Now that we are on the road, tell us something profitable that occurred on earlier pilgrimages.

GREAT. Indeed. I suppose you have heard how Christian of old met Apollyon in the Valley of Humiliation? And the hard work he had going through the Valley of the Shadow of Death. You must have heard how four villains as deceitful as a man could ever meet on the road, Madam Wanton, Adam the First, Discontent, and Shame, put it to Faithful.

HON. Yes, I have heard this. Good Faithful was hardest put by Shame; he was an unwearied one.

GREAT. Yes, as the pilgrim well said, he of all men had the wrong name.

HON. Sir, where was it that Christian and Faithful met Talkative? He was also notable.

GREAT. He was a confident fool, but many follow his ways.

HON. He almost fooled Faithful.

GREAT. Yes, but Christian put him into a way to quickly find out.

They continued on until they came to the place where Evangelist met Christian and Faithful. Their guide said, This is where Christian and Faithful met Evangelist. Here Evangelist prophesied the trouble they would meet at Vanity Fair.

HON. Is that so? I dare say it was a hard chapter he read them.

GREAT. It was, but he also gave them encouragement. What do we say about them? They were lion-like men. They set their faces like a flint. Do you remember how undaunted they were before the judge?

HON. Faithful suffered bravely.

GREAT. He did, as brave as could be. Hopeful, and others, were converted by his death.

HON. Continue, for you are well acquainted with the story.

GREAT. Above all that Christian met, after he passed through Vanity Fair, By-ends was the worst.

HON. By-ends? Who was he?

GREAT. An insidious man, a downright hypocrite, one that would be religious. Yet he was so cunning that he would never lose or suffer for it. He had his style of religion for every new occasion; his wife was as good at it as he. He would turn from opinion to opinion, yes, and argue with you about it. So far as I could learn, he came to a bad end with his by-ends. Nor did I ever hear that his children were valued by any that truly feared God.

They were now within sight of the town of Vanity, home of Vanity Fair. When they realized they were so near the town, they discussed how they could best pass through. Some said one thing and some another. Finally, Mr. Great-Heart said, I have, as you know, often guided pilgrims through this town. I am acquainted with Mr. Mnason of Cyprus (Acts 21:16), an early disciple with whom we may lodge. If you wish, we will turn in there.

Agreed, said old Honest. Agreed, said Christiana. Agreed, said Mr. Feeble-mind. They all agreed. It was evening when they reached the outskirts of the town. Mr. Great-Heart knew the way to the early disciple's house. They arrived and he called at the door. The old man immediately recognized his voice, opened the door and they all came in. Mnason, their host, asked, How far have you come today? They answered, from the house of Gaius our friend. I tell you, said he, you have gone a good stitch. You must be weary. Please sit down.

GREAT. Come, what cheer, good sirs? I dare say you are welcome with my friend.

MNAS. I welcome you. Whatever you want, just ask. We will do all we can to get it for you.

HON. Our great need is shelter and good company. I hope we may have both.

MNAS. Shelter, you see what it is. Good company, that will be decided.

GREAT. Will you show the pilgrims to their lodging?

MNAS. I will. So he took them to their respective rooms. He also showed them a nice dining room where they might fellowship and eat until it was time for bed.

When they were seated, Mr. Honest asked the landlord if there were any good people in the town.

MNAS. We have a few, indeed they are few when compared with other towns.

HON. How can we meet some of them? The sight of good men on a pilgrimage is like the moon and stars to those that sail the seas.

MNAS. Mr. Mnason stamped his foot and his daughter Grace came in. He said, Grace, go and tell my friends, Mr. Contrite, Mr. Holy-man, Mr. Love-saints, Mr. Dare-not-lie, and Mr. Penitent, that I have a friend or two at my house who would like to see them this evening. Grace called on them and they came. After introductions were made, they sat down together at the table.

Mr. Mnason said, My neighbors, I have, as you see, a company of strangers that have come to my house. They are pilgrims from afar, going to Mount Zion. But who do you think this is? He pointed his finger at Christiana. This is Christiana, the wife of Christian, the famous pilgrim, who with Faithful his brother was shamefully handled in our town. They were amazed and said, We never expected to see Christiana when Grace called us. This is a delightful surprise. They asked of her welfare and if the young men were her sons. She replied that they were. They said to the boys, May the King whom you love and serve make you as your father and bring you where he is in peace.

HON. Then Mr. Honest (when they all sat down) asked Mr. Contrite and the rest about the present condition of their town.

CONT. You may be sure that we are full of hurry at fair time. It is hard keeping our hearts and spirits in good order when we are in a burdened condition. He that lives in a place like this and has to do with such as we have, has need of an item to caution him to pay attention every moment of the day.

HON. Are your neighbors more peaceful now?

CONT. They are more moderate. You know how Christian and Faithful were abused in our town. Lately, I would say, they have been far more moderate. I think the blood of Faithful lies as a load on them. Since they burned him, they have been ashamed to burn any more. In those days we were afraid to walk the street but now we can show our heads. Then the name of a believer was odious. Now, especially in certain parts of town (for you know our town is large), religion is honorable.

Mr. Contrite asked, How is your pilgrimage going?

HON. It happens to us as to all wayfaring men. Sometimes our way is clean, sometimes foul, sometimes up hill, sometimes down hill. We are seldom certain. The wind is not always at our back, nor is everyone we meet a friend. We had some notable fights. For the most part, we find the old saying true, A good man must suffer trouble.

CONT. You talk of fights, what fights have you had?

HON. Ask Mr. Great-Heart, our guide, he can give the best account.

GREAT. We were attacked three or four times. First, two ruffians harassed Christiana and her children; they feared for their lives. Then Giant Bloody-man, Giant Maul, and Giant Slay-good, attacked us. We actually attacked the Giant Slay-good. After we spent some time at Gaius's house, he was our host, we were asked to take our weapons and see if we could find any of the pilgrims' enemies. We heard that there was a notable one around. Gaius knew where he lived, so we looked and looked until we finally found the mouth of his cave. This pleased us and lifted our spirits. We approached the den. He had dragged this poor man, Mr. Feeble-mind, into his net. He was about to kill him. When he saw us, he thought he had another prey. He left this poor man in his hole and came out.

The fighting was desperate. But, in conclusion, he was brought to the ground, his head cut off and set by the wayside for a terror to those who practice such ungodliness. I tell you the truth, here is the man himself to affirm it, he was as a lamb taken out of the mouth of the lion.

FEEBLE. I found this true, to both my cost and comfort. To my cost, when he threatened to pick my bones. To my comfort, when I saw Mr. Great-Heart and his friends fight for my freedom.

HOLY. There are two things necessary for a pilgrimage: courage and an unspotted life. If they do not have courage, they can never hold to their way. If their lives are loose, they will make the very name of a pilgrim reek.

LOVE. I hope this caution is not necessary with you. There are many that go on the road who declare themselves strangers to a pilgrimage, rather than strangers and pilgrims on earth.

DARE. It is true. They have neither the pilgrim's clothing or the pilgrim's courage. They do no walk uprightly but go amiss with their feet, one shoe goes in, the other shoe goes out. Their stockings are loose, here a rag, there a tear, to the detraction of their Lord.

PEN. They should be concerned about these things. Pilgrims are not likely to have that grace put on them and their progress until the way is cleared of these spots and blemishes. They sat talking until supper was on the table. They ate, refreshed their weary bodies, and went to rest.

They stayed at the house of Mr. Mnason a great while. During this time he gave his daughter Grace to Samuel, Christian's son, for a wife, and his daughter Martha to Joseph.

The time, as I said, that they stayed there was long. When the pilgrims became acquainted with many of the town's good people, they gave them what service they could. Mercy worked for the poor. Their bellies and their backs blessed her; she was an ornament to her profession. Grace, Phebe, and Martha, were all good-natured and did much good. They were also fruitful so that Christian's name, as was said before, was like to live on in the world.

While they were here, a monster came out of the woods and killed many of the town's people. It carried away their children and taught them how to nurse its whelps. No man in the town dared so much as to face this monster. All fled when they heard him coming.

The monster was not like any beast on earth. Its body was like a dragon, it had seven heads, and ten horns. It made great havoc of children, and yet a woman governed it (Rev. 17:3). This monster propounded conditions to men. Men who loved their lives more than their souls accepted the conditions.

Mr. Great-Heart, together with those who came to visit the pilgrims at Mr. Mnason's house, entered into an agreement to battle this beast. They planned to deliver the people of the town from the paws and mouth of this devouring serpent.

Mr. Great-Heart, Mr. Contrite, Mr. Holy-man, Mr. Dare-not-lie, and Mr. Penitent, with their weapons, went out to meet him. The monster at first was furious. He looked on these enemies with great disdain. They, being sturdy men at arms, pressed the attack and made him retreat. Then they returned to Mr. Mnason's house.

The monster, you must know, had certain times to attack the town's children. At these times our valiant worthies continually assaulted him to the point that he was wounded and made lame. He now created less havoc among the children. Some believed that this beast would die from his wounds.

This made Mr. Great-Heart and his fellows famous in the town. Many people still wanted their taste of evil things but had a reverent admiration and respect for these men. Because of this, the pilgrims were not harmed here. Yes, there was some of the baser sort that could see no more than a mole, nor understand more than a beast. They had no reverence for these men and ignored their valor and adventures.

THE SEVENTH STAGE

Well, the time passed and the pilgrims had to be on their way. They prepared for their journey, sent and conferred with friends, and committed each other to the protection of their Prince. Their friends brought them things for the weak and the strong, for the women and the men, and necessities for the journey (Acts 28:10). Their friends honored them in many ways and accompanied them for a short distance. After they again committed each other to the protection of their King, they parted.

The pilgrims went on with Mr. Great-Heart leading. The women and children, being weak, walked slowly behind. Mr. Ready-to-halt and Mr. Feeble-mind, had great sympathy with the women's condition.

After leaving town and friends, they came to where Faithful was killed. They stayed and thanked him that had enabled Faithful to bear his cross so well. They were fully aware of the benefits of Christian's manly suffering.

They walked on, talking about Christian and Faithful, and how Hopeful joined Christian after Faithful was killed.

They came to the hill Lucre, where the silver mine took Demas from his pilgrimage and By-ends fell and perished. When they came to the old monument, the pillar of salt, that stood by the hill Lucre, within view of Sodom and its stinking lake, they marveled. How could men of such knowledge and maturity be so blind as to turn aside here. They realized that nature is not affected by the harm that others have met, especially if that thing on which they look has an attracting virtue to the foolish eye.

I saw that they came to the river on this side of the Delectable Mountains. The river's banks have fine trees. Their leaves, if eaten, can cure digestive problems. The meadows are green year round. Here they can lie down in safety (Ps. 23:2).

By this riverside, in the meadows, there were sheepfolds. A house built for feeding and raising those lambs, the babies of women on a pilgrimage. Here was a trusted one with compassion. "He will feed His flock like a shepherd; He will gather the lambs with His arm, and carry them in His bosom, and gently lead those who are with young" (Heb. 5:2; Isa. 40:11).

Christiana advised her four daughters to commit their little ones to this man. At these waters they would be housed, sheltered, helped, nourished, and none would lack in the future. This man, if any of them went astray or were lost, will bring them back. He will bind up what was broken, and will strengthen those that are sick (Jer. 23:4; Ezek. 34:11–16). Here they will never want for food, drink, and clothing. Here they are safe from thieves and robbers, for this man will die before one of those committed to his trust will be lost. Here they will have good nourishment, counsel, and will be taught to walk in right paths. And that is a favor of no small account.

Here, as you see, are delicate waters, pleasant meadows, beautiful flowers, and a variety of trees that produce wholesome fruit. Not the type of fruit that Matthew ate from Beelzebub's garden. This fruit produces health; it continues and increases where it is. So they were content to commit their little ones to him. This was a great encouragement for this would be charged to the King. It was as a hospital for children and orphans.

They went on and arrived at By-path Meadow. Here they saw the stile that Christian and his friend Hopeful walked over, only to be captured by Giant Despair and put into Doubting Castle. They sat down and discussed if it would be best to fight the giant, demolish his castle, and free any pilgrims in it? They were strong and had Mr. Great-Heart for their leader. One said one thing and another disagreed. One questioned if it was lawful to walk on unconsecrated ground. Another said they might, provided their objective was good. Mr. Great-Heart said, The last assertion is not universally true. I have a command to resist sin, overcome evil, and fight the good fight of faith. I ask you, with whom should I fight this good fight, if not with Giant Despair? Thus, I will attempt to take his life and demolish Doubting Castle. Then he asked, Who will go with me? Old Honest said, I will. We will too, said Christiana's young and strong four sons, Matthew, Samuel, Joseph, and James (1 John 2:13, 14). They left the women in the road with Mr. Feeble-mind and Mr. Ready-to-halt with his crutches to be their guards. The Giant Despair lived so close, a little child might lead them (Is. 11:6).

Mr. Great-Heart, old Honest, and the four young men, went to Doubting Castle to look for Giant Despair. When they arrived at the castle gate, they knocked loudly. The old Giant came to the gate with Diffidence his wife. He asked, Who and what knocks so loudly as to trouble the Giant Despair? Mr. Great-Heart replied, It is I, Great-Heart, one of the King of the Celestial country's conductors of pilgrims. I demand that you open your gates. Prepare to fight, for I have come to take your head and demolish Doubting Castle.

Giant Despair, because he was a giant, thought no man could defeat him. I have conquered angels, should I be afraid of Great-Heart? So he put a cap of steel on his head, a breastplate of fire around him, iron shoes on his feet, and a great club in his hand. The six men attacked. They surrounded him. When Diffidence, the giantess, came to help, old Mr. Honest cut her down with one blow. They fought for their lives and finally Giant Despair was knocked to the ground. He did not want to die. He struggled hard. It seemed he had as many lives as a cat. But Great-Heart did not leave him until he had severed his head from his shoulders.

It took seven days to demolishing Doubting Castle. In it they found Mr. Despondency and his daughter, Much-afraid almost starved to death. They were saved alive. It would have made you wonder to see the bodies that lay here and there in the castle yard, and how the dungeon was full of dead men's bones.

After Mr. Great-Heart and his companions performed this exploit, they took Mr. Despondency and his daughter Much-afraid into their protection. They were honest people, though they were prisoners in Doubting Castle of that tyrant Giant Despair. They also took the head of the giant (his body they buried under a pile of stones) down to their companions. They showed them what they had done. When Feeble-mind and Ready-to-halt saw it was Giant Despair's head, they were joyful. Christiana could play the violin and Mercy could play the lute, so they played a dance. Ready-to-halt took Despondency's daughter, Much-afraid, by the hand, and they danced in the road. True, he could not dance without a crutch in his hand, but I promise you he footed it well. The girl was to be commended, for she answered the music handsomely.

As for Mr. Despondency, the music didn't do much for him. He would rather eat than dance because he was almost starved. Christiana gave him some of her bottle of spirits for immediate relief and prepared something for him to eat. In a little while the old gentleman began to be finely revived.

I saw in my dream, when these things were finished, that Mr. Great-Heart took Giant Despair's head and placed it on a pole at the side of the highway. It was beside the pillar Christian erected to caution the pilgrims.

Then he wrote on a marble stone these verses:

This is the head of him whose name only
In former times did pilgrims terrify.
His castle's down, and Diffidence his wife
Brave Mr. Great-Heart has bereft of life.
Despondency, his daughter Much-afraid,
Great-Heart for them also the man has play'd.
Who hereof doubts, if he'll but cast his eye
Up hither, may his scruples satisfy.
This head also, when doubting cripples dance,
Does show from fears they have deliverance.

After these men had bravely shown themselves against Doubting Castle, and had slain Giant Despair, they went forward until they reached the Delectable Mountains. It was here that Christian and Hopeful refreshed themselves. The men were well acquainted with the shepherds and were welcomed by them, just as they had welcomed Christian, to the Delectable Mountains.

Now the shepherds seeing so large a group following Mr. Great-Heart (for they were well acquainted with him) asked, Good sir, where did you find all these people?

Mr. Great-Heart replied,

First, here is Christiana and her train,
Her sons, and her sons' wives, who, like the wain,
Keep by the pole, and do by compass steer
From sin to grace, else they had not been here.
Next here's old Honest come on pilgrimage,
Ready-to-halt too, who I dare engage
True-hearted is, and so is Feeble-mind,
Who willing was not to be left behind.
Despondency, good man, is coming after,
And so also is Much-afraid, his daughter.
May we have entertainment here, or must
We further go? Let's knew whereon to trust.

The shepherds said, This is a comfortable company. You are welcome for we have both the feeble and the strong. Our Prince watches what is done to the least of these. Infirmity must not stop our entertaining them (Matt. 25:40). They invited them to the palace door where they said, Come in, Mr. Feeble-Mind, come in Mr. Ready-to-halt, come in, Mr. Despondency, and Mrs. Much-afraid his daughter. Mr. Great-Heart asked the shepherds to call them by name, for they are the most likely to fall back. Then Mr. Great-Heart said, This day I see grace shine in the faces of you that are my Lord's shepherds. You have not pushed the sick aside but have strewn their way into the palace with flowers (Ezek. 34:21).

The feeble and the weak went in, followed by Mr. Great-Heart and the rest. After they sat down, the shepherds said to the weaker ones, What would you like to have? For all things must be managed here to support the weak and to warn the unruly. They made a feast of pleasant things to the palate, easy to digest, and nourishing. After they ate, each one went to his room to rest.

When morning broke, the mountains were high and the day was clear. It was the shepherds' custom to show the pilgrims some valuable things. After they refreshed themselves and were ready, the shepherds took them to the fields and showed them what they had shown Christian.

They took them to some new places. Mount Marvel where in the distance they saw a man speaking to the hills. They asked the shepherds what this meant. They said this man was the son of Mr. Great-grace. You read about him in the first part of the Pilgrim's Progress. He was sent there to teach pilgrims how to remove and throw mountains into the sea (Mark 11:23, 24). Mr. Great-Heart said, I know him. He is a man above many.

Then they visited Mount Innocence where they saw a man clothed in white. Two men, Prejudice and Ill-will, were constantly throwing dirt on him. Amazingly, the dirt would fall off and his garment was clean. The pilgrims asked, What does this mean? The shepherds answered, This is Godlyman. His clothing shows the innocence of his life. Those that throw dirt at him, hate his doing good. But, as you see the dirt does not stick on his clothes. So it is with him who innocently lives in the world. Whoever tries to make such men dirty, labors in vain. God will cause their innocence to break forth as light, and their righteousness as the noonday.

They took them to Mount Charity where a man had a roll of cloth. He cut coats and garments from the cloth for the poor that stood around him. Yet his roll of cloth was never reduced in size. They asked, How can this be? This, said the shepherds, is to show that he who has a heart to give his labor to the poor will never want. He that waters will be watered. The cake that the widow gave to the prophet did not reduce the amount of flower in her barrel.

They took them to the place where they saw Fool and Want-wit washing an Ethiopian, in an attempt to make him white. The more they washed, the blacker he was. They asked the shepherds what this meant. They were told, Every method used to give a vile one a good name will only make him more abominable. It was this way with the Pharisees; it will be the same with all hypocrites.

Mercy, the wife of Matthew, said to Christiana, Mother, I would like to see the hole in the hill, commonly called the By-way to hell. Her mother spoke to the shepherds and they went to the door on the side of the hill. They opened it and invited Mercy to listen. She heard one saying, Cursed be my father for holding my feet back from the way of peace and life. Another said, If only I had been torn in pieces to save my soul! Another said, If I were to live again, I would deny myself, rather than come to this place! Then it was as if the earth groaned and quaked under the feet of this young woman. She was afraid, turned pale, and came away trembling. She said, Blessed are they that are delivered from this place!

When the shepherds had shown them all these things, they went back to the palace and entertained them. Mercy, being a young married woman, wanted something that she saw, but was embarrassed to ask. Her mother-in-law asked what ailed her, for she did not look well. Mercy said, There is a mirror hanging in the dining room. I cannot get my mind off it. If I can not have it, I think I will miscarry. Her mother said, I will mention your want to the shepherds; they will not deny you. But she said, I am ashamed that these men might learn what I long for. No, my daughter, said she, it is no shame to long for such a thing as that. Mercy replied, Then mother, if you please, ask the shepherds if they are willing to sell it.

The mirror was one in a thousand. It would reflect a man's features. But turn it but another way and it showed the face of the Prince of pilgrims himself. I have talked with them that know. They have seen the crown of thorns on his head looking in that glass. They have also seen the holes in his hands, his feet, and his side. Yes, this mirror is so excellent that it will show him to anyone who has a mind to see him, whether living or dead; whether in earth, or in heaven; whether in a state of humiliation, or in his exaltation; whether coming to suffer, or coming to reign (James 1:23; 1 Cor. 13:12; 2 Cor. 3:18).

Christiana went to the shepherds (the shepherds' names were Knowledge, Experience, Watchful, and Sincere), and said, There is one of my daughters, a pregnant woman, that longs for something she has seen in this house. She thinks she will miscarry if you deny her.

EXPERIENCE. Call her, call her, she shall surely have what we can give her. They called her and asked, Mercy, what is it that you want? She blushed and said, The great mirror that hangs in the dining room. Sincere ran, brought it, and with joyful consent it was given her. Then she bowed her head, gave thanks, and said, By this I know that I have obtained favor in your eyes.

They gave the other young women the things they wanted. They gave their husbands commendations for joining Mr. Great-Heart in killing Giant Despair and demolishing Doubting Castle.

Around Christiana's neck, and the necks of her four daughters, the shepherds put necklaces. They put earrings in their ears, and jewels on their foreheads.

When they decide to leave, they let them go in peace. The shepherds did not give the customary cautions that were given Christian and his companion. The reason was they had Great-Heart for their guide. He was well acquainted with things and could caution them when danger was approaching. Many of the cautions that Christian and his companion received from the shepherds were lost by the time they needed to put them in practice. This was the advantage this company had over the others.

They went on their way singing,

> Behold how fitly are the stages set
> For their relief that pilgrims are become,
> And how they us receive without one let,
> That make the other life our mark and home!
> What novelties they have to us they give,
> That we, though pilgrims, joyful lives may live;
> They do upon us, too, such things bestow,
> That show we pilgrims are, wherever we go.

THE EIGHTH STAGE

After leaving the shepherds, they came to where Christian met Turn-away from the town of Apostasy. Mr. Great-Heart, their guide, reminded them of this. All I have to say concerning this man is that he would not listen to any counsel. Once he was determined, nothing could stop him. When he came to the cross and sepulchre, he met one that asked him to look. He ground his teeth, stamped his foot, and said he was determined to return to his town. He met Evangelist before he came to the gate. Evangelist offered to lay hands on him and turn him back to the way. Turn-away resisted, went over the wall, and fled.

They went to where Little-Faith had been robbed. A man stood there with his sword drawn and his face covered with blood. Mr. Great-Heart said, Who are you? The man answered, My name is Valiant-for-truth. I am a pilgrim, going to the Celestial City. Three men attacked me and offered three choices: 1. To become one of them. 2. Go back where I came from. 3. Or die on the spot (Prov. 1:11–14). I answered,

I have been a true man for a long time. Therefore I could not be expected to join thieves. They demanded an answer to the second question. I told them I had no trouble where I came from. It was not suitable or profitable for me. I left it for this way. Then they asked me what my answer was to their third question. I told them my life was far too precious to lightly give it away. Besides, you have no right to force me to choose. Meddle at your peril. Then these three, Wild-head, Inconsiderate, and Pragmatic fought me, and I fought them. We fell to it, one against three, for more than three hours. They have left me, as you see, with some of the marks of their valor. They also carried away some of mine. They just left. I suppose they might, as the saying goes, have heard your horses and fled.

GREAT. Those were terrible odds, three against one.

VALIANT. It's true, but odds are nothing when truth is on your side. "Though an army may encamp against me, my heart shall not fear; though war may rise against me, in this I will be confident" (Ps. 27:3). Besides, he said, I have read in some records that one man has fought an army. How many did Samson slay with the jawbone of a donkey?

GREAT. Why didn't you cry out? Someone might have come to help you.

VALIANT. I cried to my King, who I knew could hear me and give invisible help. That was sufficient.

GREAT. You have behaved well. Let me see your sword. So he showed it to him.

After he had taken it in his hand and looked at it, he said, it is a great Jerusalem blade.

VALIANT. It is. Let a man have one of these blades, a skilled hand to wield it, and he may venture on an angel. There is no need to fear, if he can just apply it. It is sharper than any two-edged sword, piercing even to the division of soul and spirit, and of joints and marrow (Heb. 4:12).

GREAT. You fought a great while, why were you not weary?

VALIANT. I fought until my sword clung to my hand. Then we were joined together as if the sword grew out of my arm. When the blood ran through my fingers, I fought with most courage.

GREAT. You have done well. You have resisted unto blood, striving against sin. You will stay with us, come in and go out with us, for we are your companions. They took him, washed his wounds, gave him whatever food they had, and they went away together.

Mr. Great-Heart was delighted (for he greatly loved one who was a warrior). Because many in the company were feeble and weak, he questioned him about many things. First, what country was he from.

VALIANT. I was born in Dark-land. My father and mother still live there.

GREAT. Dark-land! Is that on the same coast as the City of Destruction?

VALIANT. Yes, it is. What made me go on a pilgrimage was when Mr. Tell-true came into our parts. He told how Christian left the City of Destruction and his wife and children to become a pilgrim. It was confidently reported that he had killed a serpent that resisted him in his journey. He reached his intended goal and had been welcomed at all his Lord's lodgings, especially at the gates of the Celestial City. There, said the man, the sound of trumpets played by a company of shining ones received him. He also told how the bells in the city rang for joy at his entrance, the golden garments he was dressed in, and many other things that I will not relate. That man told the story of Christian and his travels and my heart burned in haste to follow him. Father or mother could not stop me. So I left and have come this far on my way.

GREAT. You came in at the gate, did you not?

VALIANT. Yes, yes, the same man told us that all would be nothing if we did not begin at the gate.

GREAT. Look, said the guide to Christiana, your husband's pilgrimage is spread far and near.

VALIANT. Is this Christian's wife?

GREAT. Yes, and these are his four sons.

VALIANT. All going on a pilgrimage?

GREAT. Yes, they are following.

VALIANT. It makes my heart glad. How joyful Christian will be when he sees those who would not go with him enter the gates of the Celestial City.

GREAT. Without a doubt it will comfort him. Next to the joy of being there, it will be a joy to meet his wife and children.

VALIANT. Since you mentioned it, let me hear your opinion. Some question if we will know one another there.

GREAT. Do you think they will know themselves there? Will they rejoice to see themselves in that bliss? If they think they will know and do this, why won't others know and rejoice in their own welfare? Relations are our second self, though that state will be dissolved. So why is it not rational to conclude that we will be happier to see them there than to see them missing?

VALIANT. I perceive where you are on this. Have you any more things to ask about my pilgrimage?

GREAT. Were your father and mother willing for you to become a pilgrim?

VALIANT. No! They used every means imaginable to persuade me to stay home.

GREAT. What could they say against it?

VALIANT. They said it was an idle life. If I was not inclined to be lazy, I would never contemplate a pilgrim's life.

GREAT. What else did they say?

VALIANT. They told me that it was dangerous, the most dangerous way in the world is the way of the pilgrims.

GREAT. Did they show why this way is so dangerous?

VALIANT. Yes. They gave specific examples.

GREAT. Name some of them.

VALIANT. They told me of the Swamp of Despond, where Christian almost suffocated. They told me that archers were standing ready in Beelzebub-castle to shoot those who would knock at the narrow gate. They told me about the woods, dark mountains, the hill Difficulty, the lions, and the three giants, Bloody-man, Maul, and Slay-good. They also said that a foul fiend haunts the Valley of Humiliation; that Christian almost lost his life there. They said that I must travel the Valley of the

Shadow of Death, where the spirits are, where the light is darkness, and where the way is full of snares, pits, traps, and nets. They told me of Giant Despair, Doubting Castle, and the number of pilgrims that meet their ruin in that valley. They said I must go over the dangerous Enchanted Ground. And after all this I would find a river over which there was no bridge between me and the Celestial country.

GREAT. Was this all?

VALIANT. No. They also told me that this way was full of deceivers, and people that waited to turn good men from the path.

GREAT. Where did they get that information?

VALIANT. They said that Mr. Wordly Wiseman was there, waiting to deceive. They also said that Formality and Hypocrisy were continually on the road. By-ends, Talkative, or Demas would gather me up. The Flatterer would trap me in his net. That with Green-headed Ignorance, I would presume to go to the gate but would be sent back to the hole in the side of the hill and made to go the by-way to hell.

GREAT. This was enough to discourage you. Did they end it here?

VALIANT. No! They told me of many that had tried the old way for a great distance. They tried to find something of the glory that so many had talked about. Yet, they came back considering themselves fools for having set a foot in that path. They named several who did this, Obstinate and Pliable, Mistrust and Timorous, Turn-away and old Atheist. They said that some of them had gone far to see what they could find. But none found any advantage.

GREAT. Did they say anything else to discourage you?

VALIANT. Yes. They told me of Mr. Fearing, a pilgrim. He found the way so lonely that he never had a comfortable hour. They talked about Mr. Despondency, who almost starved. Yes (I almost forgot), Christian himself, about whom there has been such a noise concerning his adventures for a celestial crown. They said Christian was surely drowned in the Black River and never went another foot regardless of how it was covered up.

GREAT. Did any of these things discourage you?

VALIANT. No, they were so many nothings to me.

GREAT. How did that come about?

VALIANT. I still believed what Mr. Tell-true said. That carried me beyond them all.

GREAT. Then this was your victory, even your faith.

VALIANT. It was. I believed, came out, got into the way, fought all that set themselves against me, and by believing I have come to this place.

> Who would true valor see,
> Let him come hither;
> One here will constant be,
> Come wind, come weather.
> There's no discouragement
> Shall make him once relent
> His first avow'd intent
> To be a pilgrim.
> Whoso beset him round
> With dismal stories,
> Do but themselves confound;
> His strength the more is.
> No lion can him fright,
> He'll with a giant fight,
> But he will have a right
> To be a pilgrim.
> Hobgoblin nor foul fiend
> Can daunt his spirit;
> He knows he at the end
> Shall life inherit.
> Then fancies fly away,
> He'll not fear what men say;
> He'll labor night and day
> To be a pilgrim.

By this time they reached the Enchanted Ground, where the air tends to make one drowsy. It was grown over with briars and thorns, except here and there where there was an enchanted arbor. A man sat on it, or in it, and slept. There is a question, some say, whether he will ever rise or wake again in this world. Over this forest they traveled. Mr. Great-Heart went ahead, for he was the guide, and Mr. Valiant-for-truth was the rear-guard, in the event that some fiend, dragon, giant, or thief would attack their rear. They went on, each man with his sword drawn. They knew the place was dangerous. They cheered one another as well as they could. Mr. Great-Heart commanded that Feeble-mind should follow him and that Mr. Despondency would be under the eye of Mr. Valiant.

Now they had not gone far, when a thick fog and darkness fell on them. For a great while, they could scarcely see one another. They were forced to feel one for another by words. They walked not by sight. You would think that this was sorry going for the best of them, but much worse for the women and children whose feet and hearts were tender! Yet through the encouraging words of him that led and him that brought up the rear, they made pretty good time.

The way was through dirt and mud. They grew weary. Nor was there, on all this ground, so much as one inn or eating-house to refresh the feeble. There was grunting, puffing, and sighing as one tumbled over a bush, another was stuck in the mud, and some of the children lost their shoes in the mire. One cries, I am down. Another responds, Where are you? A third yells, The bushes have hold on me, I cannot get away.

Then they reached an arbor. It was warm, promising, and refreshing to the pilgrims. It was finely made, beautified with greens, furnished with benches and seats. It had a soft couch where the weary could lean. This, you must think, was tempting for the pilgrims already began to collapse from the terrible conditions of the way. Yet not one of them made so much as a motion to stop. As near as I could perceive, they continually listened to the advice of their guide. He faithfully told them of danger and the nature of the dangers when they were close to them. They all raised their spirits and encouraged one another to deny the flesh. This arbor was called The Slothful's Friend. It was made to allure some of the pilgrims to rest there when weary.

I saw them in my dream as they traveled this lonely ground where a man is likely to lose his way. When it was light their guide could readily tell how to miss the ways that were wrong. But in the dark he had to stop. He had a map in his pocket of all the ways leading to or from the Celestial City. He struck a light (for he never goes without his tinderbox), looks at his map, tells them to be careful, and turn to the right. Had he not been careful to look at his map, they would have, in all probability, been suffocated in the mud. For just ahead, at the end of the cleanest way, was a pit, none knows how deep, full of mud. Its purpose was to destroy the pilgrims.

I thought, who would go on a pilgrimage without a map? It is necessary to find the best way.

They continued in this Enchanted Ground until they came to another arbor that was built by the side of the highway. There were two men in that arbor, Heedless and Too-bold. These two were on a pilgrimage, but being weary they sat down to rest and fell sound asleep. When the pilgrims saw them, they shook their heads. The sleepers were a pitiful case. They debated whether to go on and leave them asleep, or try and wake them. They decided to wake them if they could. They were cautious to make sure that they did not sit down or embrace the comforts of that arbor.

They spoke to the men, calling each by name, for the guide knew them. There was no response. The guide shook them, and did what he could to disturb them. One of them said, I will pay you when I get my money. The guide shook his head. I will fight so long as I can hold my sword in my hand, said the other. At that, one of the children laughed.

Christiana asked, What is the meaning of this? The guide answered, They talk in their sleep. If you strike them, beat them, or whatever, they will answer you this way. The wise one said, Yes, you will be like one who lies down in the midst of the sea, or like one who lies at the top of the mast, saying, They have struck me, but I was not hurt; they have beaten me, but I did not feel it. When I awake, that I may seek another drink (Prov. 23:34, 35)? When men talk in their sleep, they say any thing. Faith or reason does not govern their words. Their words are incoherent, just as they were between going on their pilgrimage and sitting down here. This is the mischief of it. When heedless ones go on a pilgrimage, it is twenty to one they are so served.

This Enchanted Ground is one of the last refuges of the pilgrims' enemy. It is, as you see, placed almost at the end of the way. So it stands against us with a greater advantage. When does the enemy think these fools will most want to sit down? When they are weary. And when are they most likely to be weary? When they are almost at the journey's end. This is why the Enchanted Ground is placed so close to the land Beulah and so near the end of the race. Let pilgrims watch, lest it happen to them as it has to these. They have fallen asleep and no one can awake them.

The pilgrims wanted to go on. They requested their guide to strike a light that they might travel the rest of their way with the help of a lantern. So he struck a light and they went the rest of the way, even though the darkness was very great (2 Pet. 1:19). The children began to be weary, and they cried out to him that loves pilgrims to make their way more comfortable. When they had gone just a little further, a wind arose, drove the fog away, and the air became clear. They could now see one another and the way they should walk.

When they were almost at the end of this ground, they perceived that just ahead of them was a noise, as of one that was much concerned. They went and looked. They saw a man on his knees with hands and eyes lifted up, speaking, as they thought, earnestly to one that was above. They drew close but could not tell what he said. They were quiet until he finished. Then he got up and began to run toward the Celestial City. Mr. Great-Heart called, Friend, let us have your company if you are going, as I suppose you are, to the Celestial City. The man stopped and they approached him. As soon as Mr. Honest saw him, he said, I know this man. Mr. Valiant-for-truth said, who is it? It is one that comes from close to where I lived. His name is Standfast. He is a right good pilgrim.

They came together. Standfast said to old Honest, Father Honest, are you there? Aye, said he, I am as sure as you are there. Right glad am I that I have found you on this road. And as glad am I, said the other, that I saw you on your knees. Mr. Standfast blushed and said, You saw me? Yes, I did and my heart was glad at the sight. What did you think, said Standfast? Think! said old Honest, what could I think? We have an honest man on the road and we should have his company. If you thought correctly, said Standfast, how happy am I! But if I am not, it is I alone who must bear it. That is true, said the other, but your fear further confirms that things are right between the Prince of pilgrims and your soul. For he said, "Happy is the man who is always reverent" (Prov. 28:14).

VALIANT. Well brother, what was it that caused you to be on your knees? Was it that some special mercy laid obligations on you, or what?

STAND. Why, we are on the Enchanted Ground. As I was coming along, I thought of how dangerous this place is. And how many have come this far on a pilgrimage only to be stopped and destroyed. I thought about the way death destroys men. Those that die here do not die from violent distemper. The death they die here is not distressing to them. He that goes away in sleep begins that journey with desire and pleasure.

HON. Did you see the two men asleep in the arbor?

STAND. Yes, I saw Heedless and Too-bold there. For all I know, they will lie there until they rot (Prov. 10:7). Let me go on with my tale. As I was musing, there was an old one dressed in pleasant attire. She offered me three things, her body, her purse, and her bed. Now the truth is, I was both weary and sleepy. I am also as poor as an owl. Perhaps the witch knew that. Well, I repulsed her once, but she ignored my repulses and smiled. Then I became angry, but that didn't matter. She offers again and said that if she could rule me, she would make me great and happy. She told me, I am the mistress of the world; men are made happy by me. I asked her name, she said it was Madam Bubble. This put me further from her, but she still followed me with enticements. Then I, as you saw, fell to my knees and with hands lifted, I cried and prayed to Him that said he would help. Just as you came up, the gentlewoman went her way. I continued to give thanks for this great deliverance. I believe she intended no good, but sought to stop me in my journey.

HON. Without doubt her designs were bad. Now that you have talked about her, I think that either I have seen her or read some story about her.

STAND. Perhaps you have done both.

HON. Madam Bubble! Is she a tall, attractive lady, with a swarthy complexion?

STAND. Right, you hit it. That's her.

HON. Does she speak smoothly and give you a smile at the end of a sentence?

STAND. You hit right on it again. These are her very actions.

HON. Does she wear a great purse by her side? Is her hand often in it fingering her money, as if that was her heart's delight?

STAND. It is. If she stood here all this while, you could not have more amply described her and her features.

HON. He that drew her picture was a good portrait painter, and he that wrote of her was true.

GREAT. This woman is a witch. It is by her sorcery that this ground is enchanted. Whoever lays his head down in her lap might as well lay it down on the block over which the axe hangs. Whoever watches her beauty is counted as an enemy of God. This is she that maintains in splendor all those that are the enemies of pilgrims (James 4:4). Yes, she has taken many a man from a pilgrim's life. She is a great gossip. She and her daughters are always at a pilgrim's heels commending the excellence of this life.

She is a bold and impudent slut. She will talk with any man. She always laughs poor pilgrims to scorn, but highly commends the rich. If one is cunning enough to get money in a place, she will speak well of him from house to house. She loves banquets and feasting. She is always at one full table or another. She has said in some places that she is a goddess, and some worship her. She has her time and open places of cheating. She will say and avow that none can show a good comparable to hers. She promises to dwell with children's children if they will love her and make much of her. She will throw gold from her purse like dust in some places and to some people. She loves to be sought after, spoken well of, and to lie in the bosoms of men. She is never weary of commending her commodities. She loves them most that think best of her. She will promise to some crowns and kingdoms, if they will take her advice. Yet she has brought many to the noose, and ten thousand times more to hell.

STAND. What a mercy that I resisted her, for where might she have drawn me!

GREAT. Where? Only God knows where. But in general she would have drawn you into many foolish and hurtful lusts which drown men in destruction and perdition (1 Tim. 6:9). It was she that set Absalom against his father, and Jeroboam against his master. She persuaded Judas to sell his Lord, and prevailed with Demas to forsake the godly pilgrim's life. None can tell of the trouble she causes. She makes variance between rulers and subjects, between parents and children, between neighbor and neighbor, between a man and his wife, between a man and himself, between the flesh and the spirit. And so, good Mr. Standfast, be as your name and when you have done all, stand.

At this there was a mixture of joy and trembling among the pilgrims. But at length they broke out and sang,

> What danger is the Pilgrim in!
> How many are his foes!
> How many ways there are to sin
> No living mortal knows.
> Some in the ditch are spoiled, yea, can
> Lie tumbling in the mire:
> Some, though they shun the frying-pan
> Do leap into the fire.

After this, I watched until they came into the land of Beulah where the sun shines night and day. Here, because they were weary, they rested. Because this country was common for pilgrims, and because the orchards and vineyards belonged to the King of the Celestial country, they were allowed to enjoy any of his things. In a little while they were refreshed.

The bells rang, the trumpets continually sounded melodiously, and they could not sleep. But they were as refreshed as if they had slept soundly.

Here the conversation of those who walked the streets was, More pilgrims have come to town! And another would answer, And so many went over the water and were let in at the golden gates today! They would cry again, There is now a legion of shining ones that just arrived and so we know there are more pilgrims on the road. Here they come to wait for them and to comfort them after all their sorrow. Then the pilgrims got up, walked back and forth, but now their ears were filled with heavenly noises and their eyes were delighted with celestial visions! In this land they heard nothing, saw nothing, felt nothing, smelled nothing, tasted nothing that was offensive to their stomach or mind. Only when they tasted the water of the river over which they were to go, did they think that it tasted a little bitter, but it proved sweeter when it was down.

In this place a record was kept of the names and the famous acts of the pilgrims of old. Here they frequently discussed how some thought the river had flowed and how it ebbed when they went over. It had been almost dry for some, while it overflowed its banks for others.

In this place the children went into the King's gardens and gathered bouquets for the pilgrims that were presented with great affection. Here also grew Camphire, with spikenard and saffron, calamus and cinnamon, and trees of frankincense, myrrh, aloes, and spices. With these the pilgrims' rooms were perfumed; their bodies anointed to prepare them to cross the river at the appointed time.

While this company stayed there and waited for the good hour, the messenger arrived with mail from the Celestial City. This was of great importance to Christiana, the wife of Christian the pilgrim. He found the house where she was staying and the letter was presented. The contents were, Hail, good woman; I bring you news that the Master calls for you, expect to stand in his presence in clothes of immortality within ten days.

When he had read the letter, he gave her a sign that he was a true messenger who had come to tell her to make haste to be gone. The token was an arrow with a point sharpened with love, let easily into her heart. By degrees, it worked so effectively that at the time appointed she would be gone.

When Christiana, the first of this company to go over, saw that her time had come she called for Mr. Great-Heart her guide. He told her he was heartily glad of the news and would have been equally pleased had the letter come for him. She asked advice on how all things should be prepared for her journey. So he told her, Thus and thus it must be. We that survive will accompany you to the river.

Then she called her children and gave them her blessing. She read with comfort the mark that was set in their foreheads, was glad to see them, and pleased that they had kept their garments so white. She gave what little she had to the poor. Finally, she commanded her sons and daughters to be ready when the messenger would come for them.

When she had spoken to her guide and her children, she called for Mr. Valiant-for-truth. Sir, she said, you have in all places shown yourself true-hearted. Be faithful unto death and my King will give you a crown of life (Rev. 2:10). I would also beg you to keep an eye on my children. If at any time you see them faint, speak comfortably to them. My daughters, my sons' wives, have been faithful, and the promise will be fulfilled on them. She gave Mr. Standfast a ring.

She called for old Mr. Honest and said, "Behold an Israelite indeed, in whom is no deceit!" (John 1:47). He replied, I wish you a fair day when you set out for Mount Zion. I will be glad to see you go over the river with dry shoes. She answered, Come wet, come dry, I long to be gone. Regardless of the weather on my journey, I will have time enough when I arrive to sit, rest, and get dry.

Then that good man, Mr. Ready-to-halt, came to see her. She said, Your travel has been with difficulty, but that will make your rest sweeter. Watch, be ready, for at an hour when you think not, the messenger may come.

After him, Mr. Despondency and his daughter Much-afraid, came. She said, You should, with thankfulness, forever remember your deliverance from the hands of Giant Despair and Doubting Castle. That mercy has brought you safe this far. Be watchful, throw fear away, be sober, and hope to the end.

She said to Mr. Feeble-mind, You were delivered from the mouth of Giant Slay-good, so that you might live in the light of the living and see your King with comfort. I advise you to repent of fear and the doubt of his goodness. Lest, when he comes, you are forced to stand before him blushing.

Now the day arrived when Christiana must be gone. The road was full of people to see her take her journey. All the banks beyond the river were full of horses and chariots that had come down from above to accompany her to the city gate. She entered the river with a farewell wave to those that followed her. Her last words were, I come, Lord, to be with you and bless you! So her children and friends returned to their place, for those that waited for Christiana carried her out of their sight. She entered the gate with all the ceremonies of joy that her husband Christian had received. At her departure, the children wept. But Mr. Great-Heart and Mr. Valiant played the well-tuned cymbal and harp for joy. Then all departed to their respective places.

In time the messenger came to town again. His business was with Mr. Ready-to-halt. He said, I have come from Him whom you have loved and followed on crutches. My message is to tell you that he expects you at his table for dinner in his kingdom the day after Easter. Prepare for your journey. Then he gave him a token that he was a true messenger, "The silver cord is loosed, the golden bowl is broken" (Eccl. 12:6).

Mr. Ready-to-halt called his fellow-pilgrims. I am sent for. God will surely visit you. He asked Mr. Valiant to make his will. All he had to give those that would survive him was his crutches and his good wishes. He said, These crutches I leave to my son who will walk in my steps with a hundred warm wishes that he may prove better than me.

He thanked Mr. Great-Heart for his conduct and kindness and prepared for his journey. When he came to the brink of the river, he said, Now I will have no more need of these crutches, since yonder are chariots and horses for me to ride. The last words he said were, Welcome life! So he went his way.

After this, Mr. Feeble-mind had news that the messenger sounded the horn for him. He came in and said, I have come to tell you that your Master has need of you. You, in a very little time, will see his face in brightness. Take this as a token of the truth of my message: "Those that look through windows grow dim (Eccl. 12:3). Then Mr. Feeble-mind called for his friends, told them what errand had been given him and the token he had received of the truth of the message. Then he said, Since I have nothing to bequeath to any, why should I make a will? As for my feeble mind, I leave that behind me. I will have no need of it where I go, nor is it worth giving to the poorest pilgrims. When I am gone, Mr. Valiant, I want you to bury it in a garbage pile. The day of his departure he entered the river. His last words were, Hold out, faith and patience! He went over to the other side.

After many days Mr. Despondency was sent for. A post arrived with this message. Trembling man! These are to summon you to be ready with the King by the next Lord's day. Shout for joy for deliverance from all your doubts. And, said the messenger, to prove that my message is true, take this. He gave him a grasshopper to be a burden (Eccl. 12:5).

Mr. Despondency's daughter, Much-afraid, said that she would go with her father. Mr. Despondency said to his friends, My daughter and me, you know how troublesome we have behaved in every company. My will and my daughter's is that our depression and slavish fears are never given to anyone. I know that after my death they will offer themselves to others. They are ghosts we entertained when we first were pilgrims. We could never shake them off. They will walk about and seek entertainment from the pilgrims. Shut the doors on them. When the time came for them to depart, they went to the brink of the river. The last words of Mr. Despondency were, Farewell, night, welcome, day! His daughter went through the river singing but no one could understand what she said.

Then it came to pass that there was a post in the town that inquired for Mr. Honest. He came to the house where he was and delivered these lines. You are commanded to be ready in seven nights to present yourself before your Lord at his Father's house. As a token that my message is true, "All the daughters of music are brought low" (Eccl. 12:4). Mr. Honest called his friends and said, I die, but will make no will. My honesty will go with me. Let him that comes after be told of this. When the day he was to leave arrived, he went to the river. It was overflowing its banks in some places. Mr. Honest, in his lifetime, had spoken to Good-conscience to meet him there. This he did. He lent him his hand and helped him over. The last words of Mr. Honest were, Grace reigns! So he left the world.

After this, Mr. Valiant-for-truth received a summons from the same post. This was his token that the summons was true, "The pitcher shattered at the fountain" (Eccl. 12:6). When he understood, he called his friends and told them, I am going to my Father's. Though with great difficulty I reached here, I do not regret the troubles I have had. My sword I give to him that succeeds me in my pilgrimage. My courage and skill I leave to him that can get it. My marks and scars I carry with me as a witness that I have fought the battles of him who will now be my reward. When the day arrived, many accompanied him to the riverside. As he entered the water, he said, "Death, where is your sting?" As he went deeper, he said, "Grave, where is your victory?" (1 Cor. 15:55). He passed over and all the trumpets on the other side sounded for him.

Then there came a summons for Mr. Standfast, whom the pilgrims found on his knees in the Enchanted Ground. The post brought it open in his hands. It said that he must prepare for a change of life. His Master was not willing that he should be so far from him any longer. Mr. Standfast was silent. The messenger said, You need not doubt the truth of my message, here is a token of the truth, "The wheel is broken at the well" (Eccl. 12:6).

He called Mr. Great-Heart, their guide, and said, Sir, although I was not frequently in your good company during my pilgrimage, in the time that I have known you, you have been profitable to me. I left a wife and five small children behind. Let me plead with you, at your return (for I know that you go and return to your Master's house (to be a guide to more holy pilgrims) let my family know all that has happened to me. Tell them of my happy arrival and of the blessed condition I enjoy. Tell them about Christian and how Christiana his wife and children followed her husband. Tell them about her happy end and where she is now. I have little or nothing to send my family, except prayers and tears to help them prevail.

When Mr. Standfast had set things in order, and the time had come for him to leave, he went down to the river. There was a great calm on the water. When Mr. Standfast was about halfway across, he stood and talked with his companions that waited for him. This river has been a terror to many. Yes, the thoughts of it have frightened me. Yet it is easy to stand. My foot is fixed on that which the feet of the priests who carried the ark of the covenant stood while Israel went over Jordan (Josh. 3:17). The waters are bitter to the palate and cold to the stomach. Yet the thoughts of what I am going to, and the convoy that waits on the other side, warm my heart like glowing coal.

I see myself at the end of my journey. My toils are ended. I am going to see the head that was crowned with thorns and the face that was spit on for me. I have lived by hearsay and faith. Now I go where I will live by sight, to be with him in whose company I delight. I have loved to hear people speak of my Lord. Where I have seen the print of his shoe in the earth, there I have tried to set my foot. His name has been honey, sweeter than all perfumes. His voice has been sweet. I desire his appearance more than the light of the sun. His words I gathered for food and an antidote against fainting. He has held me and kept me from iniquities. My steps he has strengthened in his way.

While he was talking, his appearance changed. His strong man bowed under him. He said, Take me, I come to you. He ceased to be seen by them.

It was glorious to see the open region filled with horses, chariots, trumpeters, pipers, singers, and musicians with stringed instruments, all welcoming the pilgrims. They followed one another through the beautiful gate of the city.

As for Christiana's children, the four boys, their wives and children, I did not stay until they went over. Since I left, I heard one say that they were still alive and increased the church where they lived.

Should it be my lot to go that way again, I may give those that want it an account of what I am silent about here. Meantime I bid my reader

FAREWELL.

THE END.

Nelson's Royal Classics Series

Pilgrim's Progress
John Bunyan
ISBN 0-7852-4222-8

Imitation of Christ
Thomas à Kempis
ISBN 0-7852-4224-4

Confessions
St. Augustine
ISBN 0-7852-4225-2

**The Practice of the Presence of God/
The Way of Perfection**
Brother Lawrence/Teresa of Ávila
ISBN 0-7852-4227-9

The Christian's Secret of a Happy Life
Hannah Whitall Smith
ISBN 0-7852-4275-9

In His Steps
Charles M. Sheldon
ISBN 0-7852-4223-6

Additional volumes will be forthcoming to add to your collection.